She met his gaze with eyes wide and innocent, trying to look serious and sincere, but the corners of her luscious mouth were turning upward. "You ought to be ashamed of yourself."

"I am," he said.

He took her face in his hands and bent his head to kiss her. She closed her eyes.

Raney felt herself opening to the heat of Creed's kiss as if his mouth were the sun.

They'd both been waiting for this—exactly this. Everything they'd said and done since then had been leading up to this moment.

Now, the waiting was over . . .

Other **AVON ROMANCES**

GENELL DELLIN

The Captive

Cherokee Warriors

AVON BOOKS

An Imprint of HarperCollinsPublishers

AVON BOOKS
An Imprint of HarperCollins*Publishers*
10 East 53rd Street
New York, New York 10022-5299

First Avon Books paperback printing: November 2004

For Sam Lytal,
Cherokee Warrior

Prologue

Texas
April 1868

Creed Sixkiller pushed the last cow/calf pair into the gather and wheeled his horse away from the herd. Searching through the settling dust for Robert Childress, he saw him resting his horse in the shade of a live oak tree and rode straight to him. Now was the time to ask Raney's father for her hand so he could talk to her about marriage at the dance tonight.

"Is that the last of them?" Childress called as Creed approached.

"All but Tolliver's four hundred head for the beef herd," Creed said. "They're coming up the Navasota Road right now."

"Y'all will have two big herds to handle," Childress said. "I hope you've hired enough drovers."

"Come on and ride with us," Creed said. "We're bound to hear the owl hoot before we get it done."

He was only joking. He couldn't imagine the older man without his servants to bring juleps to him and a rocking chair on the gallery.

Childress turned down the offer in the same spirit in which it was offered.

"Well, thank you kindly for the invitation," he said, "but trailing cattle from Texas to Kansas is a young man's game. I didn't get enough sleep last winter to stay in the saddle all summer."

Creed, smiling at the sally, stopped his horse facing the big Tennessee Walker that was Childress's favorite mount, one of a distinctive line of horses the Childress family brought from Georgia to Texas.

"Mr. Childress," he said, "I apologize for not making a call on you at home for this conversation, but we've decided to move out at sunup and I don't want to leave Texas without speaking to you and to Raney about my intentions. I love your daughter, sir. I believe she loves me. I'd like your permission to marry her."

Robert Childress's face flushed from his white goatee to his hairline. He stared at Creed with his blue eyes wide.

"You insult me, boy," he said. "You're an *Indian*. Don't you know that?"

2

Shock hit Creed's blood like a cold drink on a hot day.

"Why, you're lucky I even let you *speak* to my daughter! Your father's my neighbor, and I've tried to be tolerant, but if I'd known of your intentions, you would never have been allowed to the same social events as her in your life."

"You'd have played hell trying to stop me," Creed said.

That made Childress's ruddiness go mottled with white.

"You don't *know* hell until you fool with me about Raney. You're nothing but a wild young buck of a *redskin*, for God's sake. My daughter's descended from some of the oldest families in Georgia."

Creed kept his fury off his face and held his body still in the saddle.

"My people were in Georgia long before yours were sent there from an English prison," he said.

The older man turned entirely pale and began sputtering.

"Why, that kind of talk is an *outrage . . .*"

Creed turned his back and rode away.

To hell with Robert Childress. He would marry Raney without her father's blessing.

Creed didn't wait for the dance. He thought about it while he unsaddled and watered his horse, turned him into the remuda, and caught and saddled another one. Robert Childress was so arrogant, he'd think his warning Creed away from Raney would be sufficient to keep them apart.

But, just to make sure they didn't see each other, the old hypocrite might take her home before the dance.

Every single man in the county wanted to court Raney Childress, and some of the married ones had trouble keeping their eyes off her, too. Any time she swung onto the dance floor at a social or floated into a room with her hair spilling like sunshine over her pretty shoulders, every male in the place turned to look at her. Now he, Creed Sixkiller, was going to be the one she would choose to marry, and the others would all envy him.

He would feel like king of the hill, yes, but this wasn't a turkey hunt or a wrestling match. It was love. He loved Raney, and not just for her beauty. She was the most carefree, fun-loving girl he'd ever known.

And what girl wouldn't be? His sister Maggie told him Raney received everything she wanted on a silver platter the minute she wanted it. She never did a lick of work in her life, so why wouldn't she be carefree and always looking for amusement? But Maggie loved Raney, too, and for those very same reasons.

And that was part of Raney's appeal. At seventeen, she was an innocent about work—about life, really—and at twenty-five, he was already mature. He would help her grow up.

But he would still spoil her with everything she

wanted, the way her parents did, and that would keep her happy. The Sixes and Sevens was a huge, successful ranch, and the Sixkillers had as much or more wealth than Robert Childress did, so that would not be any sacrifice at all.

Of course, his two sisters and his mother all did a lot of work. Each had her own responsibilities on the ranch, and they would give Raney some jobs of her own.

Well, she might not like it at first, but she could learn to do *some* work. That would be part of his helping her grow up.

As he rode the rest of the way to the shady grove, Creed didn't smell the fresh grass or see the horses scattered over the rolling pasture. All he could see was Raney in his arms, in his bed, with her bright hair falling over the pillow and making him drunk with its flowery scent.

Before he even reached the trees, he spotted her. She and Maggie were on the edge of the river that flowed through the ranch, down the slope where the bluebonnets were blooming. The girls played in the shade created by the hundred or more big trees, dipping their toes in the cool water, laughing and talking. Creed dismounted and walked toward them.

Maggie saw him first. With a look and a gesture, he told her to leave Raney and go back to the other women deeper in the orchard who were busy preparing the tables full of food. She smiled, bent over and said something to Raney, then picked up her shoes and ran off through the grass.

But he wasn't really paying attention to his sister. All he could see was Raney, turning to watch him walk toward her, one hand lifting the skirt of her blue dress, wet at the hem, out of the water, and her blond hair sweetly disheveled. She had to be the most beautiful girl in Texas.

She gave him that smile of hers that would melt a frozen river.

"Hello, Creed. Are y'all comin' in for dinner already?" She glanced toward the tables. "I was supposed to help Mama. Etty's sick, so we didn't bring her today . . ."

There was such a surge of desire in him that he could hardly hold it in.

He walked up to her and stood between her and everybody else. Raney met his gaze, letting her skirt fall. Creed reached out and took her hand.

"Raney, I love you," he said. "Will you marry me? I'll see to it that you never want for anything."

Surprise lit her eyes.

"But you're an *Indian*," she said.

The sharp cut he felt must have shown in his face.

"Oh, Creed," she said, rushing the words to try to make amends. "You are such a handsome man, and a good one, but I can't break my mama's heart. You understand that. And I'm too young to leave home. You know it. I really am."

"You went walking out with me," he said, even though he had trouble getting the words past his lips. "More than once. You let me kiss you on the mouth."

Her eyes were the exact color of the bluebonnets tumbling down the slope behind her. She widened them even more. Raney always did have a look of pure innocence.

"Creed," she said, "you are so . . . exciting. You make every girl's breath go shallow. You are the most . . . heart-stopping man in the whole world, but I'm scared of my feelings for you and I can't . . ."

She bit her lip. The look she gave him then was full of so many thoughts and feelings, all of them plain and clear in her eyes, but they changed so fast that he couldn't catch a single one of them to give it a name.

"Ask me again in a year," she said. "Oh, Creed, ask me again next year when the bluebonnets are blooming."

"Never," he said. Against his will, his fingers tightened on hers before he turned her loose. "I'll never ask you again."

Chapter 1

April 1871

*N*o *good deed goes unpunished.*

That thought flashed through Creed Six-killer's mind just before Brassell Childress's fist smashed into his jaw. Reeling from the sneak attack, he struck back off-balance and hit only Brass's shoulder. The scared kid turned to disappear into the melee, but Creed hooked his leg with his boot and threw him to the ground.

He straddled Brass and pulled his hands together at the small of his back.

"You little idiot. I should've stayed home and let all you political fanatics shoot each other to shreds," Creed said.

He moved his jaw in an exaggerated motion, although it felt so numb he wasn't sure he should. It didn't seem to be broken.

"If you'd come at me face to face like a man, it would've helped you a little," he growled, "but you acted like a craven coward, so I'm hauling you to jail, Brassell."

"Naw!" the boy cried. "Don't do that. You *can't* do that. I'm a wounded man. You gotta take me home."

"Better not add lying to your sins for the day," Creed mumbled.

His jaw was already starting to swell.

He secured Brass's hands with his own belt, jerked it tight, and stood up, hauling the kid to his feet by his shirt collar. Creed looked around.

Things were calming down. His men were getting control, and the so-called campaign rally was over for the day. "Battle" was more like it. This rivalry between the Peckerwoods and the Chickenhawks over who would win the important county seats in the fall election was fast becoming a war.

He ran a quick eye over the crowd once more. His brothers, Eagle Jack and Young Bear, were all right. Both were confiscating weapons and throwing them into the wagon. The Sixes and Sevens foreman, Nat Straight, had a man captured and sitting on the wagon seat.

The Sixkillers and their ranch hands were all acting as lawmen until either the state sent in some

Texas Rangers on a permanent basis or somebody competent got elected sheriff. Whichever, it couldn't come too soon for Creed. Thank God, at least they had an honest judge in the courthouse.

He turned Brassell around and made him look him in the eye.

"As long as I can ride," he said, "this kind of lawlessness will not be tolerated in Limestone County. You boys better plan to keep your guns in your holsters the next time you have a little get-together."

"Tell that to the Chickenhawks," Brassell said belligerently. "They're the ones pushed themselves in here and crashed our meeting."

Creed ignored that and turned him around again to push him toward his horse. The whole lot of them, Peckerwoods and Chickenhawks alike, wanted to feud. They were getting caught up in the wild emotions and making this election a blood sport. Two men—one from each side—had already died, ambushed on the road.

"Mount up," he said, and the boy balanced on one foot to put the other in his stirrup.

Creed half pushed, half threw Brassell up into his saddle.

"Our families have been neighbors all my life," Brassell said, narrowing his eyes to squint at Creed. "You ought to respect that and let me go. I ain't done one thing—"

Creed interrupted. "You crept up on me from be-

11

hind, you little coward. You're lucky I didn't kill you."

"*You're* lucky my pa and my brother are gone right now," Brassell said. "If I bleed to death in jail they'll kill you."

"Shut up, Brassell," Creed said. "Another word and I'll ask Judge Scarborough to throw the book at you."

"I've been shot in the shoulder," the boy said.

Creed mounted his own horse and rode up close to look. Sure enough, there was blood on Brass's loose white shirt, but when he pulled back the cloth at the neck, it showed only a small piece of torn flesh. Bleeding, but not bad.

"You're not shot, you're only grazed," Creed said. "Quit your crying and take your punishment like a man."

"I'm a Childress," Brass said. "My pa is not going to take kindly to finding me in jail when he gets back from Fort Worth."

"You should've thought of that before you fell in with this bunch of bushwhackers," Creed said, and tied Brassell's reins to his saddle.

The boy shot looks at him that would've killed if they'd been hot lead. Creed ignored them. Brass was as bad as his sister, Raney—thought he ought to have his cake and eat it, too.

The Sixes and Sevens men rode into a loose circle around their captives and set out for town.

* * *

Maybe it was Brass, coming home.

Raney ran out onto the gallery and peered into the darkness, listening. Yes, a horse definitely was coming down the lane to the house, and coming fast. It had *better* be Brassell, since he was supposed to be chaperoning her and Leonard, and it was way after bedtime.

Of course, Etty and the other servants were there with them on Pleasant Hill, but it wouldn't look right to have no other family members there with them, Papa had said, when he and her brother Trent were leaving. As part of his orders to Brass, he had specifically told him not to stay out all night because he had to be there even though Etty was sleeping in the house, too. Etty was fierce as a mountain cat, and she would kill to protect Raney's honor but a male relative had to be there, too, to prevent any talk from sullying her reputation.

"Raney?"

Leonard followed her, letting the screen door slam. She gritted her teeth. Of all the men who'd asked to be her husband, she'd agreed with Papa that Leonard was the perfect choice. But sometimes he tended to get on her nerves because either he was lost in his own thoughts and ignoring her or he wouldn't leave her be.

And when he wouldn't leave her be, he was way too interested in controlling her every move, in her opinion. All her life she'd done as she pleased, and she didn't intend to let a little thing like getting mar-

13

ried stop that. Leonard would just have to learn.

The hoofbeats were getting louder.

"Somebody's in a real hurry," Leonard said.

"Brass, probably," she said. "Afraid he'll be in trouble for staying out so late. He knows Etty will tell Papa."

The rider came into sight around the bend of the lane. In the moonlight, his mount looked like a ghost horse.

"A *white* horse," Leonard said.

Raney said, "That's not Brass."

They recognized Douglas Hightower, a friend of Brassell's, just before he rode up to the steps.

"Sorry to disturb y'all this time of night, Miss Raney," he said, "but I have news."

Raney's hand went to her throat.

"What?" she cried. "What is it?"

"Get down and come in," Leonard said.

"Can't, thanks," Doug said, catching his breath. "Gotta get home. There was a big fight at the rally and Brassell was wounded. The Sixes and Sevens crew took him and a bunch of our other men to jail."

Raney's heart dived through the floor.

"*Wounded!* How bad is he?"

"He's escaped," Douglas said quickly. "So he's not hurt too bad. I didn't see him, but the others say his sleeve was bloody, that's all."

"When did he escape, Doug?" she cried. "He's not here yet. He may have collapsed on the way."

14

She turned to Leonard. "He's nothing but a baby. Brass's only sixteen and way too young to be running around getting into all this mess of politics and getting all shot up . . . oh, Leonard, we'd better go look for him!"

"Brass ain't *comin'* home, way I heard it," Doug said. "He's headed for San Antone, swearing he'll never be jailed again."

Raney felt the blood drain from her face. "What if he can't travel? What if he's too weak . . ."

"Creed Sixkiller is after him now," Doug said. "He'll bring him back before morning. Creed says when he puts a man in jail, he's damn well gonna stay there until he stands before the judge."

"*Creed!* And Creed put him in jail in the first place! Why, he's betrayed us. We're neighbors, and he—"

Leonard interrupted her with a hard clasp of his hand around her upper arm and a polite offer of rest and water for Doug, who refused them with thanks and rode away. Raney tried to jerk away from Leonard.

"You've got to go find Brass," she said. "And you must hurry. I can*not* tell Papa this sorry tale. It'll kill him."

Leonard wouldn't let her go. He shook his head.

"With this late a start I couldn't catch him before Sixkiller does," he said. "He'll bring him back, and we'll have Brass out on bail before your father gets home."

"No! If Brass says he won't go back to jail, he won't," she said. "And if Creed says he'll bring him back, he will. There'll be another shooting if they meet up, Leonard. Brass'll get himself killed."

Raney tried again to pull away, but he pulled her closer.

"Calm down," he said. "Calm down right now."

"Let me go. I've got to fix you a pack of food and water," she said, hating the fact he wouldn't take his hands off her. "Or else I'll have to wake Etty so she can do it."

As she'd hoped, the mention of Etty loosened his grip.

Raney whirled on her heel and headed into the house.

Leonard followed and grabbed her by the shoulders before she'd crossed the parlor. She struggled to get free, but he held her still and looked straight into her eyes in the lamplight.

"Brassell has too much of a head start," he said—speaking slowly and firmly, as if speaking to a child. "I can't catch up with him."

He spoke as if she were too stupid to understand the situation. Fury swept through her on the heels of the fear.

"Creed is a faster, better shot," she said, mocking his condescending tone. "If *he* finds him first, Brass will end up dead. That would kill my papa."

She saw for the first time how Leonard's mouth

could set in a hard, straight line that looked as if it would never break. He was getting angry, too.

"I can*not* catch up with Brass," he said.

His fingers were biting into her flesh. They were surprisingly strong for a merchant who had soft, white hands. It made her frantic for her freedom.

Raney took a deep breath and forced herself to relax and smile up at him. She tilted her head prettily.

"Why, I know you can do anything at all you set your mind to, Leonard Gentry," she said. "And I know you want to do something good for my papa, since he helped you get your business started and extended Pleasant Hill's hospitality to you so we could get acquainted—ever since you came to Texas from Louisiana."

Leonard smiled back at her but he didn't say a word. That gave her hope.

"Papa's still deep in grief over Mama's passing," Raney went on, "and if he lost his son now, it wouldn't be long before we'd have to bury him, too."

Leonard loosened his grip on her shoulders to pat her on the back.

"Creed won't kill him," he said.

"Unless Brass tries to draw on him," she said. "Which Brass will, foolish boy that he is. If we could just get Brassell home and hide him, Papa would get this all straightened out."

Leonard appeared to be truly listening to her at last, so she rushed on.

17

"It'll spare Papa a terrible shock when he gets home if he can see Brass is safe," she said.

She felt the tears flood her eyes, but she wouldn't let them fall.

"My mama's gone," she said softly, "And I can't bear to lose my baby brother and my papa from a heart attack, too. You can be my hero, Leonard."

He smiled down at her, put his arms around her, and pulled her head to his chest. She forced herself not to resist because she seemed to be getting further with him by using charm instead of insistence.

"Your baby brother is grown enough to get himself involved in this mess of feuding," he said, as he stroked her hair.

That condescending tone and touch made her want to scream and run. But she controlled herself.

"All Brass was doing was defending himself from those hateful Chickenhawks," she said. "Why, if he shot anyone it was an accident, because Brassell is too vain to wear his eyeglasses most of the time and he has terrible aim. Everybody knows that. They shouldn't even have shot back at him."

Leonard chuckled at that. Good. She was making some progress.

"Creed knows that, too," she said, "and that's what makes me so mad at him for even arresting Brass. That and the fact he used to be a beau of mine."

Leonard pushed her away from him so he could stare down at her. "An *Indian* was courting you?"

"No, well . . . just for a very short time," she said, quickly. "But even so, he ought to have some consideration for my feelings."

She ran the tip of her fingers along the button placket of his shirt.

"He should be like you, Leonard," she said, even more softly. "*You* think about my feelings. Why, I know when you realize how much I want you to go after Brass, you'll do it."

He smiled.

"I'm thinking about your feelings, all right, Raney," he said. "I'm glad you realize that, because what I'm going to do is hold you in my arms all night long and comfort you and be with you until we get word that Brass is back in jail. Then I'll take you to town to see him."

The shock of those words in her ears made her put her hands on his chest and push back from him. He let her go.

"Well, you had *better* turn me loose," she said. "Another instant, and I'd get Etty in here to help me."

"Etty knows her place," he said. "I am your betrothed, Raney. I have a right to hold you and kiss you and comfort you."

"But you are not *married* to me," she said, "so you will not hold me all night long."

"Then I will not go after your brother," he said,

looking at her arrogantly as if he could snatch her back into his embrace at any moment, "and I will not get involved in this feud."

"You *wouldn't* be getting involved in it," she cried. "You would only be rescuing my brother."

"Who is on the run because of the feud."

She let the tears of frustration spill from her eyes.

"Leonard! Everyone would know you're family— or soon will be—and that you wouldn't be taking sides in the feud."

"Tears won't move me," he said. "And words won't, either. I have a store to run in town, a business for our future. I have no time to run all over the country looking for your hotheaded brother and no desire to alienate half my customers, either."

That just flew all over her. She stepped back and looked at him, her face heating fast with anger.

"I am appalled at your attitude," she cried. "I cannot believe that you would put your business before family, Leonard."

"It's *our* business, Raney. *That's* our business, and Brassell's actions aren't. He's nearly a grown man who makes his own decisions."

"But he's *wounded*. He's bleeding! He needs help and you're refusing to help him!"

"If he can escape from jail and head for San Antonio, his wound isn't serious."

Speechless with shock, Raney stared at him. Then she turned and ran for the stairs.

"I can't believe you are so heartless."

She threw the words back at him over her shoulder.

"Think about it," he said. "You'll see that I'm right."

Nothing would move him, she knew that now. And nothing would move her to ever feel the same about him again.

Although, at this moment, she couldn't have named one feeling that she'd had for him in the first place. When she had accepted his proposal of marriage, she had thought that she loved him, at least in a quiet kind of way. Papa approved of Leonard, and he was her own kind.

But he'd never made her thrill to his kisses the way Creed Sixkiller had done. And Creed surely wasn't heartless. He had been genuinely hurt when she'd refused him. *He* had feelings, at least, even if he was out there hunting down her brother like a dirty dog at this very moment.

She slammed the door of her room behind her, and the sharp clap it made gave her satisfaction even though it ran the risk of waking Etty in her small room at the back end of the hall. Maybe she *wanted* Etty to come to her, asking questions, because there were questions Raney certainly needed to ask her.

Something was wrong with Leonard, wasn't there? Her husband was supposed to love her enough to do anything for her, wasn't he? And, incidentally, he was supposed to love her enough not to be trying to hold her in his arms all night before the wedding.

She shivered. If he'd really wanted to comfort her, he would've gone to help Brass. Why, he might've even been planning to force some of his man's needs on her that Etty had warned her about. With no respect for the fact they weren't married!

But, even without that—what would the rest of her life be like if Leonard wouldn't accede to a request to save her brother's *life*, for heaven's sake? What was the *matter* with him? Couldn't he see that it would kill her papa if something happened to Brassell right on top of her mama's death six months ago?

She was *not* going to let that happen. She'd show Leonard!

Raney went to the armoire, pulled out her big reticule, and began to pack a few things.

When had she *ever* not been able to wrap a man around her little finger? Not since she failed to keep Creed Sixkiller on the string after Papa refused him her hand. Which, she finally realized, was an impossible thing to even try. She only did it for the challenge, since she always hated to let go of any of her beaux, but Creed had too much pride.

Well, she also did it because there was something so thrilling and dangerous about Creed, which was why she'd been infatuated with him way back when she was very young. But Papa had always said Indians weren't like white people. *And* Papa had said that Creed wasn't good enough for her because he was an Indian.

His rude behavior of putting Brass in jail only proved Creed's lack of breeding, and now this stubbornness about returning him to a cell showed his Indian blood, for sure. Didn't they always track their quarry relentlessly?

She had to admit, though, that *that* was really an individual trait of Creed's. He was well known for having no quit in him. The only thing he had ever quit was flirting with her.

It still miffed her a little that he never had smiled at her or danced with her or even looked directly at her at any social or play party after she had turned him down. And she had seen him several times, too, because the Sixkillers were invited everywhere, seeing as how many of the neighbors treated them just like everybody else.

Before she could talk herself out of actually going through with what she was thinking, Raney put a fresh blouse into her bag, picked out a jacket, and stuffed the gold coins she'd been saving since Christmas in the pocket. She wouldn't need to change into a riding skirt, since she'd have to take the buggy in case Brass wasn't able to ride, and she wouldn't need any more than this because she'd probably find him at Stoney Creek and have him home by daylight.

Just in case, though, she wanted a clean blouse. Etty scolded her sometimes, but Raney always, always had to have a freshly washed one every morning, even if she had only worn the first one since supper.

She lifted her chin. She *would* find Brass tonight. She would find him before Creed did, no matter what Leonard said.

Without even sitting down at her writing desk, Raney uncapped the inkwell, dipped her pen into it, and wrote a quick note. Then she blew out her lamp, tiptoed out of her room and down the stairs to the dining room, where she left the note on the table under Leonard's upside-down plate. She smiled. That would be a nice breakfast surprise for him before he went off to town to his *business*.

Chapter 2

Raney's anger surged as she slipped out the back door onto the moonlit gallery and let the door ease closed behind her.

She was insulted. How could Leonard be so crude and so heartless? If he *tried*, he wouldn't be able to find an excuse for his lack of gallantry—both in the implications he'd made and the refusal to go to Brass's rescue.

If Papa came home while she was gone, he would be *furious*. After all, a man was responsible for the safety of his betrothed, wasn't he? And whoever heard of *anyone* refusing to help his own future brother-in-law when he was in dire straits?

And for the sake of his *business*! If that didn't

sound like a Yankee storekeeper, or worse yet, a Carpetbagger, she didn't know what did.

She tiptoed across the plank flooring and down the steps, praying the dogs wouldn't bark. If Etty woke up now, she'd pitch such a fit, they'd hear her in the next county.

Raney picked up her skirts and, ignoring the flat stone path, ran straight across the grass to the separate kitchen building. It had lots of windows to let out the heat from the stove and the fireplace, but the moonlight didn't reach everywhere, and inside it was full of shadows.

Slightly spooky shadows, to tell the truth. Something shifted in the corner where the stove was and she jumped. Just a stove lid settling. She couldn't think about being scared, and she wouldn't. She'd think about finding her little brother and how fast she needed to get to him.

Feeling around in the top of the corner cupboard, she found a canteen and filled it at the pump. Hanging it on her shoulder with her reticule, she ran to the pie safe and dumped the leftover ham biscuits into the cloth Etty had used to cover them, stuffed the packet into her reticule, and was out the door.

She dashed across the kitchen yard and barn lot and into the stables where the horses roused from their dozing to nicker at her. The moon lit the entryway only. The darkness made her clumsy, but she threw her things into the buggy and fumbled it out into the beams of light before she took Tally from his stall.

Halfway through the hurried hitching up, tears of frustration stung her eyes, but she gritted her teeth and kept on going. Every minute counted, and she was not going to turn back now. If she hurried, surely she could get to Stoney Creek by the time Brass did.

He had been out of jail long enough for Douglas to ride to Pleasant Hill from town, yes, but surely she could catch him.

"You're an angel, Tally," she told the horse, who stood patiently between the shafts. "You know I've never done this before. Just hang on."

With trembling fingers she fastened every buckle of every chain and strap she could find and led the horse forward. She gave a great sigh of relief. The buggy came, too, and it appeared to be securely connected to the horse.

A quick satisfaction warmed her as she looped the lines around the brake handle. If she could hitch Tally up like that, surely she could drive and find Brass, too.

Raney climbed up over the wheel in the most un-ladylike way she could ever imagine but she didn't even care. It couldn't be helped. She had never gotten into a buggy without help before, either.

When she'd straightened her skirts under her and settled into place, she picked up the lines and smooched to Tally. He took off across the field at a

27

brisk road gait, ears up, happy to be out and going somewhere in the moonlight.

Raney smiled again. Who would ever have thought she was so resourceful? Why, she hadn't even known it herself! This would make Leonard sit up and take notice.

When they reached the road, Tally took the ditch at an angle that hardly jostled her at all, and before she knew it, they were up and rolling along, heading south, raising a cloud of dust behind them. Thank goodness, he was well trained and gentle. She could forget about him and concentrate on finding Brassell.

When they reached the Four Corners, she tugged on the left line, and Tally turned gracefully with a wide arc onto the San Antonio Road without breaking gait. Brass would take this way, she was sure, since it was the fastest way *and* the safest because the feuding Chickenhawks who weren't in jail would be roaming all the back roads of the county.

If only she could get ahead of Creed somehow and get to Brass before he did.

The light dimmed, and Raney looked up to see clouds drifting across the moon. They threw shadows that rose up out of the trees everywhere and reached across the road like dark fingers. The wind was rising, too.

She pulled her hat down more securely, then tucked the lines under her hip and sat on them so she could have both hands free to tie its braided straps under her chin. Actually, the breeze felt cool. She should have taken her shawl out of her bag, and her gloves, too. She was going to ruin her hands driving without them, but she didn't dare let go of the lines to put them on.

Tame as Tally was, the night might spook him.

A shiver ran through her. A tree branch from a big live oak hung low over the road up ahead, and for one, scary moment she'd thought she saw something—an animal—lying along it. Like a cougar, maybe, waiting to pounce.

Raney smooched Tally into a faster pace and deliberately made herself take in a deep, deep breath to try to slow the pounding of her heart. This was no time to be jumpy. Poor Brass was the one she should worry about, for he might be getting weak from his wound. What she had to do was watch for the place where the Stoney Creek trail met the San Antonio Road.

Another smooch to Tally and they were moving even faster through the moonlight, which had defeated the clouds for the moment. It wasn't very far now, she knew it. She tried to judge exactly how much farther it would be but she'd never paid attention to things like that before.

Raney began scanning the road, watching it a good distance ahead, looking for landmarks that would tell her she was coming up on the low hill that hid the bridge from this direction. The wind rose even more. It rattled the branches of the trees and made mysterious noises in the brush.

She rounded a bend and saw she was almost to the tall sycamore tree where people often stopped to rest in the shade. It wasn't far to the creek now, because that tree stood at the foot of the hill.

"It won't be long now, Tally," she said, just for the comfort of hearing her own voice. "We'll find Brass and then we'll all go home."

A mounted man rode out from the dark shadow of the tree. Rode right out into the middle of her way.

Her heart lurched, then stopped. Brass? Could it be Brass? But surely not, if he had followed the creek. He would've turned the opposite way when he got to the road.

The rider sat there, silent, waiting. Tally's hooves and Raney's heart were all pounding like hammers. Panicked, she sawed on the lines, trying to stop before she got to him. He must be a highwayman.

"Whoa, Tally," she called, "whoa, now."

Then she changed her mind. She couldn't turn around fast in the narrow road. She didn't even know how to turn a buggy around at all. There always was the danger of tipping it over. She would race past him.

Raney straightened up in the seat, grasped the lines in a death grip, and brought them down on the horse's back.

"Hi *ya!*" she shouted, as she'd heard Ned, her driver, do.

She was shaking all over inside but frozen on the outside, clinging to the lines for dear life. And Tally, *gentle* Tally, ran a little way, then shied, reared, and jerked the buggy sideways behind him, throwing one wheel into the ditch.

In spite of trying not to, she screamed, and that made Tally panic even more. When his front feet came back to earth, he was all over the place, kicking at the traces and scrabbling for footing, slipping and sliding on the wet grass, half into the ditch himself.

Through all the commotion, she could hear hoofbeats coming toward her, and that made her tighten up even more.

"Raney! Cut him some slack."

The deep voice, the sound of her name with the accompanying shock that the rider knew who she was—and the knowledge that it wasn't Brass—all rushed through her at the same time. Creed. It was Creed.

Something—an unseemly excitement—sprang to life in the pit of her stomach. She squashed it. This was no time to remember the times she'd walked out with him into the night air. When it smelled of honeysuckle. Or of dried sage and cedar in the winter.

She'd found Creed instead of Brass. Creed was no longer that dangerous young man whose kisses melted her into her shoes. He was her enemy now.

31

"Stop it," he ordered. "Let the lines go loose."

For a minute, her hands wouldn't listen to her mind, and then they did. Only then, when her arms went slack, did she realize how hard she'd been jerking on poor Tally.

Creed rode up and took her horse by the bridle. Tally stood suddenly still, trembling.

"What the *hell* are you doing out here?" Creed said.

"Turn loose of my horse," she said, surprised that she could even talk with her blood rushing so fast and her lips stiff. "You scared the *life* out of me."

He clucked to Tally and started backing his own mount, murmuring low, coaxing Tally to come with him. The buggy canted sideways so that she was nearly falling out the low side, but Creed pulled it right on up out of the ditch, and none too gently, either. Once both wheels were on the road, he rode in a semicircle, still leading Tally, and straightened her out.

With Tally's head pointed back the way they had come.

That just flew all over her. She slapped the ends of the lines against her leather seat in frustration.

"Creed Sixkiller, you make me so mad! You've got me headed the wrong way now and I don't know how to turn this buggy around."

"You're headed right. Go home."

He was wheeling his horse around as he spoke.

"I will *not*. And you leave my brother alone. You

have no right whatsoever to be locking him in jail in the first place, much less be chasing him down to put him back in there."

"No right?"

He was so cold. She'd never heard his voice so cold—except when he said "never" to her the last time they parted. Well, she could be cold, too.

"Our families have been neighbors for years and years," she said evenly. "Brass being jailed at your hand is unacceptable—"

"Neighbor doesn't mean the same as friend," he said, and in the shadows she could see the flash of white from his eyes. "You and your pa taught me that."

Raney sucked in a quick breath and bit her lip.

"It's extremely rude of you to bring that up," she said. "This is different."

"Yes," he snapped. "It is. That was personal. This is the whole county. If we don't get some law and order here, we're all sunk."

"Well, you're taking the law into your own hands, and all Brass is doing is trying to get better people elected to make the laws."

"Brass is part of a band of murdering thieves. I'm riding at the request of the law-abiding people of Limestone County. The ones who have a grain of sense, the ones who haven't succumbed to the bloodlust that's driving this damn feud."

"I don't appreciate that kind of language," she

said, her anger rising at his calling Brass blood-thirsty. "Why, the very idea! You're no gentleman, Creed."

"Of course not. I'm an Indian, remember?"

With that, and without so much as a by-your-leave, he loped off down the road toward San Antonio, toward the creek where Brass would come out from the trail.

Her heart started beating like a hammer. She had to get there before Creed and warn her brother.

It was the hardest thing she'd ever done, but she did it. She pulled on the line to turn Tally around, her blood pushing hard against her skin, her heartbeat urging hurry, but knowing she would be in dire straits if she didn't take enough time so as not to go into the ditch again.

She backed the buggy and drove it forward and backed it again until she had it headed south. That victory poured delight into her blood to mix with the anger. If she could do that, what else might she be able to do if she had to?

"Get *up*," she called to Tally, and they rolled after Creed at a fast, rattling trot.

He, too, would figure that Brass would come from town on the trail that followed the creek. When they were little, all the Childress and Sixkiller children had played up and down Stoney Creek. Obviously, Creed had been lying in wait for Brass when he'd heard her rig coming down the road.

34

She would warn Brass. She would lie in wait, too, and as soon as she heard him in the brush beneath the bridge, she'd call out to him.

The moonlight caught Creed as he topped the hill, then he vanished. She urged Tally faster, and when she rode over the hill herself, he still was nowhere in sight.

He was lurking again, no doubt, ready to pounce. He could lurk all he wanted but it would do him no good. She would ruin his little trap. She smooched to Tally and went careening down the hill straight to the end of the bridge, where she drove off the road just to the edge of the brush where the moonlight hardly reached.

Yes, Creed was hidden. There was no sign that anyone was there.

She listened. The creek running was the only sound.

The moon went behind a cloud, and the darkness deepened.

Then, a little way down the creek, she saw a flash of light, like a firefly in among the brush. But it was way too late for the lightning bugs to be out.

She stared at the small light dancing low in the dark among the branches. It disappeared, and hard as she looked, she didn't see it again.

Raney deepened her breathing and tried to think. It was probably the glow of a match. Someone was using the light to find the way—or maybe to look for tracks.

Yes. It might be Creed, looking for Brass's tracks. If so, he must be pretty sure that Brass had already come this way.

But what if it wasn't Creed?

True fear came over her. She wanted to scream, she needed to yell for Brassell, she even wanted to call Creed to her, hateful thing that he was. She was *alone*. She needed somebody *with* her. Right now.

She had not even had the presence of mind to bring matches, whether for a light to see by or for building a fire. Why hadn't she taken a thought or two before she jumped up and left home in the middle of the night?

Because she was always used to somebody doing things for her. And now here she was, with no help at all. Creed was being so rude and he wouldn't help her, especially now that she'd disobeyed his order to go home.

The truth hit her like a lightning bolt. She was out here now where she was going to have to do everything for herself.

Raney stood up and tried to see into the darkness on down the creek. She held her breath and listened for the sound of Brassell's horse walking on the rocky bank or the splash of his hooves in the water.

She turned to look down the road, hoping for a glimpse of something moving that might be Brassell, if he had already come by here. Once she thought she saw something, but then it was gone and she couldn't be sure.

So she turned, on her weakening knees, and tried to see into the darkness all around her. Tally gave a big shudder and blew out a long breath like a sigh. Somehow the sound of it made her shiver, too.

She dropped back onto the seat and forced herself to sit still. What should she do? Go on down the road in case Brass was already on it, or stay here hoping he would come?

What if she waited here all the night long and he never came? What if she went on toward San Antonio and he fell into Creed's hands?

"Raney."

She let out a yelp because it scared her badly, but she knew in the same instant it was Creed. She clamped her lips together and cut off the scream, so as not to give him the satisfaction of scaring her a second time as he materialized out of the dark right by the buggy, so close that she could have touched him.

"You can't scare me away from my brother," she said.

He kept his back to her and walked into the brush not a stone's throw away from her. It wasn't two heartbeats until he came back leading his horse. It scared her even more to realize she'd been here that close to his mount and she hadn't known it. Why, he or any other man could've been sitting right there on that horse unbeknownst to her. Wasn't it Tally's job to whinny at another horse?

"Your brother's gone," Creed said, as he stopped, parted his reins, and brought them back on each side of the horse's neck to the saddle horn. "He got past me. Go home. I'm not going to be responsible for you."

"I wouldn't *let* you take care of me if you tried," she said, anger and fear flowing through her like ice water. "How do you know he's gone?"

She picked up the lines. If Creed was leaving, so was she.

Her arms and hands were so tired they ached. The narrow strips of leather seemed far heavier than before. She'd never known driving was such work.

"Fresh tracks of a pacing horse," he said. "It's Brass, all right."

He stuck his toe in the stirrup and mounted.

"What if you're just telling me that to make me go home? I know Indians are supposed to be the best trackers, so you'd probably know a pacing horse tracks if you saw some, but Papa says y'all are tricky, too."

The words sounded so harsh and ugly that she clamped her mouth shut. She was miles and miles from another human being, and Creed Sixkiller *was* known as a dangerous man.

But he settled into his saddle and took up his reins without any change in his expression. It was a good

38

thing the moon floated free right then and she could see his face, or she'd really have been worried.

"Hmm," he said, sounding as if he were talking to himself. "So that's what Papa thinks."

He said it without the slightest resentment or even real interest in his voice. Carelessly. As if what Papa thought didn't make one bit of difference.

"Cherokee women are taught from the minute they're born to think for themselves," he said. "Women have always run our clans and held authority in our councils. A long time ago, they even fought in our wars if they wanted to."

That remark surprised Raney so much she just sat there. Cherokee women decided everything for themselves? They didn't care what their papas thought?

Then she realized he was moving out, and she turned the buggy to follow him. He looked back at her.

"Don't *even* say it," she said, "because I'm not going home. I'm not letting you out of my sight. You won't catch Brass if I can help it."

"You'll play hell trying to keep up," he said, and rode up onto the bridge.

He crossed it at a long trot that echoed against the rock wall of the hill.

She took out after him, clucking to Tally, who was trying his best not to start working again so soon. In fact, he kept turning his head toward home as if he wanted to go back to his stall, and he went so slow that she had to pop the whip twice. They hit the north end of the bridge just as Creed left the south end.

Raney lifted the lines and brought them down hard and used the noise of the whip to make Tally race after Creed. He was already out of sight.

When she rounded the next bend, though, there he was, waiting for her in the road. She slowed.

"If you don't stop laying in wait for me like some stubborn ghost—"

He interrupted her. "At this pace, you'll kill that old horse," he said. "Raney, show some common sense."

Creed glared at her as if that could drive her away. In the moonlight, his face was dark and shadowy beneath the brim of his hat, but she knew exactly how it looked. Papa would rant and rave if she said it out loud, but Creed Sixkiller was the handsomest man she'd ever seen, even when he was glaring.

This was the showdown, and she knew it. He was under control now, but he was really angry. She had to think, fast, and keep him talking, or he was liable to ride off and leave her for good. Tally was too old and the buggy too clumsy to keep up with Creed's horse.

"I'll go on to San Antonio," she said, "but you needn't feel any responsibility for me. I can manage just fine."

40

"No, you can't," he snapped. "You don't know a huckster from a preacher from a pickpocket."

"Our family has friends there," she lied. "I'll go to them."

"You couldn't *get* to them," he said. "You'll attract every lowdown road agent, reprobate, and outlaw along the way."

"Well! I don't know quite how to take that," she said. "Are you saying I look like a woman of questionable repute?"

"What you look like to any of those *cabrons* is a country girl who's never been off the farm," he said.

"*What?* Why, I've been to Memphis. And to Fort Worth twice, and—"

He chopped his hand through the air to silence her. He listened, then turned the other way to listen some more.

Raney's heart began to thunder in her ears. She listened, too, but she couldn't hear a thing but a breeze in the leaves of the grove of mulberry trees and brush alongside the road. That and some night birds calling.

Creed rode closer to the buggy. "Move over," he said.

Before the command could really sink in for her, he stepped from his stirrup onto the seat of the buggy. She had to scoot over or be stepped on.

"What are you *doing*?"

"Be quiet."

He sat down on the seat beside her, tied his mount

41

to the whip holder, and took the lines from her un-suspecting hands.

It changed the whole world. Not just because he took control of her horse and her vehicle, but because he was Creed and he was so close that he filled up all the space with his big body and his big presence.

He was always like that. Creed didn't talk a lot or charm everyone like his brother Eagle Jack, but wherever Creed was, he took command.

"Get out of my buggy right now," she said, grab-bing to take back the lines.

But his hands were like iron, and they were huge and in charge. Her efforts had no more effect on them than two mosquitoes flitting around and land-ing on the leather he held between his fingers.

"Somebody's out there," he said. "Be still."

Her heart stopped, first with fear and then again with hope. Could it be Brass?

"I don't hear anything," she said.

"Those 'birds' aren't whip-poor-wills calling," he said. "Let's see who they are."

Only then did she hear the muffled beat of horses' hooves against the ground. Creed murmured to Tally, the buggy's wheels slowly creaked, and they drove into the grove of trees.

As soon as they were hidden from the road, he stopped and listened some more. She leaned toward him to try to hear what he heard and bumped the hard bulk of the holstered six-shooter he wore on his hip.

Oh, Lord, please don't let him shoot Brass with that gun.

"If it's Brassell, don't try to warn him," he said, his words so low and quiet that she thought at first she'd imagined them. "He'll be jumpy, and you know I'm a faster draw."

He was right. The first thing Brass would do if she startled him would be go for his gun. Surely, since he was traveling alone, he'd be wearing his glasses. Too vain to wear them when others were around, he usually carried them in his pocket. Maybe the better vision would give him a fighting chance, if it came to that.

But what if it was someone else they knew and that person saw them? Would word get out that she was out in the countryside, unchaperoned, buggy riding in the middle of the night with an Indian? Would people think she and Creed were courting, taking advantage of the fact that Papa was gone to Fort Worth?

They might. Some girls' papas didn't forbid the Sixkiller men to come calling, and some of their mamas encouraged it because the Sixes and Sevens was a big, important ranch. But for other neighbors who thought as Papa did, this could be worse on her reputation than Leonard in the house and no chaperone but Etty.

The wind moved in the trees again, but Creed sat remarkably still. Raney heard the hoofbeats again, but she couldn't tell if they had come closer or not.

This was such an irony. First she'd been determined not to let Creed out of her sight so she could help Brass, and now here she was his captive wanting to get away so she could help her brother.

It would be terrible if this rider really *was* poor, unsuspecting, wounded Brass and Creed shot him and she *hadn't* warned him. She would never get over that.

Raney lifted her chin, and her determination hardened. No matter what Creed said or did, she had to help her brother. Why else had she come out here in the middle of the night and got herself into this mess?

She'd risked Leonard's and Etty's wrath, harnessed her own horse, drove her own buggy, and even turned it around in the road in order to help her little brother. If she could do all that, she could warn Brass and save him, too. She would grab Creed's arm if he tried to draw his gun and yell at Brass to ride away as fast as he could.

If Brass escaped, she'd have to stay with Creed, though, to try to stop him from keeping on with the search. Creed was the one who never quit. That's why everyone always said he was the most dangerous of the Sixkiller brothers.

He was dangerous, all right. His closeness was invading her, filling her with his scent, the one masculine aroma that was Creed underneath the smells of dust and horse and leather. It stirred up her whole body, just the way his kisses had done so long ago, and it made her feel weak and helpless.

His thigh pressed against hers now, his heat reaching her skin even through her skirts. He shifted his heel to get purchase on the footboard, and the gun bumped her again. But all she really felt was his long, hard saddle muscles flexing against her leg.

That touch went all through her. It made her want something, though she didn't quite know what.

She scooted away from him, to the very end of the seat. She had to be thinking about Brass and saving him from jail, not about Creed Sixkiller and what sitting next to him did to her senses.

But she had to be close enough to spoil his aim, no matter how furious that might make him. As she moved back toward him, he handed the lines to her.

"I'll keep the horses quiet," he said.

Her heart dropped when he stood up, stepped over to the hub of the wheel and then to the ground, all without making a sound. Now all she could do for Brassell was yell a warning and let him draw and get shot.

Creed untied his horse, led it to Tally, and stood with an arm around each of their muzzles. He watched the road through the screen of trees. Raney stood up in the buggy and tried to see, too.

The hoofbeats were coming closer, hitting fast and hard against the road in an uneven rhythm. A horse came into view, a black shape in the moonlight. The rider appeared to be taller and thinner than Brassell.

He stopped and turned as the whip-poor-will sounded again. He answered with the same call. A second rider came out of the brush on the opposite side of the road.

"No sign of 'im?" the first one asked.

He kept his voice low, but Raney could still make out the words.

"Not yit," said the other, in a normal tone, "but we soon will. Danny Wayne's searchin' the creekbed now, and when he finds some more tracks, we'll be hot on his trail. That little Childress whelp will never see sunup."

The ugly words knocked Raney's knees out from under her. She dropped back onto the seat, clapping her hand over her mouth to keep from crying out.

Why, these men were out to kill her brother, and they didn't hesitate to say so, right out loud! How foolish she'd been all this time—thinking that Creed was the only danger to him.

The Chickenhawks talked to each other a little more, unaware that Creed was listening, then they turned their horses' heads toward Stoney Creek. To help Danny Wayne or whatever his name was try to find Brass's tracks and then go kill him, no doubt.

Creed gathered his reins and stepped back to his stirrup. He looked at Raney.

"Keep your head down," he said, and mounted.

"Hey, Chickenhawks," he yelled. "Creed Six-killer here. Hold up. I want to talk to you."

Through the moving leaves of the trees, Raney saw the two men halt and stiffen. They turned their horses around, toward the sound of his voice.

Creed's horse was moving at a fast trot, but still in the cover of the trees.

"Think about it," he yelled. "I can kill you both before you can draw. Hands up."

Raney had to lean over to see between the branches. Both men had their hands on their guns, but as she watched, they slowly lifted their arms into the air.

Creed rode toward them and stopped with only a few yards of the road in between.

"Take your feud and go home," he said. "Y'all don't want to tangle with me."

"You're outta Limestone County, now, Sixkiller," one of the Chickenhawks said. "You got no authority when you're over the line."

"I just overheard you two plotting cold-blooded murder," Creed said. "That's against the law all over Texas."

One of the men made the mistake of reaching for his gun. He was fast, or so it seemed to Raney, because his gun was out and gleaming in the moonlight before she even realized he had reached for it, but Creed shot the six-shooter right out of his hand before he had time to fire. The man squealed like a

47

stuck pig and dropped his other arm to grab his hand up against his stomach.

"Next one is through your heart," Creed said. "Your choice."

There was no doubt he meant it. He sounded mean and cold and heartless. She believed he would kill them.

The Chickenhawks must have thought so, too, because they turned tail and left at a high lope. The dust clouds they raised hung in the moonlight for a moment or two before the wind blew them away. Creed watched until they were all gone before he turned and rode back to Raney through the trees.

"You'll have to travel with me," he said, and she could hear the irritation in his voice. "Those Chickenhawks want your brother bad."

"No," she said. "They've gone home now."

He shot her a disgusted glance as he rode up to Tally and untied him from the tree.

"Only two of them have gone," he said. "We don't know how many more are scattered all over this country hunting for Brass."

"I can take care of myself."

"What's your objection? It hasn't been thirty minutes since you promised not to let me out of your sight."

Her stomach was turning as fast as her mind. She was accustomed to having someone take care of her. She didn't want to be alone on the road in the night. Yet Creed would have shot that man through the heart without blinking an eye.

She'd heard it said before, but she'd never really believed it until now. Creed Sixkiller *was* a dangerous man.

Chapter 3

Scared or not, Raney had no choice because now it was Creed not letting *her* out of *his* sight. He took her horse by the bridle and led him up onto the road, headed for San Antonio, then put his mount into a trot, so Tally would follow.

Her arms felt like lead when she took over the lines. Her bottom was aching to get off the buggy seat. She would tell Papa that they should get a softer padding for it and maybe a thinner leather over it because her haunches felt blistered, too, even through her skirts and petticoats.

"Keep him moving," Creed said, in a voice full of impatient aggravation.

"Go on if that's the way you feel," she said. "I can take care of myself."

"Have some sense," he snapped, and took off down the road.

The buggy swayed on the rough places and whacked rocks with its wheels, and Tally moved right along with Creed as outrider. But it wasn't any time until Tally began thinking about his stall again and trying to slow down.

When she smooched to him to keep him going, her parched lips stuck together. She lifted the lines and brought them down on his back.

"Slow *down*," she called to Creed. To her dismay, her voice cracked. Her throat was as dry as her lips.

Creed dropped back to ride beside her.

"We're exposed out here on the road in the moonlight," he said. "We're moving targets."

"We're going too fast to look for Brass. He could be right near here somewhere, too exhausted or hurt to go any farther."

"He's not."

Creed rode on ahead, slapping Tally on the rump with his hat as he passed.

Hateful, hateful, hateful. There was no way he could know that—not while they were flying down this road like their hair was on fire. He hadn't given up on finding Brass, or they'd be going in the opposite direction.

What was he *doing*?

He was keeping a close eye on her, Raney was sure, making certain she kept up the pace. He motioned for her to come on, drive faster, and she slapped the lines on Tally's back. Once. Her arms were too sore to do it again.

Her head ached. She'd been jolting around, stuck in this buggy, for what seemed like hours and days.

What in the world was she doing, letting Creed take over like this? But what could she do about it? Escape when she got a chance, that was all. And she probably should wait until they got to a town because he could catch up to her easy as anything.

She was so tired she thought she would fall off the seat and into the middle of the road. Maybe if she did, Creed would stop, but then again, maybe not.

Raney shifted on the seat and let the lines slide a little looser through her hands. Her right palm had a sharp, raw pain. A blister! Oh, dear mercy, she had a blister and it would leave a *callus* on her hand. Mama would have a fit.

Then she remembered. Mama was gone. Gone to heaven. Tears filled her eyes and then more tears. Grief, frustration, and exhaustion all claimed her at once and she wanted to cry. She wanted to cry and wail and scream and pitch a fit the way she used to do when she was a tiny little girl.

She clamped her jaw shut, took off her hat to get rid of the strings tied under her chin, and turned to reach behind her for her reticule. A drink of water might help. Putting on her gloves might help.

The lines sagged heavy in her lap. Tally slowed from a fast trot to a walk and meandered toward the right. That back wheel crunched off the road into the lumpy patches of grass and then up onto it again.

Creed was there in front of her face when she turned around.

"What's wrong?" he said.

"Nothing."

She turned away from him and fumbled with the cap of the canteen.

"Go on," she said, fighting the tears. "Don't let me slow you down."

"You can't do this," he said.

"Do what?"

"Drive so far. You're accustomed to being driven."

"I'm *accustomed* to getting what I want," she said baldly, in a terrible breach of good manners, "and I want my brother. I'll do anything to find him."

Brave words. Her hands were as shaky as her voice.

She finally got the stubborn stopper out. Turning up the canteen to drink directly out of it, since she did not have a cup or a dipper, she let the cool water run down her throat. It did make her feel better but she was nearly at the end of her rope. Her whole arm was shaking as she drank.

If she'd had to work all her life like Etty's daughter did, she'd be much more able to do something like this. Clearly, a lady couldn't deal with *every* situation solely through her appearance, charm, and grace.

"We'll have to stop till daylight."

Creed sounded disgusted and angry and disappointed. Well, good. Maybe Brass would escape from him if he had the rest of the night to flee.

What a good idea! Maybe she'd been wrong. Maybe she *could* deal with this problem of Creed and save Brass by using her charm and grace to delay Creed. And her wits. Creed never did take suggestions very well.

"Don't stop on my account," she said, and drew her handkerchief from her pocket to wet it from the canteen. "Go on ahead and see if you can find Brass. I want his wound to be seen to, no matter who does it."

Surely he wouldn't obey.

She touched the wet, fine cloth to her wrists and temples, then held it against the blister on her hand. It stung like fire.

"Don't be ridiculous," he snapped. "I can't leave any woman of my acquaintance defenseless on the road."

Worried as she was about Brass, that stung her pride.

"*Any* woman?" she cried. "I'm no more than *any* woman? Once you said you loved me, Creed Sixkiller!"

He was already turning his horse away.

"I was mistaken," he said.

That cut her even worse.

She picked up the lines, although she had to force her arms to move. They felt like they might be going numb.

She wished her heart would, too. No one had ever been so rude to her as to take back a declaration of love.

"*All* my old beaux still love me," she said. "They tell me so."

"More fools they," he said.

She bit her lip. "You're just jealous, Creed," she said coolly. "All my old beaux are jealous, too."

He glanced back over his shoulder as he motioned for her to follow him off the road into a trail that angled off to the west.

"Jealous of what?" he drawled. "Luther or Lycurgus or whatever your storekeeper's name is?"

"It's Leonard," she said haughtily. "You know that as well as I do."

"Hardly," he said. "This may come as a shock to you, Raney, but I give very little thought to the names of your beaux."

"I only have one, now," she said primly. "Leonard and I are betrothed."

The sound of her fiancé's name brought her no comfort, though. She didn't even want to think about him. Leonard's unacceptable behavior was

what had put her in this miserable spot to begin
with.

"And I'll have you know I'm not defenseless.
Papa keeps a weapon in every vehicle, and there's a
gun right here underneath my seat."

"That's good," he said sarcastically, "since I'm
sure you know how to use it. Your stubbornness is
going to get you in big trouble someday, Raney."

"That's the pot calling the kettle black," she
cried, leaning away from some branches trying to
reach into the buggy from beside the overgrown
trail. "*Your* stubbornness is beyond the pale. The
very idea of hounding poor Brass to the ends of the
earth while he's bleeding to death!"

The moon went behind a cloud, making the narrow trail suddenly very dark. The thought of not
finding Brass soon enough to take him home before
daylight, the recollection of that perilous intent in
Creed's voice when he threatened the Chickenhawks, and the heavy aches and pains from one end
of her body to the other, all combined with the
night's blackness to send despair washing over her.

"Where are you taking me?"

"Don't worry," he said dryly, "your virtue is safe
with me."

She felt herself blushing and was thankful for the
dark. But then, she needn't worry. He couldn't have
any way of knowing the feelings that had surged
through her when he was sitting beside her.

"I'm not worrying," she said. "I'm only trying to think for myself."

He laughed. It was only a short, low grunt of a chuckle—or maybe it was a rude snort.

"This is still the Sixes and Sevens," he said. "I know a good place to camp in the bend of Bad Horse Creek."

Panic struck her. Had she made the wrong choice in trying to hold Creed back here long enough for Brass to escape?

"I thought we were only going to rest a little while," she said, "not camp and build a fire or anything."

"Right. But I'm talking about a safer place than the side of the road, and it's not far."

But going there would, no doubt, be going away from Brassell. Tired as she was, now the thought of leaving his trail seemed like deserting him. She felt torn about what she should do, and she was too tired to think.

"Oh," she said, fighting back a sudden sob, "I hope Brass isn't out there bleeding on the side of the road."

"Hardly," Creed said.

He sounded so callous it made her furious.

"You don't *know*," she said.

"I do if he hasn't managed to get in another scrape since I've seen him."

"Did you see any blood back there on the ground by his horse's tracks?"

"Raney," he snapped, "your foolish little brother didn't bleed a thimbleful when that bullet grazed him."

She wanted to clap her hand over her heart in relief but it was too much trouble. Her strength was gone and her stiff, tired fingers seemed forever frozen around the lines.

Then she thought about his tone of voice.

"You don't have to sound so disappointed that Brass wasn't shot all to pieces," she said.

Her voice broke on the last word.

"He thought he was," Creed said.

That disdainful dismissal roused her fury.

"You listen to me, Creed Sixkiller. Anything that breaks the skin can kill a person, and I cannot bear it if anybody else in our family dies right now. Mama's only been gone six months and we all miss her so much we can't stand it."

She began truly to cry, then, although she tried her best to do it without making a sound.

"I'm sorry for the loss of your mother, Raney," he said. His words rushed out as if to be done with it. "And I'll do my very best not to kill your brother."

Creed's low voice stirred her, way down deep, the way it used to do. Because she heard the edge of his sincerity beneath his impatience. Creed was honest to a fault, she'd always known that. He didn't say things he didn't mean.

He didn't want to admit it, but he meant to comfort her. He empathized with her feelings.

Which was more than she could say for Leonard.

Creed sat beneath the live oak tree, leaning back against his saddle propped against its trunk, waiting for dawn. The dark had given way enough that he could see Raney's small, sleeping form outlined underneath the buggy. He put her there to keep the dew off and give her a little protection, since she probably had never slept in the open before. Even while traveling, he knew her family always purchased accommodations, and always the best ones available.

Her parents had spoiled her and the boys, too. Brassell and Trent both were in this feud up to their necks, and probably neither could even say what it was all about. Politics, yes, but neither side of that fight knew what they believed in—except that they hated the other.

Well, it had fallen to him to put an end to it. Limestone County was full of good men who had worked for years to build their ranches—his folks foremost among them. They had added to the original Sixes and Sevens until the ranch spilled over into three counties, but its headquarters and the majority of the land was in Limestone County. They would have law and order there or the judge would call for a contingent of Texas Rangers. Creed didn't want that. He was the one who had started putting an end to this lawlessness, and his pride demanded that he be the one to finish it.

Right this minute, though, he wished he'd never heard of the feud. He wished he were at home in the rambling log and stone big house on the headquarters of the Sixes and Sevens, gathered around the breakfast table with his parents and his grandfather and his two sisters and his sister-in-law, Susanna; and her husband, who was his brother Eagle Jack; and his five unmarried brothers. They were all back there, dressed in fresh, starched clothes and booted and spurred, eating biscuits and sausage and gravy, drinking strong coffee, laughing and talking and lining out the work for the day.

And here he was, out in the middle of nowhere with no breakfast, saddled with the care of the most difficult girl in Texas, going down a long, long road. Sometimes life just wasn't even nearly fair.

But he was no quitter. He had no choice but to give it all he had. If he put a man in jail, he aimed for him to stay there.

He reached for his gear bag. The faintest, palest touch of color was coming to the sky. It was time to go to water.

The thought of using the power of his people to find a Childress made his lips curve in an ironic smile. It was Robert Childress's prejudice against

Indians that had turned Creed to his purpose of becoming the best man he could be, and also the most Indian.

If it hadn't been for Robert's and Raney's rejections he might never have started studying Cherokee lore and history, never mind the medicine, with his grandfather. Their scorn of Indians had made him want to truly live in the Indian way, and now that knowledge might be the way that he could bring Brassell back to them.

He stood up and reached to the bottom of the soft leather pouch for the Grandfather Medicine, the twist of specially grown tobacco his grandfather had given him. His hand closed around it.

Before he left he glanced at Raney again. The ceremony had to be done without an observer. She surely wouldn't wake until he was done, since she'd been exhausted enough to go to sleep leaning against a tree while she waited for him to stake the horses.

She had barely known it when he carried her to his bedroll spread out for her. The foolish woman had brought none of her own.

For a heartbeat or two, he couldn't take his eyes away from her. She lay still as a wounded bird, looking even smaller than she was. That's what she was, a wounded bird, with her mother gone and her brothers in trouble. He didn't know if she had the strength to recoup.

But he couldn't let himself think about what she needed over time. That wasn't any of his responsibility. His obligation to her was only temporary and had to do only with her physical safety, not with the state of her mind or her feelings. He'd have to take care of her all the way to San Antonio, but once he delivered her to her friends there, he would be done with her.

Here he was, still on the Sixes and Sevens with a long, slow trip ahead of him, not to mention a long search in a big town. He was sure he would already have Brassell Childress in hand and be on his way back to the Concho jail with him if he'd been free to ride all night. He had wanted to ride off and leave Raney on the road but there was no way he could have done that.

Creed's mother's father, Standing Bear, believed everything happened for a reason. Creed was coming to believe that, too. He turned and began walking toward the sound of the creek running over its rocky bed. Dawn was the time in the day when the curtain between the natural and the supernatural was thinnest and men could send the creative power of their minds into the spiritual realm.

He walked quickly, half by old memory of the terrain and half by the growing gray light, to a spot on the curving bank that faced exactly east, then he strode out into the water, feeling with his bare feet through its coldness for the smoother stones, reaching with his toes for purchase to step on them.

When the current rose to run just below his knees, he stopped. This would be the deepest for this creek, except in times of flash flood.

First, he held his face to the sun and blew the night out of his lungs. Then he breathed the early morning into his body, again and again, willing his mind to clear, also. He began to dwell on the state of being he wanted to augment. Peace. Peace and power for peace.

He waited, as Standing Bear had taught him, letting the generative strength of his mind begin to focus. He smelled the water and the dew-damp grass, he listened to rustlings of small animals in the woods, he felt the thick, braided plug of magical tobacco with his fingertips and rolled it in the palm of his hand. He tasted the hint of cedar in the air and looked up at the flowing, changing, moving colors of the sky.

Creed held up the tobacco to the rising sun and began the old incantation. Its purpose was to strengthen the arm of the law. He would say it four times. Once the tobacco was remade, he would bathe in its water, blow his breath on it and then mix it with his saliva, the very essence of his life force.

He spoke in the ancient language of his people.

"Now! Listen! Little Red Hawks! Very quickly all of You fly so no one can climb over.

"He hides and goes through the treetops.

"Now! Big Red Hawks! Here, here, here! I come trailing him.

"Now! You come to show him to me right now in the Hawk places, I will be saying. His clan is Childress. His name is Brassell."

Creed held his arms to the sky and filled his eyes with the red glow of color beginning in the east. Very red, the color of victory.

Raney heard Creed's voice and dropped her hands, spilling the last of the water she was using to wash her face. She scrambled to get up off her knees to look for him. This was embarrassing. Had he been this close when she came into the bushes for lack of an outhouse? Surely not.

And someone was with him! Who could he be talking to? He sounded very near, but she couldn't make out the words he was saying.

Maybe he'd found Brass! Could it be possible that her brother had chosen the same creek to rest beside in the night?

She began to work her way toward the sound of his voice, trying to move quietly, so as to see them before they saw her. This was still the Sixes and Sevens, he'd said, even though it was a different county. Maybe some of Creed's family had come out here.

She had a sharp, yearning wish that it would be his sister Maggie. She and Maggie had been friends since they were children and even more so since they'd grown up. But for these three years since Papa had refused Creed's offer for Raney's hand, she and Maggie had no longer been close. Maggie had taken Raney's refusal to marry Creed as an insult, and after she had told Raney that, she wouldn't talk to Raney anymore.

Creed *was* very near. As she came out of the trees at the bend of the creek, she saw him.

She stared. He was alone. And he was standing out in the middle of the water. Naked! No, but nearly. He wore a leather breechcloth with a beaded design on it.

He was looking at the sky, straight into the pink and purple streaks of the dawn, holding his arms open to the new sun. Its light reflected off his wet skin like tiny flames off a copper candleholder. He held something up in one hand.

The sight of him like that stopped her breath in her throat. He was so beautiful. His muscles flexed and moved beneath his skin like powerful, knotted ropes. In his arms and shoulders and across his back, they looked big enough for him to lift the world.

His stance shifted, then, and turned his profile to her. The sun limned the chiseled bones of his face, the strongest face she'd ever seen, and showed the line of his hard jaw and the jut of his high cheekbone over the arrogant arch of his nose. She'd been right every time she ever thought he was the handsomest man in the world.

No one else was there. He was talking to the sky, in what must be his Cherokee Indian language. She had heard some Spanish in town and on the plantation from Mexicans, and she spoke French because her mama had been French from Louisiana. This was neither of those.

His voice resonated in the air. Its richness, the cadence and mystery of the words, the purpose, and the clear melody in them threw a hush over the creekbed. As if he were a priest saying a prayer.

Then her own name struck her ears like the sudden peal of a bell. In English. Plain as day. "Childress."

Something else in Cherokee and then "Brassell."

This chant was about *Brassell*?

Yes. That was no mystery—he had plainly said it. And Creed would not be saying a prayer for God to *bless* Brassell, that much was sure.

Papa always said some Indians could throw spells on people and conjure magic. Was this like the witches doing gris-gris that people sometimes whispered about back in Louisiana?

Her mind racing, she watched Creed bend his knees, scoop up water in his hands, and pour it over his shoulders. They glistened in the sun while he stood straight again and brought whatever was in his hand to his mouth. It looked like . . . a plug of tobacco?

Fear and anger swirled up in her stomach and began to rise to her throat. Her heart thudded with panic.

It must be an Indian rite. A curse. With Brassell's name in it!

He turned and began wading toward the bank. She rushed to meet him.

"Creed," she cried. "Don't come out. Stay. Take it back. That's not fair—Brassell doesn't know how to defend himself from black magic. You know that. You should be ashamed of yourself!"

She waded out into the water, slipping and sliding on the rough creekbed, heedless of everything but removing this further danger from her brother.

Creed glared at her. His face was terrible.

She stopped where she was, teetering on rocks that were as sharp through the thin soles of her shoes as if she were barefooted. She had some of her skirts gathered up into her arms, but she could feel the back part of them trailing in the water, soaking it up, trying to pull her down.

Creed lifted his eyes above her head and stalked toward the bank, moving as fast as if he were on solid ground. Clearly, he meant to ignore her. He was going to pass her by. He was looking straight in front of him and heading for the bank of the creek.

She went to stop him, forgetting her hurting feet and the water dragging at her skirts. His face was so terrible, it would have scared her to death at any other time, but he had already accomplished that. Nothing mattered now but saving Brassell.

"Stay," she cried. "I tell you, stay in this water if

that's part of your black magic. Take back that curse you put on Brass."

He whirled to face her.

"*You* take back *your* ignorant remarks," he snapped. "I held the Grandfather Medicine up to the sun. I held the ceremony at dawn. Neither would be true of an incantation said for a sinister purpose."

He turned his back on her and, moving faster than she could have thought possible on the horrid rocks, headed again for shore.

She twisted around to start after him, her screaming feet trying to find new footing. But she slipped and fell backward so fast, she could barely get a breath to scream before she hit the water.

It knocked the breath out of her completely—the smooth rocks hitting her so hard and the sharp ones cutting her, plus the incredible coldness of the water. It rushed through her hair to freeze her scalp. It soaked her to the skin, and for a horrible instant she thought it might drown her before she could regain the ability to move and lift her nose up into the blessed air.

Creed's face appeared above her. He grabbed her and threw her over his shoulder as unceremoniously as if she were a sack of flour, and carried her to the bank.

His body moved as easily as the water flowing around his feet. She was helpless, completely helpless against its power, and she didn't care. Something about his muscled arm thrown over the small of her back, her belly pressed against the mountain of his shoulder, and the surefooted way he moved infused heat into her blood and made her want to stay there.

Once on dry ground, he didn't set her down. He kept on striding right along with her upside down in his iron grip. The blood was rushing to her head now and hurting.

Finally, she managed to gather a scrap of a breath into her lungs and a shred of good sense into her brain. She beat on his back with her fists. His flesh was so hard, she couldn't even get his attention.

"Put me down," she said, meaning it to be an order, but her voice came out as a feeble croak.

She tried again. "I can walk. Turn me loose."

Without a word, he kept right on. The heat of his back seeped into her breasts, even through the cold cloth of her wet blouse. As the long muscles of his back moved against them, a whole new sensation spread through her and centered deep at her core.

She made a mighty effort to free herself and accomplished absolutely nothing.

When he reached the buggy, he stopped and set her down.

He stepped back and looked at her, head to toe. She must look horrible. Soaked completely, hair stringing and dripping all over, clothes shamelessly

70

clinging to her like a second skin. That was one fleeting thought, born of habit.

Then she was looking at him, too. She couldn't raise her eyes to his face for staring at the broad, beautiful chest right in front of her eyes, with the fascinating indentation in the middle where the muscles crossed. She wanted to touch him there and run her fingertips over his smooth skin.

His broad shoulders and chest tapered sharply to his waist. The breechcloth hung from a thin strip of soft leather. It rode low on the bones of his hips. She tried to decipher the design in the middle of it, which was made of many-colored beads . . . maybe an animal . . . or a bird . . . The breechcloth moved slightly, although he wasn't even breathing hard.

Raney caught herself and jerked her gaze away. Mercy! Goodness! What was the *matter* with her? First worrying about her appearance and then thinking about how Creed looked and having embarrassingly wanton thoughts about him.

She had to get a grip. She was here for Brassell's sake. Here to stop Creed from ruining him.

She forced her scattered mind to think. Creed was proud of his honor. Hadn't he said it was the reason he didn't leave her on the road? She would shame him into living up to his own code and his own words.

So she lifted her chin and stiffened her spine as best she could with her heavy wet skirts pulling her down.

"Go undo that curse you just did, Creed. Last night, you promised you wouldn't kill my brother if you could help it, and here you are the very next morning deliberately doing it in the most cowardly way possible."

He grabbed her shoulders with iron fingers, and for an instant she thought he would shake her. Instead he held her perfectly still and bored into her eyes with his gaze as sharp as those rocks that had cut her feet to ribbons.

"What I *did* was say an incantation meant to strengthen the arm of the law," he said, from between clenched teeth, "and all you spoiled, rich white planters had better be praying that it succeeds. If this feud grows and really blows up, every family in Limestone County will be hurt in one way or another."

He was telling the truth. Looking into his fierce eyes, she could do nothing but believe that statement.

The sight of him, the sound of him, out there in the water holding up his arms to the dawn-streaked sky came back to her. He had been saying a prayer, just as her intuition first told her.

She had let Papa's thinking override her own.

Chapter 4

❦

reed let her go and turned away. What did he care whether she believed him or not?

"All right," Raney said, "I believe you, Creed. You don't lie. I know you."

"You don't know me," he said. "You never have."

He went to get the horses. It was plenty light enough to travel now and they had a long way to go.

"What am I going to do?" she called. "I'm soaked to the skin."

"Change your clothes, of course," he snapped, throwing the words back at her over his shoulder. "And do it fast."

"I didn't bring any more," she said, a little more loudly because he was farther away. Even so, he could hear her teeth chattering a little as the morning breeze freshened. "Except for a clean blouse."

Her voice broke on the last word.

He stopped and wheeled to look at her, standing there with water still dripping off her and a desperate look on her face as she pulled the wads of soggy cloth away from her legs. She had to use both hands.

"These skirts are so heavy I can't even move my limbs."

In spite of her hair being plastered to her head, she looked beautiful, more beautiful than ever—if a man looked at her as a woman. Well, he wouldn't do that. She was an ignorant, spoiled girl who had run out of the house in the middle of the night without any preparation, expecting the world to take care of her. Why shouldn't she? Someone had taken care of her all her life.

"That's what you get for spying on me."

All he could do was hope that her intrusion on the strengthening ceremony hadn't lessened its power. He turned and started for the horses again.

They were grazing on their stake ropes in the tall grass, washed in the new sunlight. They'd be rested and full-bellied, which was good because they had many a mile to travel.

He pulled up the stakes, coiled the ropes to carry over his shoulder, watered the horses in the creek, and led them back to camp. Raney was spreading out her petticoats in the back of the buggy. She had on a dry blouse but she still wore the dripping skirts.

"I know you think I did this backward," she said, "but my petticoats are just as wet as my skirts."

"We're leaving as soon as I'm ready," he said.

"I can't drive in these wet skirts."

"Then wear my blanket."

He had done without it and his tarp last night so she could be comfortable. They were still lying there under her buggy. She wasn't accustomed to making up her bed any more than she was to doing her own packing.

"The *blanket*? *I'm* not an Indian."

His anger surged. There it was again. He had to remember that she was an ignorant girl only mouthing what she'd been taught. He would ignore it.

"All I need is to come down with the ague," she said.

He spun on one boot heel to glare at her.

"All *you* need?" he said furiously. "If you had the ague, I'd be the one to pity."

"*You?*"

"Yes. I'd be the one responsible for taking care of you. Not only do you take to the road all alone after dark in the middle of a feud, you don't bring a bedroll or a change of clothes. How about food and water?"

Spots of high color blossomed in her cheeks.

"I thought I'd find Brassell and be back home by

morning," she said. "I didn't *plan* to go all the way
to San Antone."

He left her and went to the bushes to change into
his clothes. After he'd stepped into his jeans and
boots, he slapped his hat on his head, stuck his arms
into the sleeves of his shirt, and returned to camp,
buttoning it as he went. He picked up his bag and
put away his breechcloth.

Raney was in the process of hitching up her
horse, which surprised him, since he'd assumed
she would wait for him to do it. She shivered from
time to time because she was still wearing the wet
skirts.

"Hurry it up," he said. "We should already be on
the road."

"I *am* hurrying," she said. "I can't go any faster
with twenty pounds of wet cloth dragging me down."

She came around her horse's head to fasten the
traces on that side of the buggy and looked at him.

"I don't know what to do," she said. "I have to be
able to move my limbs enough to brace against the
footboard and use the brake."

He reached into his gear bag and jerked his spare
pair of jean pants out of his roll of clothes.

"Here you go," he said, and threw them to her
across the short distance between them. They fell at
her feet.

Finished with the last strap, she straightened up
and gaped at him.

"I can't wear *pants*," she said. "I can't dress like a *man*."

"You'll be able to move your *legs* even better than in skirts," he said.

She gasped, shocked that he'd said the word "legs" instead of the euphemism "limbs," which was always used in mixed company.

He turned his back and got busy with his own outfit. That was her last choice, if only she knew it. She was so used to other people solving her problems, she probably expected him to make her a skirt out of the blanket.

"I don't care how well I could move! It would be a scandal if anybody saw me."

What had he ever seen in her that gave him the urge to ask for her hand in the first place?

He tied his gear bag to his saddle strings with such force, he'd never get the knots undone.

"Don't you know we won't get to San Antonio today?" he asked.

"Oh, I hope we find Brass before we go *that* far," she said.

She was completely unreasonable. A baby. A spoiled one, too. It was hard to believe Brassell was the youngest in her family.

Creed went to the buggy, snatched up his tarp and blanket she'd used, and went back to his saddle to ready his bedroll.

"I'll keep my back to you," he said. "If you go

into the bushes to change, you're liable to fall in the creek again, and then I'd have to give you the pants I'm wearing."

"That's all right," she said sarcastically, "you're accustomed to going without them."

"That's right," he said, in the same tone. "When we aren't wearing blankets we go naked, but you civilized white people always wear your pants while you sneak around and spy on us."

"I was not *spying*."

He stopped his tongue. He wouldn't talk about the ceremony anymore—he'd already told her what it was, and that was too much talk about it. One should never talk about magic to anyone but another practitioner who could make medicine.

Creed went to saddle Marker, the big bay stallion he'd won in a poker game four winters ago. The professional gambler who lost five hundred dollars to Creed left the horse with him as a marker but he never redeemed him. Which was fine with Creed, although there were few horses that would sell for that much money.

This one just might, though. Marker had heart to spare and limitless bottom. He was fast, too, when he needed to be. Creed loved the ornery animal best of all his mounts. He wouldn't take a thousand dollars for the horse.

He would never sell the bay, but while he threw the saddle blanket on him and added the saddle, he thought about how much the horse might bring instead of about whether his ceremony had been weakened by her intrusion. All generative power resided in thoughts.

He could control his thoughts. He would think of his horse and finding Brassell. He would not think about Raney. Anger and irritation would only disturb his peace and distract him from his purpose.

She was heedless in her words because she was hurt and lost. She truly was a wounded bird who might not be able to recover from her fall from the disintegrating nest. If he kept that in mind, he could hold his temper and do what he had to do.

But when he was saddled up and ready to ride, his anger surged up all over again. Raney was nowhere in sight. Creed went to Tally and checked to see that he was hitched properly.

"Raney!" he called. "Hurry up. We're burning daylight."

He was trying the last of the fastenings that hitched her horse to the buggy when she appeared. The first glimpse of her made him forget what he was doing.

His jeans and the lacy blouse she'd changed into emphasized every curve of her body. She'd had to roll the legs of the pants because he was so much taller, but except for the waist being too big, they fit her. Like another skin. She walked across the grass with gingerly steps, holding her wet skirts away from her at arm's length.

At that moment, he forgot all about the wounded bird. He couldn't help but look at her as a woman. He couldn't do anything but look at her. He couldn't *believe* she had done something so improper as to step into the jeans, proper little lady that she was.

"Didn't you trust *me* not to spy on *you?*" he asked, taking refuge in sarcasm.

She flashed him a look. "Of course I did. Didn't I tell you I know you don't lie?"

"Then how come you're taking up good traveling time hiding in the bushes?"

"I was looking for something I thought I'd lost."

"What?"

"Never mind," she said, and walked past him. "I found it deep in my sodden pocket."

He waited while she took her skirts to the buggy and spread them out beside the petticoats, but she didn't say anything more.

"Then you *were* changing clothes—if you had your skirt with you."

"All *right*," she said. "I went to the bushes for both reasons. *I'm* not accustomed to stripping off my clothes out in the open."

She went to the front wheel, put her foot up on the hub, and took hold of the sideboard to climb in.

"We'll eat on the road," he said, going to help her up onto the seat, "so put your breakfast where you can get to it without stopping—if you have any."

"I do," she said. "In my reticule."

Then she waved his help away, saying, "Thanks, but I can do this."

She sprang up into the buggy before he could touch her.

Creed mounted up and led the way back down the winding trail the way they had come. Gradually, he broadened the distance between them so he could scout the road before she got there with the buggy. No sense just barreling right out into the open when there could be Chickenhawks around.

When he got to the end of the trail, the sounds of hooves plopping on the dew-damp sandy road and low-pitched voices made him pull up. He waited, just behind the curve in the cover of some mesquite, where he could see the road.

Three men, two on horseback and one mounted on a mule, rode into the space in the road that he could see. They didn't notice him, partly because the brush was so thick between him and them and partly because they were engrossed in their conversation and not looking around them at all.

They looked peaceable enough, but not prosperous. If they lived in Limestone County, he had never seen them before. They each had a bedroll and bundles tied behind a well-worn, and in one case raggedy, saddle, so they might be on a long journey. However, their pace was leisurely, and so was their conversation.

They seemed harmless enough. He was as certain of that as he could be without knowing who they were.

Creed studied them until they were out of sight. They had just vanished when he heard the rattle of the buggy coming up behind him, hell-bent for leather.

Great. She must've lost control of the horse, which would be another problem she would expect him to take care of for her.

Raney was holding the lines tightly in both hands and she had her legs—shockingly encased in Creed's blue jeans—propped securely against the footboard. She was yelling at Tally as loud as she could, but he was already trying to turn toward home before he even got off the little trail. Thank goodness Creed was there, blocking the entrance to the road. Maybe that would slow him down.

This horse was getting out of control and that was scaring her half to death. Surely Creed would stop him for her.

But the next thing she knew, Creed was sitting his horse out in the middle of the road and Tally was picking up speed with every step he took. Tally jerked her and the buggy out onto the road angling to the north, trying his best to go home. She pulled harder on the lines and harder still, but she only succeeded in turning his head an inch or two. She didn't have the physical strength to force him around.

The fear that had started when Tally first began to ignore her hands on the lines turned into panic. From the corner of her eye, she saw Creed moving.

The next instant, he was at Tally's head, grabbing the bridle and pushing his horse up against hers. He pulled him around to head south.

"You better get a handle on him," he barked.

Her cheeks burned with embarrassed frustration.

"I told you to ride on and leave me last night," she said. "I can take care of myself."

His only answer was a scornful grunt.

Raney wanted to cry. He'd been downright hateful to say she'd been spying on him, and now he was so snappish about her horse running away. Well, she couldn't help that. If she wasn't physically strong enough to hold him she couldn't help it. Horses were a lot stronger than people.

Deep down, though, she felt glad that he was there. Her arms were sore from all the unaccustomed work, she'd been way too tired to travel on last night, and she would've been scared to death to stop and rest without him. And now Tally had already scared her this morning, plus pulled the lines through her hands so hard he'd broken the bad blister on the palm of her hand.

"I'm sure Leonard will be along sometime this morning, and he can drive the buggy," she said, to try to regain her dignity.

And maybe to try to make Creed just a little bit jealous. He had certainly lost a lot of his gallantry. Why, he hardly ever smiled at her anymore.

"Why didn't you bring him along in the first

place?" Creed asked. "Or better yet, why didn't he come and you stay home?"

Now she wished she hadn't said anything.

"Raney? Why didn't Leonard go after Brassell? I know Trent and Robert are away in Fort Worth."

"He has a business to run," she said, and set her face to her driving.

Creed said, "Raney."

He was riding along beside her, and when she turned, he captured her eyes with his inscrutable dark ones.

"I left him a note," she said, "and told him I was going after Brassell."

"Can he read?"

"Well, of course! He can do anything you can do, Creed."

His gaze held hers for a long heartbeat, and then it drifted from her eyes down to her lips. Suddenly her mouth remembered the taste of his.

"Somehow," he drawled, "I doubt that, Raney."

He met her eyes once more, then he loped off to ride ahead of her.

Raney watched his broad shoulders and the way they narrowed to a V at his waist; she watched his small, muscular bottom and the way it sat the saddle. Naked, his body was the most powerfully beautiful one she had ever seen.

How did Leonard look without his clothes? He was a man of utmost propriety, so she'd never seen him without his shirt. Leonard wasn't as big as Creed, and even his face was softer because he worked indoors. Leonard wasn't half as handsome as Creed, either, even if Creed did look very Indian.

A poignant regret seized her. It was a terrible shame that he was an Indian and she wasn't.

Raney realized that Creed was glancing down at the ground even more often than usual. She looked, too, and saw that there were tracks in the sandy soil. Quite a few of them, in fact.

She lifted the lines and brought them down, urging Tally to speed up.

"Do you think these tracks are from Brassell's horse?" she called.

He shook his head, and when she got up even with him, he said, "I know they're not."

Sharp disappointment stabbed her.

"How do you know?"

Creed dismounted, went to the tracks, and knelt down on his right knee. He touched one, ever so lightly, so as not to mess it up, and then another.

"They're fresh," he said. "See how the sand on the sides of the tracks is still stacked up? These riders aren't more than fifteen or twenty minutes ahead of us."

"Brass was right ahead of us last night," she said. "Maybe he rested overnight, too, and this morning he started riding along with some other people . . ."

She stopped talking to watch his bizarre behavior.

He bent over, took off his hat, and smelled the earth. He laid one hand, palm down, on a place between the hoofmarks and frowned at it thoughtfully. Then he moved back a little, bent over completely, and put his ear to the ground.

After listening a moment, he got up and brushed himself off.

"Well?" Raney said.

He motioned to her to be quiet. He looked off down the road into the far distance for a long time.

Then he went to his horse, looked at her, and spoke.

"Three men," he said, "all strangers to me. One's wearing overalls and a blue shirt. He's on a gray mule. The others, who're both wearing waist pants, are on horses—a sorrel and a dun. Not a pacer among the three. The mule's saddle has a jug of whiskey tied to the strings."

Astounded, she stared at him.

"How can you tell all that just from these tracks? A jug of whiskey? You can't possibly know that."

Creed swung up into the saddle. "I might be wrong. It could be a jug of sorghum molasses."

He clucked to his horse and they started moving.

Raney was so astounded, she just let the buggy roll along beside him without really driving it at all.

No one could really know all that from some tracks, could he?

She stole a glance at his face to see if he was teasing her, but it was set straight ahead. All she could see was his chiseled profile.

Was this another kind of Indian magic? Was he a real medicine man? The way he'd looked standing there in the creek at dawn, with the water glittering around his feet and the new sunlight burnishing his copper skin, she had felt a sense of real power in the air.

But could it really be true that Indians could know such secret ways?

He clucked and put his horse into a longer, faster trot. She urged Tally to keep up with him but Creed stayed a bit ahead. Tally seemed peaceful enough and content to follow, so Raney risked taking both her lines in one hand. Her brain was tied into a knot, and besides that, she was starving.

She fumbled for her reticule underneath the seat and finally extracted a ham biscuit from the crushed bundle she'd wrapped in a napkin at the table in the kitchen house at Pleasant Hill. That moment seemed ten years ago. Pleasant Hill, where she had spent her whole life, seemed strange and far away.

It was as if her whole life had changed yet again, but this time in a way she didn't know how to name. She could only hope that she wasn't feeling that way because Brassell was gone forever, like Mama. Oh, how she hoped he wasn't dead!

In spite of everything, though, her hunger was growing by the minute. The ham biscuit looked very small, and the biscuit was in a state little better than crumbs, but she ate it greedily and reached for another one. When it was gone, she struggled to open her canteen. She would give anything for some coffee.

She *needed* coffee to clear her head.

Creed would never stop now and build a fire, and she didn't even know if he carried any coffee in his pack or not. This was another new feeling. This was the first day in her whole life she could remember actually lacking a necessity and having no way to get it.

She thought about that while she tried to keep up with Creed's brisk pace. If he was right about how old those tracks were, she might soon find out. He couldn't be. He did have a sense of humor, everyone knew that, even though most of the time he was completely serious.

However, she couldn't imagine him playing a joke on her so soon after his anger this morning.

Then he reached a bend in the road that held a tall, lone oak tree in its crescent. A good shade on the side of the road usually tempted travelers to rest, and this one was no exception—there was a small fire with people around it, and Raney saw Creed ride up to them. By the time she reached them, he had dismounted. She stopped, too.

"Howdy there, ma'am," said the man pouring the coffee. "Get down and have a cup with us."

She could smell the coffee from there.

Creed stepped to the front wheel of her buggy and, when she moved to the end of the seat, reached up, put his hands on her waist, and lifted her down as easily as if she were a feather. She had no time to even try to do it herself.

The minute he set her on her feet, she realized how naked she felt without skirts. She wished she'd never left the buggy, yet their host didn't seem to notice anything amiss.

"Y'all come far?" he asked.

He wore overalls and a blue shirt. Raney took the tin cup he held out to her, and while she inhaled the delicious fragrance of the steaming coffee it held, she cast unobtrusive glances at the other two men. They wore jean pants like Creed's—and hers, come to think of it. And they wore jean jackets. She was afraid to look at their animals. If it turned out that Creed was right about everything, he'd be too proud of himself.

And it would be too mysterious for her to understand.

"From Concho," Creed said. "What about you all?"

"We be from Tarrant County," he said, in a cheerful way, "lookin' fer San Antone. They call me Fiddler."

"I'm Creed Sixkiller," he said. He didn't introduce Raney, as was only fitting since he didn't know these men.

She looked around as she sipped the strong brew and silently gave thanks for it. It seemed to have chicory in it, like Louisiana coffee. Usually she drank it with half hot milk, but that didn't matter. This was like a miracle.

Then she realized she was staring at a mule and two horses, one a sorrel, the other a dun. The mule had a whiskey—or molasses—jug tied to the saddle strings.

The strangest feeling took her. Creed had been right on every detail. Indians really *were* different, and Creed was one of them who could make magic. What if he could read her mind?

Fiddler served everyone there, and when they were all drinking coffee, he hung the pot back over the fire.

"Yep," he said, "we're goin' to San Antone to make some music for them people. They ain't likely heard no good fiddlin' fer a month of Sundays. Gonna play so them people can dance."

"My brother's on his way to San Antonio," Raney blurted, before she even knew she would be so bold. "He has run off from . . . well, he's left us. We're looking for him."

Fiddler turned to her, and she felt all the others' eyes on her, too.

"What I mean is, he might . . . come to y'all's dance . . . or something. Brassell loves to dance and he plays the big bass fiddle. And the accordion, too, if it's Cajun music."

She could feel the weight of Creed's look more than those of the others but she refused to glance at him. This might be a way to find Brass if she had to go all the way to San Antonio looking for him. In a town that big, he would be a needle in a haystack.

She noticed that all three of the men were exchanging looks. The other two seemed mute, because Fiddler did all the talking. One of them nodded, though.

"We could use a bass player. Your brother lookin' for a job?"

"I . . . I don't know. He might be, because he'll be needing money. Brassell Childress is his name."

Creed was staring at her steadily, but she couldn't stop now. She might have hit on the perfect way to find Brass, assuming he was as lightly wounded as Creed said.

"Where will you all be playing?"

"Wherever there's a penny to be earned," Fiddler said. "Maybe on the street."

"Brassell is six feet tall and has blond hair," she said. "He's sixteen years old and lanky and his hair curls tight all over his head. He might have blood on his shirt because he's lightly wounded from . . . an altercation he had. If y'all come across him, could you let me know? It's very important that I find him."

Fiddler must have heard the desperation in her voice. His eyes crinkled in a kind smile.

"And where would I find *you*, little lady, if I see this young brother of yours?"

91

Her mind raced. She had never laid her eyes on San Antonio. Only one name came to mind.

"The Menger Hotel," she said. "Leave a message for me at the desk there if you see Brassell anywhere."

Fiddler's smile broadened. "Do I leave this message for Miss Childress or Mrs. Sixkiller or the young lady in the Levi Strauss pants?"

Both of the latter two choices struck her like lightning. She felt the heat flare into her cheeks that he had noticed her scandalous costume, and that he had suggested she might be married to Creed, but she gave no other sign.

"Miss Raney Childress," she said, and offered her hand for him to bow over with as much aplomb as if her father were the one introducing them and she were wearing her best, laciest dress. "I am pleased to meet you, Mr. Fiddler."

When she turned to Creed, he was looking at her as if he'd never seen her before.

Creed could not believe his ears. Raney was far more naïve than he'd ever realized. No wonder she'd turned him down when he'd asked to marry her—the two of them weren't living in the same world. If a Cherokee woman, or for that matter any other Indian woman, had grown up as sheltered as Raney, she'd be discarded or dead by now.

She was far more unpredictable than he'd ever realized, too. Who would've thought that Raney Childress, the belle of the county and always such a lady, would stand there wearing pants in front of a bunch of men?

And she appeared to be completely unaware of their interest in that fact. Usually she was conscious of her effect on every man within eyesight of her.

Before she could say anything else, he spoke to Fiddler.

"Last I heard, the bridge was out over Longhorn Creek. Do you know whether it's fixed yet?"

Yes, Fiddler knew everything, or thought he did.

" 'Twas a tornado took that bridge out, clean as a whistle," he said, "and ain't nobody—the county or the state—even trying to put it back. We all will still have to use the ford downstream, far as I know."

Creed wasn't sure what he meant by "we all," but he sure as hell was not going to let them join up with him and Raney.

He turned the conversation to the road and the weather. The other two men drifted over to the fire and actually chimed in a word or two. Raney, thank God, concentrated on her coffee.

"Have you crossed there lately?"

"No, sir," Fiddler said, "not since last fall. It oughtta be shallow, though, considering how little rain we've had."

Raney set down her empty cup, and Creed followed suit. They'd visited long enough to satisfy the unwritten rule that if a man partook of food or drink at another's fire, he must pay by entertaining his host. Raney had given these musicians enough entertainment to pay for a whole barbecue, much less a cup of coffee.

"We'll move on," he said. "Much obliged to y'all for the coffee."

But Fiddler hadn't forgotten about Brassell. He followed Raney to the buggy, assuring her all the while that he would keep a sharp eye out for her brother and, if he found him, would make a beeline for the hotel. She even let the old buzzard help her up onto the seat.

"Thank you, Mr. Fiddler," she told him, with her sweetest smile. "If you find my brother, I'll be ever so grateful to you. And so will my papa."

Damn! How could she not have as much common sense as a three-year-old? She was twenty. She was, supposedly, a woman grown.

The day she'd turned down his proposal of marriage had been the luckiest day of his life.

If he were tied to her for life, he'd turn into a Mexican bandit.

Chapter 5

～⌒◯◯⌒～

Creed, his jaw clenched against his anger, rode up beside Raney.

"For a while there I thought you were going to tell them where your papa's plantation is and where y'all keep the silver," he said.

She turned to him, her big blue eyes flaring wide in surprise.

"What are you talking about?"

"You. Running your mouth back there."

"I was only trying to do the right thing to help us find Brass. That's three more pairs of eyes looking for him, and San Antonio is a big place, Creed."

"Yes," he said, trying to hold on to his patience,

"it is. And that was a decent idea. You just threw yourself into it way too much."

She tossed her head to show she didn't believe that.

"I used my charm," she said. "A person can catch more flies with honey than vinegar, and I made them want to please me."

"You might've made *those* flies want a lot more than that," he said. "You don't know them from Adam's off-ox. They could be highwaymen."

Eyes wide, she stared at him.

"Why, they're not! They're good-hearted and musical and generous and hospitable to ask us to stop for coffee when anyone can see they're poor as can be."

"Raney," he said, through clenched teeth, "you told them way too much."

"And how are they supposed to look for Brass if they don't even know what he looks like?"

"That's right," he said, barely holding on to his calm tone, "but they didn't need to know he ran off or that he's wounded or that his papa has money or that he's your brother or any of those details."

She looked shocked.

"I didn't *say* Papa has money."

"You're driving a high-dollar rig and wearing lace on your blouse that some people couldn't buy with a year's wages. You implied that your papa would give a reward for him. They *could* start thinking more in terms of a ransom."

"They *won't*. Fiddler is a good person."

"You also implied that you yourself would give a reward of a different, more personal kind."

Tears sprang up, but her eyes flashed fire. She stared at him defiantly.

"You mean like kisses?"

"And more," he snapped.

Lord! How could she be a betrothed woman and still be so innocent?

"That's not what I meant!" she shot back at him.

"But that's how he took it. You have to be careful how you talk and what you say to men, Raney. Flirting all over Limestone County with decently brought-up boys is way different from being out in the world."

"I can take care of myself."

"No, you can't. You proved it just now."

"I can, too. I knew I was laying it on a little thick, but, Creed, those men can help me."

"Flirting may get you exactly what you want back home, but in San Antonio, flirting will get you more than you bargained for."

"All *right*," she said, and turned her head to give full attention to her driving.

"You don't need to get a burr under your saddle. You acted downright featherheaded back there. Learn from it and watch yourself from now on."

"Well, how about you learn to consider other people's feelings," she said, and her voice nearly broke. "Why are you being so critical of me, Creed?"

"For the sake of your own survival," he said.

He loped off and rode on ahead of the buggy. He was only trying to teach her for her own good. She had to grow up sometime, and now seemed to be a damn fine time.

However, maybe he *had* laid it on a little strong.

But there was no excuse for her being so feather-headed and soft and spoiled rotten. Most twenty-year-old women were wives and mothers with a house to manage and children to raise. Lots of them helped their husbands ranch or farm. There probably wasn't another woman Raney's age in Texas who was as naïve and helpless—or as ignorant and fearful as she was.

Yet she *had* overcome her fear to come out into the dark and travel alone for the sake of her brother. That took some courage.

And the very fact that she had spoken up to strangers and tried to do something—anything—on her own initiative put her a surprisingly high step up from where she'd been yesterday.

Raney glared at Creed's back as he rode ahead of the buggy. Featherheaded! She was not. Was she? She bit her lip and blinked her eyes fast to keep the tears at bay.

Was Creed right that she'd said so many foolish things and behaved outrageously? Was she stupid?

No. She was smart. Hadn't she figured out how to

hitch a horse to a buggy? Hadn't she figured out where Brass would come onto the road at the creek? Creed had seen the tracks at that exact spot, so she'd been right.

Creed. He just made her so mad she could scream.

The road in front of her blurred. Creed disappeared in the haze, and all she saw was the fuzzy ruts and tracks in the ground.

No one had ever talked to her like that. Good heavens, wasn't he the one who had just been saying she couldn't think for herself? Then the minute she did, he could not find one right thing about it.

Her grip on the lines hardened. She used firmer hands than she had used before. She had taught herself to drive, too, hadn't she? She was a whole lot smarter than he thought.

And she could take care of herself. She would prove it to him.

"Hi-*yah*," she said, putting the new firmness into her voice as well as her hands. "Git-*up*, now."

She slapped the lines down. Tally picked up speed, but it wasn't three spins of the buggy wheels until he started to try to slow again, which, knowing him, was to be expected. She was ready. She picked the whip from its holder and popped it over his back.

It was a matter of keeping up the pressure. That must be the trick. The more he slowed, the more he wanted to stop, so she'd make him go fast enough to keep that thought right out of his head.

She brought the lines down again and the speed increased a little more. The buggy's wheels turned smoothly and silently. A nice breeze had sprung up, and the motion of her vehicle made it blow her hair back from her face. She loosened the strings of her hat and pushed it off to hang down her back.

Creed was the one who didn't know how to behave out in the world. Didn't he know that the rest of this trip would be much more pleasant if he didn't insult and upset her? He was the one insisting on their traveling together, so he might as well be polite about it.

Didn't he know that he needed her to help him find Brassell? She knew more about Brass's likes and dislikes and what he might do in a town than Creed did.

As Tally went around a bend in the road, Raney saw Creed up ahead, off to the side, off his horse, bent over, using a hoof pick on Marker's left rear foot. Creed's neat, muscular bottom in his tight-fitting jeans held her gaze.

Even furious with him, she couldn't quite make herself take her eyes away. He surely was a handsome man. All over. From any angle.

Heat surged into her face. She was shameless, that's all there was to it. Back three years ago, when Creed had been flirting with her and she'd been letting him steal kisses, thoughts like that had shocked her all the time.

Back when he was telling her how beautiful she was and she never imagined he would call her featherheaded.

She stuck her nose into the air and sailed on by.

Creed called something after her, but she couldn't make out what he said. And she didn't try very hard, either. He could keep his advice and his opinions—*and* his insults—to himself.

Tally wanted to slow and turn back because he'd seen Marker was stopped, but she didn't let up on him.

"How come you never want to stay with Marker when he's running fast down the road?" she said. "Git-up, Tally."

She only wished it was Creed in the traces. She'd love nothing more than to be the boss of *him* the way he thought he was the boss of her.

Raney rounded another bend in the road and began to hear a constant, rushing noise. It took her a moment to identify it as running water. Maybe it was the creek Fiddler had mentioned.

She tried to remember what he had said. He had called it shallow, hadn't he? This would be the perfect way to show Creed that she did have a brain in her head, and the courage to take care of herself.

The road ran up over a little rise and, as it took her down onto the flat that led to the water, she glanced upstream and down. Upstream, the creek banks rose steep and overgrown with scrubby trees.

Downstream, the ruins of a bridge sat collapsed in the water on either side, evidently from having given way in the middle.

But at the place where the road originally had curved along the bank to lead to the bridge, she could see tracks where people had gone straight into the water. This was the ford.

In fact, she thought that some of the tracks looked very fresh, maybe made earlier this morning. There was no way to confirm that, as she was not speaking to Creed at the moment, but she felt proud, anyway. The edges of them weren't crumbling yet and that was what Creed had looked at when he'd examined Fiddler's and his friends' hoofprints.

On this side, the bank was a wide, low one and the approach to the crossing was gradual, but on the other, the only open place where people could climb out was narrow and steep. The creek itself was wide, though, and it did look shallow.

It must *be* shallow. Fiddler had said it was, and people had been driving into it. There were ruts as well as tracks in the sandy soil.

She glanced behind her but didn't see Creed yet. He was probably in no hurry because he would expect her to stop here and wait for him to catch up— since he thought she couldn't take care of herself.

Well, other people had obviously been successful in crossing the creek here, since no people, horses, or buggies were still in it. She slapped the lines on Tally's back.

Should she speed up going into the water to give the buggy some momentum or go slowly to find out what the footing would be? There at the edge, the water was clear and she could see more sand underneath it, so she decided on speed.

She clucked to Tally and was gratified when he did go faster. She was not going to wait until Creed rode up behind her and started taking charge and bossing her around. She would surprise him and already be on the other bank when he arrived on this one.

Tally tried to balk right at the edge of the water, but she yelled and cracked the whip and told him to go on. He did. The buggy wheels were large and the box sat up high, so she probably wouldn't even get splashed. This would be fun.

But as they got farther into it, the water came up higher on the wheels and higher still, until she gasped in dismay. It was up to the hubs!

She was leaning over to see better when the bottom dropped out from under the buggy with a suddenness that sucked her stomach down to her feet. A little scream came out of her mouth and her hands clutched the lines so hard she pulled Tally's head too high, and when she really looked at him, she saw he was swimming.

Oh, dear Lord! She herself could not swim a lick.

And the current was strong. It was trying its best to pull them sideways, in spite of all Tally could do. In the middle of the creek—which was also wider than it had looked at first—the pull was stronger yet.

Raney sat still, not only from fear of being jostled off the seat to fall into the water, but from panic so great she couldn't move. She didn't dare turn loose the lines to hold on to the seat, so she braced her feet against the floorboard and tried not to breathe.

They almost made it. The water was receding a little, she just knew it was—she didn't dare lean over far enough to look at the wheels, but the drag of the current seemed less. They were near enough the other shore that Tally actually got his feet under him, and Raney had the one fleeting thought that they were safe, when something caught the buggy's wheels with a grip like a giant's and jerked Tally back in the traces.

He tried to go on, then he stood still to get his breath.

She shook the lines on his back and managed to croak out, "Go. Git-up, Tally," but she knew he couldn't do any more right then.

She also knew standing still was the wrong thing to do. They would get bogged here where the current was strong enough, even outside its center, to push the buggy and try to pull it, too.

Panic began to rise in her blood. They were powerless. She and the horse could do nothing against the soft sand beneath them and the will of the water.

If it washed the sand out from beneath them, it could carry them sideways and wreck them. If she ended up in the swift part of the water, she'd drown for sure.

What a foolish featherhead she'd been not to wait for Creed! If she survived, he'd never let her forget that she'd lost her horse and buggy and nearly drowned herself.

Raney tried to breathe but she couldn't get any air in. Her arms were shaking all the way to her shoulders, and her legs felt wasted completely away.

Why did they call this a *creek*? Good heavens, it must be a river!

She tried to force her fear to recede so her mind could start working again, but all she could think was that she couldn't do one thing to help herself, even if she could figure out what she should do. Her hands were stone and her blood was ice.

"Quicksand," Creed yelled. "Don't move."

She turned to see him coming down the little hill at a lope, untying the rope from his saddle.

Raney's face flushed with heat. No. She *would* prove to him that she could take care of herself.

She bent out far enough to see the water rushing past and the bottom of the wheel sunk into sand. It was clear as day that it looked trapped down in it at least six inches, although the water's movement made everything seem to shimmer and move.

"Sit still," Creed shouted. "I'll save you."

That order in that flat, uncompromising, *superior* tone of his just flew all over her. It warmed her right up and brought her strength and her voice back to her.

"I'll *drown* before I'll let you save me," she yelled back at him. "Stay out of my business."

"*Raney*," he roared. "Do as I say for once! *Do not move!*"

She picked up the lines and slapped them down on Tally.

"Yee-*hi*," she screamed. "Get up *now*!"

Tally threw up his head and set his shoulders into the harness. He pulled and the buggy moved—it actually *moved*—but only a few inches, and then it stopped. It rocked back.

That might be the way to do it! Maybe she could rock free. Thank God the horse wasn't mired, it was only the buggy.

"Tally," she said, reaching for that firm, new voice that she'd used to get him—and her—into this mess, "Back. Back now."

He did it. The water was swirling around his feet almost to his knees, and Tally was a wise, old horse. He seemed to be getting his strength back.

"We can do it," she promised him. "We can do it."

She smooched and clucked and he pulled even harder, front and back, and on the third try, the wheel came loose with a loud sucking sound, and Tally pulled the buggy onto the shallower, harder part of the bottom. They even hit a rock or two on the way to the bank.

Raney looked back to see where Creed was. Marker was swimming easily across the strongest part of the current with Creed in the saddle, whirling the loop in his rope above his head.

She faced forward again. They still had to climb the steep bank, and she could only pray that Tally had that much heart left in him. She hated to ask it of him after all this, but they'd roll back into the creek if she didn't. There was no place else to go but up.

Ahead of Creed. Without his help.

But Creed was on a much younger horse who wasn't hitched to a heavy buggy, and he swam him out around her and Tally, moving faster through the current than she could ever have believed possible. He rode him up the bank as fast as they'd been swimming.

Well, fine. This wasn't a race, it was a contest of wills. The thought made Raney smile, and that unfroze her face. Her fear began to rush away on the creek's current that now lay behind her.

It was almost a calm feeling filling her now. No, it was a happy one. No, victorious. She had escaped from the greatest danger on her own.

She looked to her own horse and realized he was headed a little downstream from the ford. She helped him get his bearings. Then she urged speed so he'd have the momentum to climb the bank.

Tally looked up and saw it ahead of him and began a long trot, splashing out of the shallow water's edge as surefootedly as could be. The footing was good, the ground wasn't as steep as it had looked from down below, and he climbed it, doing fine.

The buggy was heavy and he couldn't go very fast, but the good old horse never faltered. Before she knew it, Raney rolled out on top of the bank.

Creed sat his horse there, waiting.

"Whoa," she said, to Tally, who didn't need to hear it because he had already stopped.

To Creed, she said nothing. She stared him in the eye and waited for him to acknowledge her feat.

He stared back. His lips were a tight line and his eyes were hard as stone. His face told her nothing but he was furious with her, she knew.

She set her own jaw just as stubbornly as his was and lifted her chin, keeping his gaze trapped by hers.

Finally, he gave in.

"Pretty salty," he said, and turned his horse away to ride in the lead again.

Creed went straight to the shade thrown by a pair of huge old cottonwoods that grew along the bank. The horses needed to catch their breath and he needed to catch his, too—after Raney's performance had taken it completely away.

He could hear the buggy creaking along behind him at a walk, but he didn't look around.

"Tally needs some rest and so do I," she said fervently. "Thank goodness we're stopping."

As if she could never do such a thing without his permission and wouldn't think of trying.

"Might've been good to stop before you drove off into quicksand," he said, before he could bite the words back.

No sense talking about it now.

What he wanted to do was think about it. He still couldn't believe what he'd seen.

"This is the best old horse," she said.

He turned around just in time to see her climbing down over the wheel, moving fast and freely in his tight-fitting jeans. One glimpse of her stepping down from the hub with her back to him made him itch to run his hands over her neat, perfect little butt.

Surely her skirts would be dry by tomorrow.

Maybe if she wore less revealing clothing, instead of her physical self he could think about her soul, her essence. Who was she? He had known her for years and he would never have predicted that she would even try to do what she had just done.

"Aren't you, Tally?" she chattered. "You're the best horse in the whole world. Creed, don't you think so? Could you believe what Tally did?"

He could believe that a whole lot quicker than what *she* did.

He couldn't believe what she'd said, either.

I'll drown before I'll let you save me.

Raney Childress, helpless little princess of Limestone County, had yelled that at him in a most unladylike manner.

She was chattering on, partly to him, partly to the horse.

"Don't you think Tally has so much heart, Creed?"

It would've been some easier to understand if she'd had no one there to help her and no choice but to act alone.

"Creed?"

He looked at her.

"Don't you think Tally has so much more heart than you ever expected?" she asked.

"No. I saw it when he was trying to turn around and go home."

That made her laugh. He always had liked to hear Raney's laugh. She didn't giggle like other girls—she wasn't afraid to really laugh.

"Well, he's not going to do that anymore," she cooed, "are you, sweetie?"

Of all things, she was hugging the horse around the neck in spite of all the sweat and lather on him. Creed felt a little stab of jealousy.

And another of bewilderment. That was not like Raney, either. She was always very particular about her pretty clothes.

"You'll ruin that lace," he said.

"Well," she said, her eyes twinkling, "you don't

have to be so grumpy about it. At least I'm not ruining your jeans."

Well, why wouldn't he be grumpy? She could've drowned right there before his eyes. And because of no other reason but her foolish pride.

Creed dismounted and loosened the cinch to let Marker blow a little.

"I'll buy some new clothes when we get to San Antone," she said.

"And you'll smell like a horse until then," he blurted.

What in the *hell* was he saying? What did he care? He wouldn't be close enough to her to smell her. Just because he had always liked her laugh *and* her fragrance—always that of roses—didn't mean he should be talking about it.

"I'll stay far away from you," she said, laughing.

She caught his eye and held it a little too long, almost as if she were laughing at him.

"How about that?"

"Fine," he growled, and lifted his boots, tied together with his belt through the pull-on straps, off his saddle horn.

"It's good you didn't get your boots wet," she said. "Was that why you took them off, or did you think you'd have to swim?"

He limped over to a protruding root on one of the trees. Big mistake. He should've had more sense than to dismount sock-footed.

"Did you get some sticker-burrs?" she called.

He sat down and began picking the pesky things out of his socks.

"No," he said, "I just like to make sure my socks are really clean before I put them in my boots."

"Good idea," she said. "You're getting wise in the ways of the world. You weren't always such a careful person, as I remember."

He couldn't see her now. She must be around behind the buggy.

The little minx. He could just shake her. He vowed to ignore her and not to answer a word she said.

"And I see you've also learned not to talk too much," she called cheerfully. "Some people think that's one of *my* failings."

That remark, in the innocent, teasing tone that she used so well, made the corners of his mouth lift in a grin. He tried to erase it. He was so angry with her, he was not going to let her charm him.

If she did, from now on she would always think that she could ignore his orders, and that was dangerous on the road.

"I'm working on correcting that fault," she said.

The grin attacked him again. He set his lips in a straight line. But he couldn't resist a retort.

"Not so as a man could notice," he drawled.

She came out from behind the buggy wearing the blouse she had had on when she fell in the creek that morning at dawn, which seemed like a hundred days ago now. And his jeans, of course, which showed her every curve. Her hair tumbled in curls to her shoulders.

"I thought your clothes were wet," he said.

"This is thin and by now it's only damp," she said. "The sun and wind will have it dry in no time."

"How are your skirts coming along?" he said, and she knew exactly what he meant.

"Wet as sop," she said, shaking her head in mock sadness. "I doubt they'll be dry for a long time. I may have to wear your jeans for several days."

The blouse held just enough dampness to cling to her breasts and—almost—to let him see through it. He jerked on the reins of his mind and tried to get it under control.

"Creed," she said, taking it upon herself to sit down beside him on the tree root, "I don't want to make you feel responsible for me or anything, but do you have some jerky or something like that I could have for a snack?"

He stuck one foot in his boot and stomped it on.

"Didn't you eat breakfast like I told you?"

"Yes, but all that driving across the river made me really hungry," she said.

"How much food did you bring with you?"

"I never dreamed you'd be so inhospitable," she said, with a teasing sadness. "Or is it that you didn't bring much food with you, either? Oh, Creed, you didn't rush off on this trip *unprepared*, did you?"

He only shook his head. His anger was fast flooding away and there was nothing he could do to hold it back, hard as he tried.

"I'll get you some jerky," he growled, and stomped his other foot into the other boot.

He just kept on wanting to shake his head in amazement the whole time he walked to Marker, got the jerky from his pack, and walked back to her. She was a pistol, all right. That girl could charm a snake out of a tree.

Which he badly needed to remember, because look what happened to Adam when Eve did that.

He handed the pouch to her.

"Oh, thank you so much," she cooed. "I just could not eat another one of those old soggy, crumbly biscuits I've got in my reticule."

He meant to go and look over the buggy to make sure the wheels were all right after what they'd been through, but he sat back down again to take off his boot and get a sticker that he'd missed. Somehow, he stayed there beside her.

"It's not polite to talk with your mouth full," he said.

"Sometimes," she mumbled, around a bite of the chewy dried meat, "I'm not polite."

She ate three sticks of jerky in rapid succession and talked to him the whole time she did it. He was too busy thinking to hear most of what she said.

That's one thing he'd loved about her back when

he thought he wanted to marry her. Raney gave her appetite free rein and she enjoyed life. She had a real zest about everything—from eating, to going on a hay ride on a frosty fall night, to dancing, to . . . kissing.

Only the fear of a consequence they wouldn't be able to hide had kept her from doing more with him than kissing. Raney was a passionate woman.

And it was true that she wasn't always polite—although most times she was the perfect young lady—and sometimes that made her company even more interesting.

There had been incidents when she was hilariously funny. Raney had a sense of humor, which was another reason he had thought he loved her.

And Raney was like him in that she kept on until she got what she wanted. Every time.

As she had proven today.

That crossing today had proved she had a lot more courage than he'd ever guessed she had.

And that she was even more unpredictable than he'd realized.

Raney possessed an indomitable spirit like his. He might not have thought about it in so many words, but deep inside he had known that even back then.

That was why he had wanted to marry her. He'd never met another girl whose spirit matched his.

He let his fingers brush hers as she handed the leather pouch back to him.

Yes, she was all those things. But her unpredictability stopped at Robert Childress's door.

The one thing that always proved true was that the man controlled his daughter. Even more so now that her mama was gone.

Raney was going to please her papa, come hell or high water.

Chapter 6

Raney drove through the rest of the day with a high heart. Creed rode on ahead to see where they could spend the night, and she held Tally to a slow trot—as if he really wanted to go any faster. They had rested the horses for a good while there in the shade on the south side of the ford, but Tally wasn't young anymore and she was taking no chances with him.

It was crazy for her to be happy with Brassell missing and Papa not even knowing that yet and no telling what kind of trouble ahead for them all. When Mama had died, Raney's first thought had been that she'd never be happy again, but here she was, six months later, thinking that she was.

At the very least, she was filled with a strong satisfaction. She had saved herself—with Tally's help, of course—in an impossible situation. That made her feel . . . powerful. Competent.

Definitely *not* featherheaded.

Creed's acknowledgment of her feat with his grudging praise, "Pretty salty," made her smile every time she thought of it. At least he was man enough to admit he'd been wrong, which she doubted Leonard would be able to do.

The sounds of a buggy approaching from the rear at a good, brisk pace caused her to pull over and drive even more slowly down the shady side of the road. Several other travelers had already come along, and she'd learned that there wasn't much extra room when two wheeled vehicles passed each other.

But this one didn't pass. When it came even with her, Raney saw that it was an open rig a lot like her own. A man and woman were on the seat. She glanced at them, then, when she realized they were deliberately driving alongside her, she recognized them.

"My goodness gracious," Mrs. Scarborough called in her trilling, high voice, "is that you, Raney dear?"

"Yes, ma'am," Raney said, realizing that, sure enough, as she had feared, someone from home—and one of her mother's best friends—was seeing her in the scandalous jeans she'd borrowed from

Creed. She wished she had a lap robe over her legs, although the late afternoon was plenty hot for this late in the spring.

Hallie Scarborough wasn't known as a terrible gossip, but Raney's situation would be so shocking that even a saint would be hard put not to mention it to anyone. And once mentioned, it would be all over the county by sundown the same day.

"Mrs. Scarborough, Judge Scarborough. How are y'all today?"

Judge Scarborough was driving his own buggy, which she'd never seen him do before.

"Fine, darling. Are you all right? Surely to heaven you aren't way down here all alone," Mrs. Scarborough said, all in one breath.

She raised the veil on her traveling hat, and Raney saw her small, sharp eyes searching the back of Raney's buggy as if she had a companion crouching behind the sideboards.

"No, ma'am, I'm . . ." What?

Traveling with Creed Sixkiller and no chaperone? Waiting for my Indian friend to come back and say where we'll spend the night tonight?

"Is one of your brothers somewhere around?"

Mercifully, before Raney could answer, the judge leaned across his wife and said, "Pull over for a moment, if you please, Miss Childress. Up ahead in the shade of that cottonwood grove will do just fine. I have need to speak with you."

"Yes, sir."

Oh, dear Lord! What did he want? Were they going to try to take her under their wing?

Well, she wouldn't be taken. She hadn't rushed off from home and nearly drowned just to be prevented from finding Brass. Because she certainly couldn't find him with them in tow. She was rescuing Brassell to hide him at home, and she would do it, in spite of all Creed Sixkiller and the Scarboroughs and the rest of the world could do to jail him again.

The judge motioned for her to go on ahead and she did, then pulled off the road to stop in the shady place he'd pointed out. Maybe she could get rid of them before Creed came back, and that would spare her a second scandal for Mrs. Scarborough to talk about.

"Honey, this is so surprising to see you here . . ." Mrs. Scarborough began, but the judge waved her to silence.

"Are you going to your brother, miss?"

He demanded, rather than asked, and Raney pressed her lips together to think for a moment. A woman who had just forded a bad-current river and escaped from a quicksand trap to boot did not have to submit to being bullied.

Not even by a judge who was a friend of her father's.

"My brother Trent is in Fort Worth," she said. "And I don't know the whereabouts of Brassell."

"When he escaped from my jail, he said he was going to San Antonio."

"I didn't know it was *your* jail, Judge Scarborough," drawled a voice from among the trees.

Creed rode out into the open with his eyes fixed on the judge.

The judge stared back.

"Sixkiller! What are you doing here?"

"Risking my hide and neglecting my cattle again," Creed said, "chasing down residents of *your* jail."

"Well, that's not too far off the mark," the judge said, defending himself with his famous charm as he relaxed into a big smile. He always tended to joke about any matter at hand, no matter how serious. "Think about it," he said. "I try to keep them locked up but I have to dispose of them somehow. Can't keep them in jail till the cows come home."

"If you could at least manage to keep them in there until they come up for a hearing, it'd help me out," Creed said. "Letting them escape the same day I bring them in plays hell with my spring roundup."

He used a jovial tone, but it had an edge of censure to it. Raney noticed that both Scarboroughs heard it, too.

Then Creed, with a smile as charming as the judge's himself, tipped his hat and nodded to Mrs. Scarborough and to Raney.

"If y'all will please pardon my language, ladies."

"Of course we will, Mr. Sixkiller," Mrs. Scarborough said, fanning herself vigorously, although she sat in the cool shade. "It's so nice to see you again."

"Likewise, ma'am," Creed said, with a sketch of a bow from the saddle. "Are y'all bound for San Antone?"

"Oh yes," Mrs. Scarborough said, fluttering her lashes at him. "The judge has some urgent business there."

"Then we must let you go," Creed said, moving his horse to the side.

Both Scarboroughs looked from him to Raney and back again with puzzlement in their eyes.

"You're traveling with Miss Childress?" asked the judge.

"I am," Creed said.

After another moment in which it seemed that both Scarboroughs tried to read the secret solution to that mystery on Raney's face, the judge spoke to her in his most persuasive tones.

"It's most responsible of you, my dear," he said, "to help Mr. Sixkiller uphold the law. It'll be greatly to your brother's benefit if he'll return to Limestone County and face the music."

Raney, silent, looked at him. She couldn't agree because it seemed a betrayal of Brassell.

"Do you have friends to stay with in San Antone?" he asked.

"Yes, she does," Creed said, "so we'll be well chaperoned. Y'all needn't worry about that."

As if they weren't going to camp by the side of the road, just the two of them, a couple of hours from now! As if they hadn't been unchaperoned last night.

But the judge wasn't worried about their morals or Raney's reputation.

"If you'll give us the address where you'll be staying," he said, "perhaps we could make arrangements to have dinner one evening with you and your friends. We always like to widen our circle of acquaintances in Bexar."

"Oh," Raney said. "I don't believe I've ever known the name of their street, but I can find their house when we get there, I'm sure."

"What part of town is it in?"

Raney thought about it frantically, but she couldn't recall ever having heard the name of any part of San Antonio. She thought there was a river running through the town, but she didn't know what to say about that.

She smiled and made a pretty shrug. "I just never do pay attention to things like that," she said. "My papa is the one who always drives us there."

They sat silent for a moment, the judge's hands moving restlessly on the lines.

"I wonder if I'd recognize the name," he said.

Raney thought fast, reaching for a common surname.

"Beauregard Jackson," she said.

Quickly, she added, "I think it's William Beauregard, but Papa always calls him Beau."

"Nooo," the judge said, "I'm afraid that doesn't ring a bell with me."

He thought about it for a little longer, then finally, he said, "We must be going."

"Don't let us keep you," Creed said.

"So nice to see you, Raney, darling," Mrs. Scarborough said, as the judge urged their team of horses into action. "You two ought to just fall in and go with us."

The judge didn't give Raney time to answer. He drove back onto the road and headed south again at such a fast clip, the dust boiled up in a cloud.

Raney and Creed watched them go. She felt so embarrassed by her newly embroidered lie that she had to distract herself. And him. She could *not* answer any more questions about the mythical Jackson family at this minute.

"I had feeling someone would see me in these pants," she cried. "Why did it have to be Mrs. *Scarborough*?"

Creed's head jerked around and he looked at her in total amazement. Then he widened his eyes in mock horror and gave her an infuriating grin.

"The judge saw you, too," he said. "Are you not worried about him, too?"

124

"I don't think *he* would've noticed if I'd been wearing your breechcloth," she said, feeling her cheeks grow warm at the boldness of saying such a thing.

They heated even more when the image of Creed in his breechcloth came back into her mind.

"The judge was too worried about his urgent business to take note of your clothes," he said, as his grin faded. "Wonder what business it is."

"That's right," she said. "He didn't even seem shocked when you implied you'd be staying with me at my friends' house."

She was so mad at herself for starting to weave this tangled web. Right now would be a good time to confess the truth to Creed, but she couldn't do it. She shouldn't. She might be able to use the fictional Jacksons to get away from him in San Antonio and find Brassell on her own.

"Right," Creed said, thinking it over. "And he wasn't shocked that they'd be willing to shelter an Indian under their roof."

She stared at him.

"I hadn't thought that far," she said.

They looked at each other.

It was strange, but there for a minute she *had* forgotten he was an Indian.

"Maybe he assumed I'd be quartered with the servants," he said.

"No, he even suggested we all have dinner together," she said, still looking at him in amazement. "I know he meant you, too."

"It's urgent business, indeed," Creed said. "I'm guessing he wasn't thinking about anything but finding Brassell."

Raney's mouth fell open. "What? He's the judge. He wouldn't go after Brass himself."

"Why else would he be so inquisitive about your friends' place? He wanted their address and their name."

She thought about that, nodding her head.

"It seems that way," she said. "But why? Why would he go to all that trouble?"

"That's what I'd like to know."

Without exchanging a word, they pulled back onto the road and set out again, Creed riding alongside the buggy seat.

Finally he said, "Can you think of anything different Brassell may have been into lately? Anything unusual he might have said? Anyone new that he's started running with?"

She considered all of it and shook her head. "No," she said. "I didn't notice one new thing about him."

Creed said, "He risked getting shot in order to escape from jail only a few hours after he'd been telling me he'd be out of there as soon as his father got home from Fort Worth. I would've sworn he'd wait for Robert to rescue him."

"Brass is a big baby," she said, and Creed looked

surprised at her admitting it. "I've been trying to figure out why he didn't come straight home. He could certainly make it home sooner than he could get to San Antone, and Pleasant Hill is plenty big enough to hide on, even if he never came to the house."

"Right," Creed said.

They thought about it a little more.

"Ever since we saw those two Chickenhawks and I sent them home, I've been wondering why they want Brassell so bad," he said. "Normally, those feudists go about their usual business and wait for their enemies to cross their paths."

Her fear rose again as she stared at him.

"Yes, they do! You're right. I've heard enough talk to know that."

"When somebody leaves the county, that's a sign he's getting out of the feud and nobody follows him," Creed said. "There were at least four Chickenhawks out there last night—and probably more—all hunting for Brassell *after* he'd crossed the county line."

"Why would that be?"

He shook his head. "Beats me."

"Were you still in town when Brass escaped?"

"No. I'd ridden all the way back to the Sixes and Sevens."

"Who sent for you?" she asked.

"Johnny Bill Dexter," he said. "He was one Chickenhawk who wasn't at the rally, and he was

127

incensed that I had jailed any of them. He sure didn't want a Peckerwood like Brass getting special privileges like escape."

"He's just mad because none of his men had sense enough to get away," she said, and they both laughed.

"All I can come up with is that Brass is a threat to somebody," he said, picking up the pace to a faster trot.

"Every Peckerwood is a threat to every Chicken-hawk," she said, trying to keep her voice from trembling.

"Yes, but the Chickenhawks are singling Brass out. How could a sixteen-year-old kid who is, as you say, a big baby, not to mention a naturally lousy shot, be a special threat to forty full-grown men?"

"Maybe it's revenge," she said, as much to herself as to him. "He might've shot someone during the fight at the rally, although it would have been an accident if he had. Brass won't wear his glasses in public and without them he's blind as a bat."

"It was a melee," he said. "It'd be doubtful if anybody knew who shot whom. Besides, it's *all* about revenge. *Any* Peckerwood they killed would be revenge—it wouldn't have to be Brassell."

Raney frowned.

"Even after he's left the county," she said, puzzling to herself, "they're desperate to get Brassell back in jail."

Creed nodded.

"I think it's just what Johnny Bill said," she said, staring at his profile, trying to read his mind to see if he agreed. "If their men have to stay in jail, they don't want Brass getting out."

"Maybe so," he said.

"And the judge is only interested because he doesn't want anyone escaping from his jail," she said. "All he was doing asking us all those questions was making polite conversation about our journey."

"Maybe so," Creed said again.

Raney had a feeling that he thought it might not all be that simple, but he didn't say any more, and she didn't ask. If Creed really believed that things were worse than they appeared to be at the moment, she didn't want to know about it.

"But if they really are after Brass especially hard," she said, "you must let him come home to hide, Creed. Until Papa and Trent can come home and defend him."

He jerked his head around, fast.

"Brass was threatening me with what they'll do when they come home," he said. "You don't need to repeat it."

"They *will* be really insulted that you jailed Brass," she said, trying to make him see reason.

"He's no better than any man involved in this feud," he said flatly.

Then he added, "No matter *how* much Southern royal blood runs in his veins."

129

"Well, you don't have to be so scornful about it," she said hotly. "Brass can't help who his ancestors are."

He shocked her then, with a hard, careless grin.

"And you can't, either, can you, Raney? But your papa insists on holding them against y'all."

He picked up his hat and put it back on, settled it a little deeper.

"You just keep coming," he said. "I'll ride on up to the spot I found for a campsite and make sure nobody else is there."

He took off at a high lope while she stared after him, thinking about what he'd just said. To the best of her knowledge and instincts, he had just insulted her whole family. Again. As in the slander that their line was started by a convict sent to Georgia on a prison ship Creed had spoken when Papa refused him her hand.

For an instant her anger flared hotter. Then it died down.

Oh, well, there was no use to take offense. Creed was her only companion, and she had miles to go and she didn't want to make him stop talking to her.

Besides, if a person was going to be really honest about it, Papa had insulted Creed's whole family first. He had told him an Indian wasn't good enough for her, hadn't he? Turnabout was fair play.

Creed bit his lip and rode off in disgust. Was he learning nothing from his grandfather Standing

130

Bear? He was ashamed of himself for being so petty as to make that jibe about Raney's father's arrogance.

Standing Bear would be ashamed of him, too.

When Robert Childress had given Creed his first real brush with true prejudice, that scorn, coupled with Raney's rejection, had cut him to the core. All of it was rooted in such deep injustice, bringing such insult to the Sixkiller family, that anger blossomed in all of them.

It was a betrayal. They had thought the Childresses were true neighbors and friends.

For a few weeks, the bitterness from that betrayal ran in all their veins, and it still lingered in his sister Maggie's heart after all this time.

What it had done to Creed was to make him think about himself as a man all the long way to Kansas on that trail drive. One of Robert Childress's reasons for rejecting him as a son-in-law had been Creed's reputation for wildness and riotous living. Somehow that rang with memories of derogatory remarks about drunken Indians, although Robert dared not use that phrase because his own sons were more than a little fond of their liquor themselves.

And his wild ways had not been a drop in the bucket compared to his race as a reason for rejection. Creed knew that. Yet he thought it all through that summer, and he came back home to Texas determined to become the best man he could possibly be.

With that, he determined to know and live his heritage. The day after he returned to the Sixes and Sevens, he went to his grandfather and asked to learn all that Standing Bear knew about the old ways.

Standing Bear told him that first he needed to learn more about life. Then Creed would be able to see how the old Cherokee ways of living life fit its realities as surely as a fox darting into its den.

The first story he'd told him, the Story of the Two Wolves, was one that he'd told to his grandchildren many times before, but this time Creed heard it as if it were new. Standing Bear sat down cross-legged in the shade of the mulberry tree and motioned for Creed to sit facing him.

"This is what the old men said when I was a boy," he began, as all stories always started.

Creed heard those words strike his deepest heart for the first time. He was one of thousands and thousands of Cherokee men who had listened to these same words, a line of men stretching back to the Blue Ridge and the Great Smoky Mountains in the east, to the center of the earth. A line stretching back over hundreds and hundreds of years.

"A fight is going on inside me," Standing Bear went on. "It is a terrible fight, and it is between two wolves.

"One wolf is Fear, Anger, Envy, Sorrow, Regret, Arrogance, Greed, Self-Pity, Guilt, Resentment, Lies, False Pride. Sometimes he is all of these at once.

"The other wolf is Joy, Serenity, Peace, Love, Hope,

Generosity, Friendship, Empathy, Truth, Compassion, and Faith."

Standing Bear fixed his wise, dark eyes on Creed's and held his gaze in their trap.

"The same fight is going on inside you, my son, and inside every other person, too."

Finally, as one of the listening children was expected to do, Creed asked the question.

"Grandfather, which wolf will win?"

"The one you feed."

Creed rode on, letting those words ring in his mind. Petty remarks going out of his mouth brought guilt and shame. They came from and they engendered regret and arrogance. They fed the bad wolf.

What had happened to make him sink so low?

He was as distant from three years ago as Texas was from the Center of the Earth. He was long past his resentment of Robert Childress. He was far removed from any feelings he had once had for Raney.

It must be his lack of sleep from keeping watch all night. Tonight he must sleep. He needed rest, and he needed dreams to help him in his quest.

He rode in a wide circle around the little tucked-away copse of live oak trees he'd picked for their camp, looking for someone with a fire built already or the tracks of someone who might have just come in there with the intention of staying the night. He wanted no one around to molest them, because there was no way to know whom he could trust.

There were no Chickenhawks or anyone else.

If his puzzling of the situation had led him to the right point so far, any Chickenhawks who had left Limestone County would keep away from him if they could. They wanted him to find Brassell. His belief was that they had been out in such numbers chasing the boy across the county line in hopes of driving him into Creed's sights.

The question was why? The bloodlust of the feud usually required its possessor to do his own killing.

He turned back and loped out to the road to wait for Raney. She was already coming toward him, holding on to the lines with all her might, trying to keep control with the old horse going at a long trot and straining at the bit.

"As soon as you and Marker were out of sight, he started trying to run off with me," she called breathlessly.

"Marker's his new buddy," Creed called back. "At least he isn't trying to go home anymore."

"No, but this is just as bad. He has nearly worn me smooth *out*."

Creed rode in front of Tally so he'd slow down and follow Marker, then led the way to the best place to put the buggy for the night. Raney drove between the trees, pulled back on the lines, and called, "Whoa." She was gasping a little for breath, and her voice sounded hoarse.

Creed stopped his horse, stood in his stirrup, and swung to the ground while he watched her. She sat there on the buggy seat, unmoving for a minute, letting the lines fall from her hands. She looked pale and exhausted.

"Raney?"

Seeing how tired she was after driving all day and getting herself out of the river, he felt small. Sniping at her father's arrogance only hurt her, not Robert. Robert was the one who'd insulted him.

The bad wolf spoke in his ear.

And so did she, Sixkiller, you and all your people. Don't forget that, just because she's a wilted flower. She still has the power to pull at your heart.

No, maybe that was the good wolf instead. It was a good warning.

"I'm all right," she said. "I just want to rest for a minute."

He bent his head to his task of unsaddling, but instead of the buckle and the latigo and the cinch, he kept on seeing her straight back and the proud way she held her head, tired as she was. Of course she was exhausted, after the day they'd had. Raney had grit, he'd have to give her that, and in spades.

From the corner of his eye, he saw her begin to stir. She wrapped the lines around the brake handle and stood up.

He pulled his saddle and blanket, threw them down, and strode toward her.

She glanced up. "I don't need any help, Creed," she said. "I'm wearing my jeans."

He kept on coming, though. He'd seen the shakiness in her legs, and when she turned her back to him and started climbing down the wheel, he saw she was shaky all over. He got there as her foot slipped on the hub. He caught her as she fell.

A tiny trembling was running all through her, and she clung to him as if to warm herself. She still fit perfectly in his arms.

"I never should've let you wear those pants," he said.

"Why not?"

"They make you cocky," he said. "I saw that when you tried to scramble down off the wheel, fast as a squirrel."

She laughed, but the sound was shaky, too.

He managed to keep his arms from tightening their grip on her, but he wasn't strong enough to make them loosen any. Raney felt warm and soft and curvy against him, just the way she used to do.

Chapter 7

They stood without moving. Raney closed her eyes and let her head rest on Creed's chest.

His arms remained around her.

She hadn't felt warm—not warm all the way to her bones as if everything was all right—since she left home. No, it'd been longer than that. She hadn't had that feeling, not once, since Mama died. Until now.

Creed's heart was beating, strong and sure, deep inside him. She could hear it. Every beat it made drove more of the trembling out of her body.

She could stay right here forever.

Always before, long ago, when they had walked out together from the socials, she had loved it when he held her. But she'd also been too nervous about letting him kiss her the way he did, to let any of their embraces go on too long.

She mustn't let him kiss her this time, though. They were all alone and she might get carried away. A tingle stirred in her breasts where they were pressed against his hard muscles. The taste of his kisses came back to her tongue. Creed was a shameless kisser.

Leonard was a . . . careful kisser.

She wished she'd never thought of Leonard. He was careful about taking to the road, too, no matter what the need might be. And careful about trying to take advantage of being her betrothed only when all her male relatives were gone.

"I don't feel very cocky," she said, against Creed's shirt.

She lifted her head to look up at him, but she didn't move away from him any.

"I will admit, though," she said, with a grin, "I did when I drove up out of that river."

He grinned back.

"See? What did I tell you? Save yourself one time and a man can't live with you."

They laughed and then their eyes held for a long time. Raney felt her smile fade away. Creed's vanished, too.

His gaze drifted down to her mouth.

Her lips waited for his. Her lips *ached* for his.

"I'd really like to kiss you right now," he said. "But I won't."

She wanted nothing more. She didn't know when she'd ever wanted anything so much.

But he meant it. He had decided, and it was almost impossible to turn Creed around when his decision was made.

Even her flirting, which was the best in the county—maybe even in all of Texas—had never caused him to change his direction. She would keep her dignity.

At least as much of it as possible with her breasts pressed against him. She made herself take a step back. A sharp disappointment darted through her when he let her go.

"Well, then," she said. "I'm not going to kiss you, either."

That startled him. It didn't show on his face, but then he *was* the best of anyone she'd ever known at hiding emotions he didn't want seen.

Realizing she knew him that well brought a little smile to her lips. He was the only beau she'd ever had that she couldn't always read.

"What we'd better do is build a fire," he said. "I noticed some wild onions out there on the other side of the creek. Want a hot supper?"

Her stomach gave a loud growl at the sound of the words.

139

"I take it that's a yes," he said. "If you'll gather onions, I'll get wood and rocks for the fire ring."

"You said the other side of the creek," she said. "Does it have quicksand?"

"What's the matter? You're not scared of a little quicksand, are you?"

She gave him her best narrow-eyed, dangerous look.

"I'm not scared of nothin'," she drawled.

Then she had to turn away. That mischievous grin and the glint in his eyes made her want to run back into his arms.

They went about their chores. Creed told her to take their canteens to refill while she was at the creek but Raney was the one who thought of taking her petticoat to put the onions in. He gave her his pocketknife to scrape the dirt off and trim them, and she felt her new self growing as she strode off with hardly a qualm in the direction he sent her. It was amazing what saving herself from drowning could do for a girl.

She thought about that while she took off her shoes and waded across the shallow stream to walk in the soft grass on the other side. She'd lied when she said she wasn't scared of nothin'—especially with Creed back there within range of the sound of her voice, which was a thought that made her smile wryly—but she was so much bolder than she'd ever thought she could be.

Amazingly enough, she even thought to wash the

onions after she'd gathered them and before she left the creek. The next thing she knew, she'd be learning to cook, and Etty would be out of a job. Etty. The poor dear would be wringing her hands this very minute, worried sick about her Raney and her Brassell.

Dear Lord, let me find Brassell and get him back home. Soon.

She returned to the campsite to find the horses staked out to graze, the fire built, and some meager camping gear spread out beside it. He took one of the canteens from her and poured some of the water into a small iron pot.

"What are we having?" she asked. "Onion soup?"

"Wild onion and salt-cured venison soup," he said. "I hope it's one of your favorites."

He took the onions and his knife from her, dropped down to sit on his haunches, and cut up the onions in the blink of an eye.

"What a coincidence—it *is*," she said. "Right now, I could eat two pots of it. Do you not have any bigger cooking vessels?"

He laughed.

"Try to control yourself. We have dessert. I've been saving some of Maggie's good lemon teacakes."

She missed Maggie so much. But she couldn't think about Maggie right now, any more than she could think about Leonard.

Nor could she think about Creed and how beautiful his face was when he smiled like that.

She had to think about Brassell.

"Creed," she said, "you know back there on the road when you said that Brass shouldn't have special privileges because he's no better than any other feudist?"

He slanted a wary look up at her.

"Yeah."

"Well, when I asked you to let him come home instead of to jail, I wasn't thinking that he should be treated special."

He didn't answer. He just waited for her to go on.

That was another way Creed was so much better than Leonard. Leonard talked too much. He never gave her time to explain herself.

"And I didn't ask because of what you and I used to be to each other, either."

He glanced up. She looked into his eyes but she couldn't see a flicker of feeling about those words.

Her cheeks reddened. She could feel the warmth of the blush surge up her throat and into her face. They hadn't been *anything* to each other. They had never been betrothed.

But he must've had some feelings for her. Hadn't he just said he wanted to kiss her? He remembered their kisses, too.

And he had, after all, once asked to marry her. So she wasn't imagining things.

"I mean *who* we used to be to each other," she said.

He nodded abruptly, as if to say, *Get on with it*.

Raney swallowed hard. "I asked you to promise me he could go home with me because of the danger," she said. "It's only common sense. Brass needs to be in a safer place than that jail."

He shrugged as he added the meat to the pot of water and hung it over the fire.

"Who knows?" he said. "We may not even find him."

It made her furious. That attitude was so false, coming from him. The whole world knew Creed Sixkiller never gave up on anything. He was famous because he always kept on coming, no matter what.

All he was doing was sidestepping her request, trying to keep from giving her that promise.

Her mouth opened to tell him so, but she closed it again. No sense making him furious with her. And no sense pitching one of her fits. That had never worked on him, ever. She had to remember the old saw about catching more flies with honey.

But she had to say *something* or burst.

"Oh yes, we will," she blurted, through clenched teeth. "Or, at least, *I* will. I'm not going home until I do."

She caught his quick look of surprise from the corner of her eye before she stalked over to the buggy and snatched up her other blouse. This would be a good time to wash it in the creek and think about the argument she would make later. When his stomach was full. Hadn't Mama always counseled not to ask a man for anything or tell him any bad news before he had eaten his supper?

By the time Raney had finished washing her blouse and spreading it on the sideboard of the buggy to dry, the food was ready. So was her strategy. She would break all the rules of wise social behavior between a young woman and a man. She would let him see into her mind. She would tell him the truth.

"I'm starving," she said, as she joined Creed at the fire.

He even had two bowls made from gourds and two spoons sitting on one of the rocks, all ready for the meal.

"How'd you know I was coming along?" she said lightly. "I thought our meeting on the road was an accident."

He filled one bowl with the fragrant stew and handed it to her.

"I left home on the trail of a prisoner," he said, in that same careless tone. "I wouldn't let him starve while I ate."

He added wryly, "Or the other way around. I couldn't deal with Brassell Childress on an empty stomach."

She laughed. "I know what you mean. I am so mad at him I could just wring his neck right now."

After he had poured the other half of the food

144

into his own bowl and had hung the coffeepot on the hook where the pot had been, they carried their food to the shade of a big tree and sat leaning back against its trunk. They both ate hungrily, in silence, until the soup was all gone.

"Thank goodness," she said, setting her spoon into the empty bowl. "It's amazing how much better hot food can make a person feel. I'm craving the coffee, though."

"It'll be ready soon," he said. "Then I'll find the tin of teacakes in my pack."

They sat quiet, looking out through the screen of trees and across the creek to the meadow on the other side. Far beyond it, the sun was lowering in the sky, but it would be a long time until twilight.

"The days are getting a lot longer," Raney said idly. "But I'm glad we stopped when we did. I wonder if the Scarboroughs are going to drive all night."

"Could be," Creed said. "They did take off like the devil was after them."

"She was worried about me," Raney said, remembering the look in Mrs. Scarborough's eyes. "My mama was her friend. She felt she should see about me, traveling with you without a chaperone."

"It didn't bother the judge," Creed said. "He was in such a hurry he forgot his gallantry."

"That whole meeting was odd," Raney said. "She asked us to drive along with them but said not a word about us all camping together tonight."

She turned to Creed just as he glanced at the coffeepot and started to get up.

"I'll pour," she said. "I need to do something to earn my keep."

"Stay," he said. "Rest. You're not used to hard days on the road."

She watched him get the tin of teacakes from his pack, tuck it under his arm, shake out two collapsible tin mugs, and fill them with coffee. Every move he made was fluid and full of natural grace, strong and sure. Every step he took was a caress of the ground beneath his boots. He walked like the Indian he was. He didn't make a sound.

His whole body was as handsome as his face. And, as the saying went, he covered the ground he stood on. There was a power about him that no one could deny.

Raney turned her thoughts back to the Scarboroughs. She couldn't let herself think about Creed or how she'd felt in his arms.

Or about how much she wanted to be in them again.

When he was settled beside her once more, with the tin of teacakes on the ground between them, and Raney had had a few sips of coffee, she organized her thoughts and broached her argument.

"You know what I'm thinking," she said, trying to keep her heart still and free of fear so her brain could work unimpeded, "is that maybe the judge *knows* that Brassell is a special danger to the Chickenhawks. He may even know why. Maybe he's trying to get him back into jail before they find him and try to . . . uh, kill him."

"Then why didn't the judge say so to me?" Creed asked. "It's *my* duty to capture a missing prisoner."

She turned and looked at him over the rim of her cup. "Maybe he doesn't want to tell you the secret—*if* he knows why they're so determined to get Brass."

He held her gaze.

"Maybe Brass found out something," she said, "that the Chickenhawks don't want him to tell. And the judge thinks that if it got out, it would cause the feud to get even worse."

His inscrutable eyes narrowed in approval, and he raised one eyebrow.

"Not bad," he said, with a teasing grin, "for a white woman who's used to hearing, 'Don't worry your pretty little head.'"

"Thank you," she said, grinning back at him. "I'm learning to think like an Indian woman."

That made his grin widen. Then it faded.

"I think you've hit the nail on the head when it comes to the Chickenhawks," he said. "They are determined to kill Brass, and it could very well be because he knows something they don't want told. But I wish I could get a direction on what that secret might be—and why the judge is so hell-bent on finding him."

"The judge is trying to stop the feud," Raney said again. "That has to be it."

"If I had a way to get word to Eagle Jack," Creed said thoughtfully, "I'd tell him to do some nosing around."

Raney set her cup down on the ground so fast that some of her coffee splashed out. Her blue eyes widened and locked on Creed's gaze.

"I know! Send him a smoke signal!"

She sounded as excited as a little girl, and it was all Creed could do to keep from laughing. Then it irritated him. When would she ever learn not to believe everything she heard about Indians? And that not all Indians were alike? And that his family had been assimilated into the ranching culture of Texas for nearly a hundred years?

If she was trying to learn to think for herself, it was time for her to know those things.

"Now why didn't I think of that?" he said, getting to his feet in a flash. "Is your skirt still damp? Is it all right if I use it?"

All excited, she scrambled up to help.

"Of course," she said, "but I thought y'all always used your saddle blankets."

"If that's all we have with us," he said, as they started walking quickly toward the buggy. "But there're lots of different circumstances. For instance, if we were on the warpath wearing only our breechcloths, and riding bareback, we would have to use the bareback riding pad if we had one or our breechcloth if we didn't."

She stopped in her tracks.

"Will this make my skirt smell like smoke? It's the only one I have with me. Maybe you should use your breechcloth instead."

He stopped, too, and frowned down at her thoughtfully.

"Well . . ."

"I mean, if that *is* possible, as you said."

"We-e-ll, as I *also* said, there're lots of different circumstances. I'll have to look at the angle of the fire to the direction we need," he said. "We don't have time to build another fire. Don't you agree?"

She frowned, too, trying to make sense of that gibberish. She was about to carry this thinking thing too far.

"The angle of direction matters and so does the weight and size of whatever we use to interrupt the rising of the smoke," he said quickly. "Let me step over here and see what I think."

She followed him over the fire and squinted with him to the north, the general direction of the Sixes and Sevens.

"What if Eagle Jack isn't there right now?" she asked. "What if he's gone to Concho?"

"Anybody in my family can read the signal and get word to him," he said absently, pretending to be absorbed in choosing exactly the right "angle."

He moved over to the other side of the fire and looked north from there. She moved with him.

He stood completely still for a couple of long heartbeats. So did she.

"My instincts tell me that on this spot we're a little south-southwest of the ranch," he said, at last. "Only by a hair. This will be the best place to work from. Exactly here."

"I'll mark it," she said, picking up a stick from the small pile of kindling he'd had left over. "Here, move over. But first, dig your boot heels in."

He did as she said, and she knelt behind his tracks to drive the larger end of the stick into the ground.

"Now," she said, "let's get the skirt and the breechcloth and see which one will work better from there."

Together they hurried over to the buggy and his packs, which lay near his saddle.

"It will make it smell like smoke," he confessed. "I hope the breechcloth will work."

"If you have to use the skirt, that's all right," she said. "I just know it's too heavy to wash it tonight and wear it again tomorrow, and I *will* not go into San Antonio wearing pants."

"You're always welcome to the breechcloth," he said sincerely.

He didn't know when he'd had so much fun. Why was it that Raney always brought out the light side of him? That must've been another reason he had wanted to marry her.

Predictably, she blushed bright pink right up to the roots of her hair. She had beautiful skin.

"I'd wear the blanket first," she said.

"Then we're making even more progress in your thinking than I had realized," he said, "if you're willing to go into San Antonio dressed as an Indian."

She flashed him a fiery blue glance he couldn't read. He wanted to take her by the shoulders and look into her eyes until she told him what that look was saying to him.

What he wanted was to kiss her.

She hadn't hesitated to say what she felt a little while ago: *Well, then, I'm not going to kiss you, either.* What had she meant by that remark? Did she really not want to kiss him?

"I just want to go into San Antonio knowing what danger my brother is in," she said. "Let's get this smoke signal in the air before dark."

"Now you're planning ahead," he said. "You're right."

They took both garments back to the fire, Creed fixed himself carefully in the right place, and picked up the breechcloth. He held it flat with both hands.

"Stir it up," he said, gazing off into the distance toward the Sixes and Sevens, "give me a little more fire to work with."

Raney stirred it with another piece of wood, then added a stick of dead tree limb that Creed had brought in. He lowered the breechcloth and held the smoke down, then whipped it away and let the smoke rise. He had no earthly idea how to make rings of smoke or different-shaped clouds of it.

The smoke rose in a narrow column, just as it had been doing.

"This isn't heavy or big enough," he said, handing the breechcloth to Raney while keeping his eyes fixed on the northern sky.

She gave him the skirt and he held it flat, waist-high, across the smoke. It was still heavy, even after it had dried, and there was so much of it, he could hardly get all the edges of it gathered up in his hands. How did a woman as small as Raney carry such a thing around?

Slowly, he bent at the knees, lowered it, and held it down. This time, when he whipped it away, he did get a round burst of smoke to rise into the sky. He waited a moment, then did it again.

"That tells Eagle Jack who this message is from and that we need his help," he said. "Now I'll tell him what we want him to do."

This smoke cloud would need to look different from the first ones.

"How do you read the puffs of smoke?" Raney asked. "And how do you make them round? You need to show me how to do this."

Damn.

"Don't think about it," he said, not daring to take his eyes off the sky and look at her lest she see his need to laugh. "I've never met a white person who could make any sense out of it."

"But *I'm* learning to think like an Indian woman."

"The women don't do this," he said quickly. "Just the men."

"Hmm," she said, considering that for a minute. "That seems really strange. For women like them, who think for themselves and go to war if they want, I mean."

Well. Instead of being simple and helpless, Raney really was too smart for her own good—or for his.

"It does," he agreed. He didn't dare to look at her. She was silent, obviously still thinking.

"Well," she said finally, "if Eagle Jack can read the message we're sending, that's all that matters, isn't it?"

"You're right," he said. "It is."

"That, and if *you* know how to say, 'Brassell Childress may have seen or heard something that makes the Chickenhawks determined to kill him as soon as they can. Please ask around and see if you can find out what that secret knowledge might be.' "

"Right again," he said.

"That's quite a lot of words," she said. "How many puffs of smoke will it take to say that?"

153

He swallowed hard and kept his face turned away from her.

"We-ell," he said. "It doesn't work quite that way. I'm sending the signals in Cherokee, not in English."

"Oh. So Cherokee doesn't take so many words?"

"It . . . its alphabet is what's called a syllabary. Syllables instead of letters."

"Oh. So you'll need a smoke signal for each *syllable*?"

This was getting to be ridiculous. He racked his brain. Fast.

"No," he said, in his firmest, most final tone. "The smoke is more in *symbols*. Ideas. One . . . no, *two* more will be enough. That'll be *plenty*."

And these two had to be different from the ones he'd just made and different from each other.

Creed stirred up the fire himself and when the smoke was boiling up, he passed the cloth across it, held it there for a count of four—one of the sacred numbers, so surely the Apportioner would help him here—and then let the smoke go up.

He added a pass around it, and it did rise in more of a tall cloud than the other had done. This was the most insane idea he'd ever had in his life. But he was truly trying to teach this girl a lesson about prejudging a whole people based on a willful lack of knowledge.

Thinking about that helped him to feel a little less foolish.

"One more," he said.

To try for a flatter, wider cloud, he sat on his haunches and held the skirt closer to the flames. For a longer time. Surely those two changes would make the smoke rise differently. He held it for a count of seven—the other sacred number—and talked while he did it.

"Eagle Jack knows everybody in the county and he can charm anyone into telling him whatever he wants to know," he said, to distract her from her thoughts *and* from examining his handiwork too closely. "He'll find out what we need to know. Don't you worry, now."

She gasped and clasped her hand to her heart.

"Don't worry my pretty little head? Surely that's not what you're saying, Creed. Why, you've been telling me all along I need to learn to think for myself and I'm trying my best and—"

He interrupted her rant with a roar. *"No!"*

Immediately he modulated his voice. "No," he said, "I'm not meaning to say that. I only mean to ease your mind about your brother."

This joke was getting to be a whole lot more trouble than it was worth.

"One more smoke cloud," he said, more firmly than ever.

He stood up suddenly and whipped the skirt away from the fire with a fine flourish. A large, rather flat cloud of smoke rose into the air.

For some reason, it had a different, more acrid

155

smell to it, too. He kept an eye on it, pretending to make sure it said what he'd intended.

"Oh," Raney cried, "oh no! My skirt. Creed, it's on fire!"

He looked down to see a bright tongue of orange flame in the middle of the expanse of pale tan cloth. Without a conscious thought, he dropped the skirt and ground the fire out of it with his boot.

With another scream, she grabbed it away from him and shook it, coughing from the dust that flew up around them. Then she spread it out to look at the damage. A black-edged hole about as big as a silver dollar glared in the middle of the fine cloth.

Raney turned her head away as if she couldn't bear to look at it. Gradually, she let her blue gaze travel from his boots on up his frame to meet his eyes. Hers were narrowed and her look was furious.

"You have ruined the only skirt I have with me on this trip," she said, biting the words out from between her clenched teeth, "and I can tell you right now that I am *not* going to drive into San Antonio dressed like a man."

"I'll buy you another skirt when we get there," he said.

Lord! He hoped he didn't have to listen to remonstrations about this all the way to San Antonio.

But that seemed to mollify her, at least a little.

"All right, then," she said. "Because I didn't bring

156

a whole lot of money with me and I may need it for food—"

"Surely not," he said. "Your friends wouldn't be that inhospitable."

"Oh. Yes. Well, anyhow," she said, as she shook the skirt out one more time, "now let's go over there and sit by the tree and watch for Eagle Jack's reply."

This time, most of the dust somehow came up in his face. He had to cough, too. Couldn't complain, though. Not since the dust was all his doing.

"Oh, Eagle Jack won't reply until he's found us an answer to our question," Creed said.

"But he *might*. He might just send a smoke signal back to us right away to say that he received our request and that he will help us."

Raney folded the skirt carefully over her arm with the burned side up and strolled toward the tree. Creed walked beside her, vowing silently to talk her out of this in a hurry because he was so restless he could ride a bucking bronc.

And he had to confess. How else would she learn anything if he didn't tell her she'd been fooled?

When should he do that? How could he do it without making himself look stupid? She was taking every bit of this way too seriously.

They sat down beneath the tree where they'd eaten supper. Raney laid the skirt aside, with the hole up.

"To let the heat out of it," she said, fanning it with her hand.

He looked at it. She reached up, took his chin, and gently turned his face to the north. Irritating as it was, the warmth of her soft hand stirred his blood. It was all he could do not to touch her, too.

Should he have kissed her? *Had* she wanted him to, or not?

"Be sure to keep watch," she said. "Smoke doesn't last long, and it'll be twilight soon."

"Raney," he said, finding his most reasonable but firm tone, "I tell you that Eagle Jack . . ."

He looked at her, a move she corrected with one fingertip along his jaw. He stared to the north again.

"I wish I had some chocolate," she said. "To go with the coffee that's left."

"I wish I had some whiskey," he said fervently.

She slanted a bright glance up at him.

"Thank goodness, you don't," she said, "you have to be sober enough to read Eagle Jack's message. *I* surely can't."

He set his jaw. Damn it, he was going to put a stop to this insanity. Right now.

"Raney . . ."

"Creed, you know what?" she said, far too cheerily for a woman whose only skirt had just been ruined.

She would really be riled when she found out it'd been ruined in a joke played on *her*. Then she truly would be so mad she'd *never* want him to kiss her.

"*What?*"

"I think y'all should teach the women to send the smoke signals and the men can just be runners to carry messages when the sky is dark or the air is foggy or full of dust. I cannot *imagine* a woman being so clumsy as to burn a hole in her skirt."

Something in her voice told him. A chortle she was trying to hide.

He looked down at her then. She met his gaze with her eyes wide and innocent, trying to look serious and sincere, but the corners of her luscious mouth were turning upward.

He couldn't stop looking at her. He wouldn't have turned his head away again if she'd put it in a vise and cranked it.

"How long have you been shucking me?" he drawled.

"You are such a disgraceful bounder, Creed Sixkiller. You ought to be ashamed of yourself."

"I am," he said.

Neither one of them broke that look while they laughed at themselves and each other.

Not until he took her face in his hands and bent his head to kiss her.

Chapter 8

Raney felt herself opening to the heat of Creed's kiss as if his mouth were the sun. The waiting was over.

They'd both been waiting for this—exactly this—ever since he'd remarked that he wanted to kiss her. Everything they'd said and done since then had been leading up to this moment. She knew that with the first touch of his lips to hers.

This need and this fulfillment and this sudden, insatiable longing for more—all the feelings now overwhelming her to her core—had all been inevitable since the instant she'd heard his voice call out her name back there on the road in the dark. Her bones and her flesh had known it all this time.

They were all she had now because her mind had left her. So had her will. Her lips parted of their own volition and the tip of her tongue went seeking for his.

The thrill of that connection sent fire into her blood. New and familiar at the same time, it took away her strength.

She gave herself to the kiss with an abandon she hadn't known she possessed. Somehow she found her arms around his neck, pressing their flesh against the power of his broad shoulders, fitting themselves to the shape of his hard muscles, and her hands in his hair, exploring, feeling to know him.

Under the tips of her fingers, his hat tilted forward to rest its brim on her cheek. To shelter them.

He kissed her fiercely, then, as if he'd only been waiting until they were hidden. She responded in kind, curling his tongue with hers in a teasing dance that made him groan deep in his throat and drop one of his big, brazen hands to close boldly around her breast.

He knocked the hat, unheeded, to the ground and ravished her mouth until they both had no breath left. Raney didn't need to breathe, not when she had the taste and the thrill of Creed's lips and tongue, but the unimagined feeling his hand created was an excitement that could carry her completely away.

She broke the kiss because she scared herself witless. She would've let him bed her. She wanted him to bed her. There were passions living in her that she had never known existed.

And she broke the kiss because she remembered. She was betrothed.

As she turned her face away, he pressed his lips to her cheek in one last caress as if he couldn't bear to let her go, and at that instant she knew something else, too. She had been a terrible fool three years ago to have ever told him no.

"No," she had said, when Creed asked to marry her.

And now she was betrothed to Leonard.

Creed got to his feet, abrupt as you please, and went to see about the horses.

She sat like a statue and watched him. He moved like a panther she'd once seen up on the ridge above the house. He could pounce in an instant. Her whole tingling body cried out for him to come back here this minute and pounce on her.

There was something woefully wanton in her that she had never known about before. No one—not Mama, not Etty, not one aunt or girl cousin or girl-friend that she had ever had—had told her a woman could feel like this: weak with wanting and muddle-headed with longing and throbbing all the way through her whole body, with desire for she did not know what.

163

Maybe they'd never felt this way. None of them, to the best of her knowledge, had ever been kissed by Creed Sixkiller.

Dear Lord, Leonard had certainly never made her feel this way.

A chill ran down her spine. Ignorant as could be, she had pledged her word to spend the rest of her life with Leonard.

Creed finished moving the stakes that held the horses to graze in one area and walked back to the fire. He sat on his haunches and stirred a stick into the short flames.

"More coffee?" he called, in a brisk tone. "In the morning we won't take time to make any. It'll be breakfast on the road again."

"I thought this feasting was too good to last," she said, thankful that her voice came out stronger and calmer than she'd expected.

Evidently, he hadn't been so undone by the kiss as she had. She wouldn't let him know how it had shaken her.

She picked up both their cups and got up, then forced her legs to carry her over to the fire.

"Do we have to leave before daylight?" she asked, holding the cups for him to refill them.

"First light," he said, hanging the pot back on the hook and standing up to face her. "First glimmer. While the morning star is still out."

She made a face at him as she handed him his coffee.

"You're a hard taskmaster," she said. "I should've taken up with Fiddler and his bunch while I had the chance."

"You'll get a second one," Creed said. "That old hillbilly will be looking you up at the Menger whether he has news about Brass or not. I could see it in his eyes."

A sudden truth hit Raney so hard she choked on her coffee. When she'd coughed and spluttered and finally managed to swallow it, she began to laugh.

"What's so funny?"

"You," she said. "You truly *are* shameless. I just figured it out—you've been fooling me all along! You didn't read all that about whiskey jugs and overalls and blue shirts in the tracks in the road. You *saw* them, Creed. You saw Fiddler and them go by before I got to the road, while I was driving down that little lane fighting with Tally."

He laughed. The glint in his eyes was approval, and he let her see it.

"I did," he said. "But don't let that fool you. I really am a pretty fair tracker. Don't try to get away from me."

A thrill ran through her at those words. She tried to ignore it. She must forget their kiss and remember that in San Antonio, once she found Brassell, getting away from Creed really was her whole purpose.

Yet it seemed strange to think that now, when it seemed she and Creed were partners, somehow.

"You couldn't track me if I was walking in mud," she said. She was laughing, enjoying teasing him. "You never sent a smoke signal in your life, and I doubt you know a horse's track from a deer's."

They bantered back and forth as they returned to the shade of their tree to finish off the teacakes. The lowering sun was beginning to throw long shadows. Gradually, they grew quiet.

The locusts began to sing in the trees and the wind rustled the leaves.

Raney felt the nearness of Creed's body to hers like a power of enchantment. She thought of his kiss again. She *wanted* his kiss again.

And she wanted him to say something to her. His voice beguiled her.

His scent—man and horse, dust and leather and, of course, smoke—made her take a quick, deep breath that she hadn't even known she needed. This couldn't happen. She couldn't let him have such power over her. If one kiss could throw her into such a state of wanting, she could never let him kiss her—not even one more time.

She turned away from him and tried to regain the light, teasing mood they'd shared. Thinking about his trick with the smoke signals—and the fact that she'd caught on to it right in the middle of his play-acting—made her smile.

"No word yet from Eagle Jack," she said lazily, squinting at the northern sky. "He must have missed a word or two of what we were telling him."

"Maybe some Comanche somewhere out west saw it and is riding in to help us," Creed said. "The Plains Peoples are the ones who used smoke to talk to each other. The Cherokee used it to talk to God."

"Then you were being sacrilegious a while ago," she said.

"The Apportioner understands that I need all the help I can get with you, Raney," he said. "He won't hold it against me."

There was a soft, low chuckle in his voice that never quite escaped his throat. It charmed her.

All the help I can get with you, Raney.

She loved the way he said her name.

"Papa always talks as if all Indians are the same," she said. "I never thought about different tribes being *that* different."

"Every *person* is different, same tribe or not," he said impatiently. "Of course we're all human beings, Raney."

She nodded.

"We Cherokee come from the same ancestral country as your people—the Deep South," he said. "But we were east of Louisiana, in the mountains."

Raney said, "I suppose that was why y'all didn't

use smoke signals. It was too hard to see them in the mountains and the trees. Especially in the Great Smoky Mountains."

They both smiled at her little joke.

"That makes a lot of sense, doesn't it?" he said, and his eyes glinted his approbation again.

"Are you proud of me for thinking of that myself?" she said.

"Yes," he said, nodding, "you might make a Cherokee woman, after all."

If I'd said yes instead of no when you asked for my hand . . . would I already be a Cherokee woman?

But she didn't dare say it. She didn't dare think it.

Marrying Creed had been impossible. It still was. He was still an Indian. And Papa was still Papa.

She had to remember Leonard, to whom she—and Papa—had given their word, and get a grip on herself. But Leonard had not shown such sterling character these past few days. Papa would not be pleased with him when he got home.

"I don't know what to think about Leonard."

The words popped out of her before she even knew she would speak. And she didn't stop there. She couldn't. Some kind of rebellion was rising in her, getting bigger and bigger with every thought of Papa and Leonard.

Creed looked at her and waited.

Anger came over her with the rebellion, all hot and prickling and upsetting to the core. She felt exactly the same way she'd felt when Leonard had refused to go look for Brassell.

Words of hurt crowded onto her tongue, all trying to spill off it at once. She had to work to keep her voice from trembling.

"Don't you think it's a bad sign when a man won't go to the aid of his own . . . family?" she asked. "Brass is his . . . future . . . family, yes, but it's the same as done. In two months' time, Leonard and I are to be wed."

She could hardly even say those words. The memory of her useless pleadings with that hard-hearted *pushy* Leonard came back to her, and the panicky worry about being betrothed to him came back with it. Could she actually marry him after all this?

"You said you left him a note," Creed said, in a tone so reasonable that it irritated her unduly, "so I take it that he didn't know you were going to look for Brassell until you were already gone."

"I had already asked him—*begged* him—to go and see about Brass," she said. "He said no because he has a business to run."

Admitting such a thing out loud humiliated her, but she was too angry to care. She only wished that Leonard were here to be embarrassed for himself.

"Well," Creed said, "that's true."

"Are you taking up for him?" she cried. "Brass was *wounded*."

"But Brass escaped from the jail and told his

friends where he was going. So Leonard knew he wasn't hurt bad."

She hit her thighs with her fists.

"That's what *he* said. But don't you see? I was asking Leonard to do it for *me*. If he's going to be my . . . husband, he should be willing to do things that are important to me for *my* sake, never mind the fact that my brother's life was at stake."

Creed waited for her to go on. Even if he'd tried to speak, she would've talked over him, because the words were pouring out of her and she was helpless to stop them.

"I don't know if that means Leonard doesn't . . . love me," she blurted. She turned to search his dark eyes as she clapped her hand over her heart. "*I* think that it does, Creed. If he really, truly loves me—even if he wouldn't do it because it's the only right, manly thing for him to do—he would do it to ease my worries."

"Do you love him?" Creed asked.

Shocked, she looked away. His eyes were searching hers, now, and they pierced her to the heart.

"I . . . I . . . well, of *course* I do . . ." She tried to keep going, but her voice trailed off.

Creed didn't speak when she fell silent. She looked at him.

"Papa thinks he's the very best man for me," she said. "For a year or more, he's said that Leonard and I would make a good match because we have so much in common."

She bit her lip and stilled her tongue. Inside, her spirits were sinking while her fear and frustration were rising. What was she doing, telling all this to Creed Sixkiller, of all people?

For a long time, he didn't say anything at all. She stared far into the distance at the sunset beginning to flame across the darkening sky.

"What do *you* think?" Creed said at last, his voice low and quiet. "In your own estimation, is Leonard the very best man for you?"

This time she was the one who sat silent.

After a while, he nudged her with words and with his gentle tone. "You're a woman learning to think for herself."

It was true. Somewhere in the back of her mind, she'd been thinking for herself about Leonard ever since he refused her pleas and then planned to comfort her by holding her in his arms all night long.

"I agreed with Papa at the time we were betrothed," she said slowly. "Our families have known each other forever, and we're all the same kind of people."

"You mean white-skinned?"

Startled, she stared at him. Then she grinned.

"Yes," she said. "And besides that, they're from one of the best, old families of the South, like ours.

171

He's only a merchant until he can recover some of his father's fortune lost in the war. And he's willing to live at Pleasant Hill after we marry so I can run the house for Papa."

"Do you like it when he kisses you?"

Shocked, blood rushing to her cheeks, she looked at him.

"That . . . that's personal," she stammered.

His dark gaze wouldn't let hers go. His eyes demanded the truth.

"Not much," she said.

Not as much as when you do. Not at all, really. There is no comparison.

"Do you like to talk with him?"

"I hardly ever get a chance," she said. "Leonard, without fail, does most of the talking."

Creed chuckled.

"It's not *funny*," she cried. "I'm supposed to marry him two months from now, and he knows I'm out here on the road by myself and he hasn't even come after me!"

Creed stopped smiling.

"Raney," he said, "you went into that betrothal with your head, not your heart."

She nodded.

"And now I don't know what to do," she said, in a voice just above a whisper.

Softly as she spoke, he heard her.

"Look into your heart," he said, "and listen to what it tells you."

He rose from the ground in one smooth motion, reaching his hand down to lift her to her feet, too.

Raney couldn't take a single step, and it wasn't because he held her there. His big hand enclosed hers loosely now but she clung to it. Because Creed wasn't moving away from her and somehow he might help her yet.

She raised her eyes to meet his.

"Raney," he said, "we Cherokee have words for the true connection of a man and a woman: 'Walk in your soul.' "

He pulled his hand from hers.

"You say you don't know what to do," he said. "Ask yourself if you can walk in Leonard's soul."

He turned and left her, gliding away on his panther's step.

Raney could not take her eyes away from him.

If she wanted to walk in *his* soul, she'd have to go against her Papa and her brothers. It would destroy their family that Mama's death had shaken so hard.

What a stab to the heart it had been for her to see that Papa was not as strong as he'd seemed, although he ran everything and everybody on the place. Mama had had a lot more power than Raney had thought she did. Maybe lots of women did.

Maybe she would, too, in her own marriage. She

173

couldn't imagine how that could be true for anyone married to Leonard.

Regrets dogged Creed as he went about the chores of readying their little camp for the night. He watered the horses and moved them to a new graze, he cleaned the pot and the bowls and put them back into his pack, he checked all the harness and his tack in the last of the light, then spread most of his bedroll in the back of the buggy for Raney, but no matter what he did or forced himself to think about, he could not shake them.

How could he be so weak? He had worked for three years to eliminate his feelings for Raney, and he had done so. Now here they were, alive and kicking him in the heart all over again.

Even while she was out of sight in the trees, washing her hair and taking a sponge bath, as she called it, in the water he'd carried for her from the creek, he could feel her presence in the dusky twilight as strongly if she were right there beside him. Tomorrow would be none too soon for them to arrive in San Antonio.

All he wanted to do was kiss her again. And see her eyes sparkle while they teased and joked with each other. Now he could look back at the time when he asked her to marry him and see that his love for her had been based on the most trivial of reasons. He'd had no idea of the woman she could grow up to be.

But he could see that woman now, and he knew her power would be irresistible. Nothing would do but that he get away from her because no flesh and blood man could keep from falling in love with her.

His heart beat even harder at the thought. He couldn't wait to leave her in the care of her family's friends. Then he would find Brassell, jail him, and forget about Raney again.

The next day, for most of the time, Creed rode close beside Raney's buggy. All morning, he told himself it was for her protection because the farther south they traveled, the closer they came to that part of Texas where Mexican raiders habitually attacked travelers and stole cattle. In the afternoon, he added the reason of the increasing traffic, since they were much nearer to San Antonio and she was such an inexperienced driver.

Finally, when they'd reached the very outskirts of town, a long string of freight wagons pulled by multiple spans of mules came up behind them. Creed tied Marker on behind and got into the buggy to drive for her.

"Tally might try to bolt," he said. "And you might sweat on your nice, clean hair from the effort of trying to hold him back."

"What do you mean, 'trying'?"

He glanced at her face to see whether she was insulted or only pretending to be. Then he couldn't look away again. She was pretending to be piqued.

Her upturned chin, her head tilted to the side, her bright blue gaze that challenged him, all radiated the charming flirtatious ways that were Raney, belle of the county.

"Have I let this horse run away with me this entire trip?" she demanded. "Answer me that."

"Not entirely," he drawled, "but I do recall a couple of times that you had to have some help, or else you'd be back in Limestone County by now."

"I only let you help me with Tally because I wanted to make you feel good," she said, flirting some more. "Etty always reminds me to accept graciously when a gentleman offers me gallantry."

"Hmpf," he said. "My guess is that your arms are tired and you want to be free to look at all the sights."

"Hmpf," she said, in return.

But she was looking around eagerly at this part of San Antonio.

"I've never been here before," she said. "They say this is the biggest town in Texas."

Creed sat right there beside her on the seat, with their thighs touching just ever so slightly, and thought about that.

"I seem to recall some remark that you made to Judge Scarborough about your papa always driving you to your friends' house in San Antonio," he said.

She turned to him, her eyes wide and startled. "Oh, did I? He had me so flustered I don't even know what I said, the way he was poking his nose into my business and all. I couldn't believe he demanded to know the name of our friends and the address."

She smiled at him as if it were three years ago and they were back in Limestone County at a neighborhood social.

"Which is it?" he asked. "Have you been here or not?"

"No, I just said that to the judge to get him to stop questioning me," she said, starting to look around her again. "Papa and the boys have talked about how to get to the Jacksons' house and they lodge with them when they come to San Antonio to sell the crops and buy supplies, but Mama and me always stayed at home."

He slapped Tally into a fast trot to keep well ahead of the freighters behind them.

"I still don't understand why you insisted on washing your hair last night," he drawled. "People will be so busy looking at the hole in your skirt, they wouldn't notice a little dust in your hair."

People would, though. The words were no more out of Creed's mouth than he saw that the two men on the seat of the buckboard meeting them on the road were both looking at Raney. When they noted his observation of them, they pretended to be deep in conversation.

"And who burned the hole in my skirt?" Raney

asked coolly. "All I can say is, it's a good thing you promised me a new one. I can't wait to go shopping."

"Hey, now, remember I didn't say I'd buy you anything else," he said. "All I damaged was one skirt."

"You owe me something for embarrassment," she said. "Look at all these people here who don't know that I usually dress respectably. They'll misjudge me entirely, and my reputation will suffer. Two blouses and two dresses might be about right."

She raised her eyebrow at him playfully.

"Nope," he said, "you don't embarrass that easy. In fact, I'm not sure you ever have been."

His tone was light but his heart wrenched, even as he spoke the teasing lie.

Every time he thought about her deep humiliation when she talked about Leonard's refusal to go after Brassell and then his neglect of her, leaving her out on the road alone in these dangerous times, it roused Creed's blood. No woman ever went out unescorted except in her home community.

Leonard was a newcomer to Texas, but he was a merchant and he heard news with every shipment of goods he received. He knew that she was heading toward San Antonio and that it was as rough a town as they come.

He wished the worthless bounder *would* come after her.

"Why, I'm mortified by my appearance right this

very minute," she said. "You just can't tell it because I'm a good enough actor to be on the stage."

"Oh yeah."

"You'll see," she said. "As soon as I get my new wardrobe from you, I may join up with a traveling company of players."

"Forget it. I didn't bring that much money."

"You can get a job," she said, and tossed back her hair to laugh at him.

No wonder those men in the buckboard stole another look at her as they passed. Her hair was catching the sunlight and falling over her shoulders in a cascade of curls. So thick it had still been wet when they started out this morning, it had dried gradually throughout the day, and now it blew around her face in the gentle breeze.

Watching her, Creed nearly forgot what their joking conversation was about.

"Raney," he said. "I can't work in town. I'm a cattle rancher. A poor one, because I'm always out chasing criminals instead of seeing to my animals and my affairs."

"Ha," she said. "You're not poor if you're from the famous Sixes and Sevens Ranch."

At the sound of more hoofbeats behind them, Creed glanced over his shoulder. Coming around the freight wagons at a fast lope was a contingent of cavalrymen.

The road was getting more crowded all the time,

and buildings were thicker along both sides of it. The road was narrow and crowded. Raney was turned around in the seat, her gaze on the approaching men.

"They look handsome in their uniforms, don't they? Do you think they're stationed here in San Antone?"

"Probably," he said, feeling suddenly irritated. "If the ranchers along the Nueces could get them to stop Cortina's raiders, they might be worth their pay."

"That's not the soldiers' fault. I heard Papa say it's the Carpetbaggers. They can't forget Texas was for the Confederacy, and—"

She stopped talking as a blush suffused her delicate skin with pink.

"It's unseemly for a woman to know about politics . . ." she said, then stopped her tongue.

He watched her out of the corner of his eye while he kept the buggy moving on the very edge of the road.

"No," she said, straightening her shoulders. "I'm going to think for myself about that, too. If I want to learn about politics and talk about them, I will. Papa will just have to get used to it."

A passing horse bumped against Marker, who kicked out sideways, and Creed turned his attention to his driving. The streets of San Antonio were far busier than they had been the last time he'd been there. He turned a corner to head toward Alamo Plaza.

Raney looked around in every direction, apparently fascinated.

There were stores and saloons, vaudeville theaters, blacksmith shops and warehouses, saddle shops and bawdy houses everywhere. Someone on the street called out in German. Mexican carters were calling out their wares in Spanish. Bearded Germans jostled cowboys. Cowmen, sheepmen, tradesmen, buyers were all moving through San Antonio. Behind the cool stone walls, great merchants and money men and real estate tycoons went about their business.

Creed eased the buggy through an opening between a cart full of firewood and a farmer's wagon and turned into the plaza.

"There's the Alamo," he said. "Over there. And, as you can see by the sign on the front of it, there's the Menger Hotel."

She looked from one to the other and nodded, but the square itself was filled and teeming. Booths were everywhere, their proprietors selling everything from hanging sides of beef to colorful Mexican clothing to leather goods to all kinds of prepared food to be eaten on the spot.

Creed drove at a snail's pace, trying to go around it all to the hotel.

"This town is a carnival from noon to midnight

every day," he said. "A man can get anything he wants in San Antonio, just as long as he can pay the price."

"What's going on over there?" Raney asked, gesturing toward a circle of shouting men.

"Probably a cockfight," he said.

On the outside of the circle, a tall young man was standing on tiptoe to see what was going on inside it. He turned away from the ring and toward them at the moment Creed noticed him. His eyeglasses caught the sun and sent back a blinding reflection as he snatched off his hat and slammed it against his leg in disgust. He had a headful of blond curls.

Raney was on her feet in an instant.

"Brassell," she screamed, although there wasn't a chance of being heard at that distance above all the braying donkeys, creaking wheels, and yelling voices.

She started scrambling to get up on the seat, holding on to Creed's shoulder, bumping against him as she struggled to untangle her feet from her skirts, yelling in his ear. He ignored her.

Creed kept his eye on the kid, who slapped his hat back onto his head, left the cockfight, and disappeared into the crowd in a heartbeat.

Raney stood on the buggy seat with her hand shading her eyes.

"I thought I saw Brassell," she cried. "Now I can't find him. Over there. Where . . ."

"I saw that kid," Creed said. "It may have been Brass and it may not."

"It *was*," she cried, still searching frantically for another sighting. "I know my own brother, don't I?"

"Get down from there," he snapped. "I'm trying to drive. You'll fall off and kill yourself if you don't watch out."

She had tears running down her face. He could just imagine what she'd do when he took Brassell back to jail.

This had not been a good idea, hooking up with her. He had never once thought he would care a whit about hurting her feelings or going against her wishes after she had hurt his three years ago.

Especially not where her brother was concerned, since he had not only a right, but a duty to put the boy back in jail. Maybe he could leave her at the Jacksons', find Brassell, and get him back to Concho without having to see her face to face.

He should've forced her to go back home.

But how could he have done that? Stubborn as she was, he would've had to drag her there and lock her up. Leonard couldn't be trusted to keep her safe, that was for sure.

She was still standing on the seat, ignoring him completely.

"Raney," he said, through clenched teeth. "Sit down or I'm going to set you down. We cannot leave the horses and the buggy here, and we certainly can't find that boy in this crowd."

Finally, she obeyed—he thought. She did sit down but then she tried to climb out over the side.

"I'm just going to go look for him—"

Creed grabbed her arm and held it as he shook the lines with his other hand.

"We're going over to the Menger right now," he said. "Somebody there can tell us where to find Beauregard Jackson. More than likely, Brassell has contacted your friends and they can tell us where to find him."

Chapter 9

～✤～

Raney stared out at the crowd while Creed drove the rest of the way around the square, but all she could see was Brassell's curly blond head shining in the sunshine. The trouble was, when she blinked and looked again, it wasn't there anymore.

She had a terrible sinking feeling in the pit of her stomach.

Not only had she missed getting results from the miracle of seeing Brassell the minute she arrived in San Antonio, now she had to do something about this lie hanging over her head. It was beginning to look, more and more, as if she'd have to tell Creed the truth.

And he was already in a foul mood.

"That was a damn-fool stunt to try to get down and into that crowd by yourself, Raney," he said.

She whirled—as best she could with him holding her by one arm—to glare at him.

"Well, it was pretty much a damn-fool stunt to see Brass right there before our eyes and do nothing about it when we've just worn ourselves smooth out and half choked to death on dust and nearly drowned just to come down here and find him, wasn't it, Creed?"

She could not *believe* she used a curse word.

Creed had all his attention fixed on driving with one hand, so he didn't look shocked, nor did he turn around to receive the full benefit of her angry stare. But he could still talk.

"Now you listen to me, Raney Childress. Don't you dare go out in this town without a male escort. You're used to going to Concho with only your maid but you can't do that here."

Furious, she ripped her gaze from his square-jawed profile and stared ahead at the big white stone building with its name, MENGER HOTEL., with a big period after it, printed in equally big black letters above the three second-story arches.

"No lady ever goes out in San Antonio without an escort," he said. "It isn't safe, and everyone knows that."

"You don't have to preach to me," she said. "I'm not a lady anymore."

That made him jerk his head around.

"What are you talking about?" he growled.

"Haven't you been paying attention?" she snapped. "I'm driving my own buggy and wearing men's pants or ragged skirts, and cussing like a sailor. This trip has destroyed my appearance *and* my behavior."

To her consternation, he threw back his head and laughed. Laughed a long, deep belly laugh that was so contagious, some people walking by laughed, too. Even Raney smiled, in spite of the state she was in.

But when he was done, he turned and looked at her with an expression in his eyes that wiped the smile off her face.

"As a woman, then, lady or not," he said. "While you're staying with your friends, do not leave the house without one of the Jackson men as escort. Do you understand me?"

She had to look away, his gaze was piercing her so.

"Raney?"

"Yes," she said, as if one lie wasn't enough of a burden to carry.

But, then, this lie was really part of the first one, and the whole mess just went on and on. Tangled web, indeed. Whoever made up that saying knew what he was talking about.

They pulled up in front of the Menger, and a boy who worked there immediately came running.

"Stable your horses, sir?"

"Hold them, please," Creed said, reaching into his pocket for a coin. "I shouldn't be long."

He stood up and stepped over the side to the ground as swiftly and gracefully as he did everything else.

"I'll wait for you," she said.

Who knew? She might be lucky. He might find the address of some Jackson family in San Antonio where she could persuade him to leave her. Once he was gone, she could simply drive away without bothering the inhabitants of the house . . .

But then where would she go? She had no money—or not much—and no idea how to draw some from a lender in Papa's name. Or what lender to go to, or . . .

No, the jig was up. And Creed was at her side, holding up his arms to help her down.

She let him and tried not to think about the feel of his strong hands on her waist. As if she knew what she was doing, she walked beside him across the sidewalk and through the big doors that another employee of the hotel—this one in a fancy uniform—held open for them.

He would be even more furious with her than he already was. Creed couldn't abide lying, everybody knew that, just like the whole county knew he wouldn't quit once he'd started something.

So it followed that he couldn't wait to be rid of her to go after Brassell without the bother of taking care of her. Not only did he feel he had to protect her all the time, he probably thought she'd beg him some more to let Brassell go home. Which she wouldn't. Creed wouldn't give in to that, and she knew it. What she *would* do was help Brassell escape from him, and they'd get home on their own.

It wouldn't be easy, though, if he wouldn't even let her sit outside in the buggy with a boy holding the horses while he went inside. Good heavens! There were great long windows all across the front of the bottom floor. All he'd have to do was turn his head and look out, and he could see her.

He was acting like San Antonio was the Wild Horse Desert or somewhere like that.

The hotel certainly wasn't a desert. It was beautiful inside. The ceiling rose two stories high, with an ornate balcony all around the second floor, reached by two graceful staircases. The floors were marble and the air was cool and pleasant because of that and the thick limestone walls. It seemed festive because flowering plants in big pots were scattered about everywhere.

Raney also could see a remarkable patio garden. Glass-paned doors ran all across the back of the lobby. The whole place was a beautiful, serene oasis in the midst of all the dust and noise and heat outside the doors.

"Creed," she said, reaching up to touch his arm just as he moved toward the desk to ask for directions, "let's walk out there into the patio garden and get the kinks out of our . . . legs. I need to tell you something."

189

He stopped and stared down at her.

"What?"

His eyes could be so piercing.

"I . . . need to talk to you in private. Let's go walk in the garden."

"You've had two days and nights to talk to me in private," he said, just a little more loudly than was necessary. "What's this about?"

"I don't have any friends here in San Antonio," she blurted, "I lied about that."

His eyes darkened and his face hardened, but not before she saw his astonishment. "Why?"

"I was trying to get you to go away and leave me alone," she said.

He searched her eyes. She wished she could shrivel up and curl into a ball like a water bug.

"How did you think you could accomplish that with nonexistent people?"

Again, his voice was just a little too loud. There weren't many people right near them, but there were several in the lobby. She spoke more softly, and he bent his head to hear.

"I would drive into some nice neighborhood and pick a likely house," she said.

She began blushing at the stupidity of the plan, which was as plain as the nose on her face when spoken aloud.

"And then what?"

"I would persuade you to leave me and when

you'd gone, I'd drive away without bothering the strangers who lived there."

"How dumb do you think I am?" he roared. "And how irresponsible? Do you think I'd go off and leave you helpless in the middle of San Antonio without seeing that you had protection? That's not thinking for yourself. It's stupidity."

He was right, but this was a fight. She lifted her chin and defended the plan that, two seconds earlier, she herself had judged completely insane.

"It is *not*! How could I possibly know that you would insist on meeting them?"

"Anybody who knows me would know it and that doesn't mean much—any worthless bounder off the street would do the same, and . . ."

"*Querelle d'amour.*"

Raney and Creed both turned toward the cultured feminine voice. A beautifully dressed woman and man were strolling past, eyeing the two of them with indulgent amusement.

Creed understood that much French, at least. He flashed a murderous glance at the woman's back.

"I agree," Raney said. "Thank *goodness* this is *not* a lovers' quarrel. Since you think I'm too stupid to live."

"I thought you were learning to think for yourself and here I find out you can't think at all!"

"That's an insult and I resent it," Raney said. "My idea could've worked if you would've cooperated."

"Yeah," he said. "If I'd lost my mind and manners entirely. *Then* it could've worked."

He pivoted on his boot heel and swept her alongside him so fast that her pitiful skirt swirled like a ball gown. He strode across the gleaming marble floor to the registration desk.

"Two rooms," he barked. "Adjoining door. This is Miss Childress of Limestone County. Send up a maid and a bath for her. Immediately."

"Yes, sir, Mr. Sixkiller," the clerk said. "Right away, sir. And will you be needing anything else?"

"Have somebody from J. Joske's bring over an assortment of ladies' clothes. Small sizes."

"Yes, sir, Mr. Sixkiller."

Creed scooped up both room keys, and they headed for the stairs.

"I feel like a Siamese twin," Raney said. "And I don't like it one bit."

"You promised not to go out alone, but now that I know you're a liar, I can't depend on that."

"You can depend on this," she said, through her clenched teeth. "I may be small-sized, but I will pay you back for manhandling me if it's the last thing I ever do."

He loosened his grip. She wouldn't try to break away. She wouldn't give him that satisfaction.

"You must drag women in here all the time," she said. "The clerk knew you, and he didn't raise an eyebrow at the fact we have no chaperone."

"That's his job," Creed said.

"Well, if you think you can distract me with a bath and clothes while you go find Brass and put him in jail, you're wrong, Creed."

"All right. I'll stay with you. Help you with your bath."

"No!"

She glanced up and found his hard gaze waiting for hers. A little shiver went down her back. He appeared to mean what he said.

"Why are we taking time for a bath and getting new clothes, anyhow?" she demanded. "We know Brassell is here. We saw him. We need to be out looking for him."

They reached the top of the stairs and Creed glanced at the numbers on the keys, then at the row of doors that lined the sunny hallway.

"And how do you propose we do that?" he asked.

He stopped in front of number twenty-four, stuck the key in the lock, and opened the door. He ushered her in and let go of her arm.

"Go back out there on the plaza right now and look for him," she said. "He's probably still there . . ."

Her voice trailed off. He was shaking his head as if she were very wrong and that was a hopeless task.

"I thought you knew how to find him," she said. "Isn't that your job?"

"It's an occupation the good folks of Limestone County have wished on me," he said, "but my *job* is running a ranch. I want to get back to it, so let's find your brother as fast as we can."

"Then why are we standing here waiting for a bath to be brought up? We're wasting time."

He looked straight into her eyes.

"We have to be partners, now, Raney, if we want to find him. You'll have to stick with me because you can't roam the town alone, and I have to stay with you to find out where to go—your family's banker, lawyer, or anyone else Brass might go to for help."

His gaze hardened.

"You understand that now, don't you? You won't try to get away from me?"

"I won't try to get away from you," she promised and silently added, *At least not until we find Brassell.*

A maid appeared at the open door with towels over her arm and knocked lightly. Creed turned and motioned for her to come in.

"Now that Beauregard Jackson can't tell us where Brass is likely to be or whether he's staying with him," Creed said, "we'll have to go to every place that your father and brothers usually do business. I know you'll not to want to wear a skirt with a hole in it."

She nodded.

"Besides," he said, "you hate to wear dirty clothes."

She nodded again. Really, even angry as she was, she had to admit that this was very thoughtful of him.

"Gotta have your mind clear to remember everything you've ever heard about San Antonio," he said briskly.

He strode across the room, unlocked the door that connected to the next one, and disappeared through it.

Once she was sitting in the wonderful bath and had sent the maid away, Raney heard Creed's last remark still ringing in her head. The minute he'd said it, she knew she'd been wrong.

He wasn't thoughtful. He was determined, as always—determined to put poor Brassell back in jail.

"Raney?"

She crossed her arms over her breasts and slid deeper down into the water.

Why would he call to her? He knew she was in her bath!

"Yes?"

"What cotton broker does your papa use? Do you recall ever hearing him mention a name?"

She stared at the door. Was he about to come in here?

"I think I should be the one to keep the key to that door," she said.

"What's the matter, don't you trust me?"

His drawl was so low and sensual, it made her blood begin to heat even more than it had when she first heard his voice. Or maybe that was just the effect of the bathwater.

"More than most," she said tartly. "But here lately, I'm having a hard time trusting any man, especially one who talks to a lady while she's in her bath."

She shouldn't be answering. She should ignore him, for heaven's sake. This was a scandal!

"Aren't you Raney Childress? Of Limestone County?"

Her eyes widened and she stared at the polished oak panel that separated them.

"You know I am."

"Then you're the one who told me, not an hour ago, that you're no longer a lady."

She felt a blush go from her head to her toes.

"Well, in some ways I'm not, but when it comes to talking to a . . . gentleman while I'm in my bath, I still am."

"Mmm," he said, in a maddeningly thoughtful way, "you could've fooled me."

She blushed even more. He *did* have good reason to say that—wasn't she talking right back to him, naked as a jaybird?

"I don't know why you wouldn't trust me," he said. "After all, we've been on the road alone together for two nights, and I have not made one assault on your virtue."

His drawl was so low and sensual it made a thrill go through the very core of her. She almost wished

196

he *would* open the door. Oh my! That thought was more deplorably scandalous than his starting this conversation in the first place.

No matter, she wasn't going to let him get the best of her. She might be from the country but she could hold her own in the town as well.

"That's no guarantee," she said. "You might like clean girls better than dirty ones."

That made him laugh nearly as much as he'd done in the buggy.

"You got that right," he said. "And I might like women better than ladies."

"I'm only a woman in *some* ways," she said primly.

This was fun, matching wits with him.

"No," he drawled, "I'd say you're a woman in *all* ways, Raney."

He said it sincerely and as if that were a good thing. It made her proud, somehow.

"Like a Cherokee woman?"

"You're getting there," he said, "once you give up your imaginary playmates."

He said it so lightly, it made her laugh.

She ought to have fun while she could. She hadn't had very much fun for a long time. Who cared if she talked to him while she was wearing no clothes? Who knew? Whose business was it?

"You can't judge me too much for lying, though," she said. "You just told a lie yourself."

"What?"

"That you never attacked my virtue."

He was silent for a moment.

"Are you talking about that kiss?"

The way he said it, she couldn't tell if it had been important to him or not.

"Yes," she said boldly.

"That kiss underneath the live oak tree when you kissed me back so hard I couldn't even get my breath?"

He had a silly, careless tone in his voice.

She giggled. "Yes."

"That wasn't an assault on your virtue."

"What do you call it?"

"An assault on *my* virtue. I feared for my chastity, I can tell you that right now."

She had to laugh, really laugh, he sounded so silly and so sincere at the same time. When she stopped, neither of them said anything for a minute.

Then Creed spoke, in that low, sensual way that made his voice rich and smooth, the one that felt like a hand stroking her skin.

"Raney," he said, "when I make an assault on your virtue, you'll know it."

She swallowed hard. Her heart began to beat against her ribs like a wild thing trying to get out of its cage.

She couldn't speak. He stayed silent, too. She didn't know what to say.

Oh! She never should've let this conversation get started. She had to put a stop to it.

"Creed, I'm on to you," she said.

"What do you mean?"

"I know why you're talking to me so much I can't even finish my bath," she said, hurrying to finish with the soap before the water got cold.

"What are you talking about?"

"You're the one who mistrusts me."

"How could that be?"

That hidden chuckle was in his voice again.

"Why would I *possibly* mistrust you, Raney?"

She really did like the way he said her name. She really did like the feel of his name on her tongue.

"I can't understand why, either, Creed," she said, in her most innocent tone, "but I think you're determined to know where I am every minute."

"I am," he said.

The way he said it made her think of a lot of other reasons that it might be true, other than that he wanted her help to find her brother.

"Would you prefer for me to keep an eye on you, instead?"

That brought the heat into her face again, and when a knock came on the door, she jumped, thinking at first that it was Creed.

But no, it was the door to the hall.

"Who is it?"

"The maid, miss. Rinse water is here."

The sharp disappointment Raney felt was gone in a flash, but it left its mark.

She'd better get a grip on her fun with Creed. Creed Sixkiller was a Cherokee Indian. Hadn't she been through this before?

Yes, but he'd been right when he accused her of not knowing him. Back then she hadn't known him very well at all. They had laughed and made jokes and had fun, but mostly she had only thought of how hot his kisses felt and how good he looked on a horse—and off—and the powerful way he held her in his arms when they danced.

Now was not the time to remember all that. All of her growing up, she had known that, in her parents' way of thinking, he was forbidden. No matter that lots of other mothers hoped their daughters would have the opportunity to marry one of the Sixkiller boys.

"Come in," she called.

She heard a knock she guessed to be at Creed's door as the maid opened hers, and a valet's voice as he brought Creed a bath, too. For one second, her mind tricked her into imagining how he would look as he stripped off his dusty shirt and jeans.

"I'll need plenty of towels," she told the maid, "until some new clothes arrive. I'm not going to put the dirty ones back on."

"Yes, miss. I done brought plenty."

Raney tried very hard to put her attention fully

on what she was saying and not on what was happening next door. And not on how she'd felt while she and Creed were talking.

"J. Joske's sent back word that a clerk will be here very shortly," the girl said.

Raney deliberately made conversation the whole time the maid helped her finish the bath. She concentrated on the feel of the water running over her back when the girl poured it from the pitcher, and the mat beneath her feet when she stepped out of the tub, and the tingling friction of the thick, snowy cotton across her shoulders and down her legs as she dried herself off.

The maid handed her the last, big, fluffy towel, and she wrapped herself up in it. Then she walked to the window and looked down at the busy street below.

None of it helped. She needed the feel of Creed's hands on her skin and the sound of his velvet voice saying her name.

Chapter 10

~~∞~~

When the waiter finished arranging the table with fresh fruit and cheeses, cool glasses of water with real ice, and a basket of crackers, he took their dinner order and left them. Creed let himself concentrate on watching Raney, sitting across the round table from him, close enough to touch.

He'd escorted her down the stairs and into the Menger's dining room with her arm through his, and ever since he let her out of his grasp, he'd felt strangely empty-handed. That teasing conversation through the closed door had been a big mistake. He never should've started it. The quick intake of her breath and the hesitant sound of her voice at first, then the saucy teasing between them, had roused his appetite for more, a wanting that wouldn't go away.

A wanting for Raney that he'd banished from his life a long time ago.

Actually, it had come back to him with a vengeance when he kissed her, and it had been with him ever since.

You're losing your mind, Sixkiller. Remember who she is.

"I still can't believe we have *ice*," she said, pausing in her examination of the room long enough to lift a bite of peach to her lips, "and this delicious fruit . . ."

"They bring it in from Mexico," he said, unable—just for a moment—to take his gaze from her lush mouth. "In San Antone, a man can have anything he wants if he can pay the fare."

Except this woman. You can't pay the fare for her.

". . . not that I didn't enjoy the jerky and warm canteen water that you gave me on the road."

She flashed a slanting, upward glance at him that made his breath—only that one breath—come short. He made an effort to hang on to the thread of the conversation.

"What about the stew? You ate a whole pot of my stew last night."

"It was delicious," she said, sparkling, flirting with him. "I don't want you to think it wasn't good or discourage your efforts at cooking, Creed, but aren't you glad we have more choices this evening?"

"I'm mainly glad I don't have to cook," he said.

"One thing I might suggest for your next campfire dinner is flowers in a vase and a linen tablecloth."

She ran her fingertips over the snowy fabric that covered their table. "These must be hand-woven."

He thought of how her hands would feel on his skin.

Her eyes looked a darker blue in the light from the chandeliers. A man could get lost in her eyes.

Now. He had to start talking now. He had to stop thinking of doing anything *but* talking with her.

"I thought you told me you've been to Memphis," he said.

She smiled at him, recognizing immediately that he was teasing her. Raney was quick-witted, which was one reason she'd been such friends with his sister Maggie.

"I have," she said. "But we stayed in the homes of friends. And whenever we stopped at a hostelry on the journey, it was an awful place—nothing at all like this. I'm a country girl, as you once pointed out, and I just find it amazing that this is a hotel and not a fine home."

"The Menger is the only hotel in Texas that serves something besides fried pork and the only one that doesn't assign guests to share common rooms," Creed said, glad for something to talk about.

"Oh, thank goodness," Raney said. "Wouldn't that be terrible—to have some stranger for a bedfellow?"

Don't even think about it, Sixkiller. Move on.

He racked his brain for something else to say.

"Fifteen years ago, when the Menger was built, all these furnishings cost sixteen thousand dollars in hard cash," he said. "And then there was the expense to haul them all the way across Texas from the port at Galveston."

"Well, it was worth every bit of that," she said, looking around at the opulence. "The owners should be congratulated for their good taste."

She wore a dress that fit her to perfection, a dress exactly the color of her hair. It made her seem different, older, somehow.

"I remember hearing Papa say that Robert E. Lee kept a room here when he was inspector general of the army," she said. "That's how I knew the name of even one place in San Antonio for Fiddler to leave a message for me."

"Let's hope he does," Creed said, seizing on their purpose as if he'd forgotten all about it. Which, to his chagrin, he had. But only since he'd seen her in this dress. "We're starting from scratch and we don't have much time."

"Not if Brassell is important enough for the judge and Mrs. Scarborough to be coming all the way down here after him," Raney said. "Of course, if they find him first, he'll be safe with them."

"Of course."

That dress would be ruined if she wore it on the road home. And so would her skin. It was cut low enough in the front that it curved over the tops of her breasts.

"That's quite a replacement for the skirt I burned."

"Remember the Frenchwoman who said we were having a lovers' quarrel?"

"Yes," he said. "Foolish woman."

"Exactly," Raney said. "But she looked wonderful and I hated being so ragtag. I got a skirt, too. One I can travel in. And some other things. Thank goodness I brought the buggy, so there's no problem taking them all with me. If I'd come horseback, I couldn't have bought much, or else I would've had to have it all shipped to Pleasant Hill, and that might take a long time."

She added crackers and cheese to her fruit plate.

"Don't worry, Creed. I had a good idea—just all of a sudden when the woman from Joske's brought all those pretty things into my room. Papa can pay you back for them. I'll ask him to do that as soon as we get back home."

"I owe you a skirt."

"Yes, but it wouldn't be proper for me to accept any other clothes from you. A lady doesn't accept gifts of clothing from a gentleman."

He imitated her tone from earlier in the day.

"Haven't you been paying attention? I'm no gentleman. I'm wearing jeans to dinner, and it's been said more than once that I'm a little rough around the edges."

She grinned.

"Well, then, we're two sorry renegades loose in the big town," she said. "And we'd better find Brassell in a hurry and get out of here before I spend so much money, Papa will disown me."

Remember that, Sixkiller. Her biggest worry is that Papa will disown her.

"We'll start looking for him tonight."

While they ate juicy steaks, fresh bread, and early spring vegetables, then finished with a dessert— crystal dishes of ice cream, a rare delicacy concocted by the hotel's French chef—they began to organize their search for Brassell. They listed every place he might go to find people he knew, either to borrow money, get a job, hide out, or arrange for credit, maybe even to travel farther away. Raney argued that her baby brother would never go farther away from home than this, but Creed wasn't so sure.

Afterward, as they left the dining room and walked across the lobby of the Menger to go out into the lengthening evening, Raney remembered the name of the cotton broker.

"It's Holloway, I recall it now," she said. "But his establishment will be closed."

"We'll go there tomorrow. For tonight, let's walk around the plaza and listen to the players. Brass might be drawn to the music."

"Yes! Remember, Creed, he doesn't know that any Chickenhawks followed him out of the county.

He won't hesitate to be out in public—in fact, when we saw him earlier, he wasn't even wearing a hat, and his hair is very distinctive."

Creed suppressed a sigh. He wasn't at all sure that it was Brass they saw, but he might as well let her believe it. He needed to believe it, too. He had to separate himself from Raney as soon as he could, and finding her brother in a hurry was all that would do the trick.

Vendors were lighting lamps all over the plaza, which was as busy and crowded as it had been earlier in the day.

"The booths selling food are all doing a good supper trade," Creed said. "Want something to eat?"

Raney groaned.

"I'd burst the seams of this dress if I ate one more bite. But what are all those women selling? Over there at the big plank table."

"They call them the chili queens. Their Canary Island people brought chili here in the seventeen hundreds, and those are some of their descendants. Each one of them makes a slightly different version of the kind called San Antonio red."

"I want some tomorrow."

"What happened to your love of luxury?"

"We'll buy some for lunch and take it back to the Menger dining room to eat it," she said, laughing. "Can't you just see our waiter's face if we came in carrying bowls of chili?"

Then they spotted some musicians getting ready to play on the other side of the square and started making their way toward them. Raney hung on to his arm and walked on her tiptoes to try to see who it was.

"Not Fiddler and his friends," she said, as if Creed weren't tall enough to see for himself. "And no Brass yet. But he may come to listen when they start to play."

They crossed the plaza with Raney clinging to Creed's arm. He tried not to think about her, but her small hands burned their imprints through his sleeve and into his skin and the rose scent of her soap reached his nostrils in spite of the much heavier aromas of roasting kid and spicy chili that floated over the earthier ones of horse manure and wood-burning fires.

Against the falling twilight, all the lanterns glowed unnaturally bright. The mix of languages that always sounded on the streets of San Antonio seemed to have even sharper contrasts than usual.

A pair of rough men came lurching up behind them, unsteady on their feet from too much to drink. Creed put his arm around Raney and drew her closer to him as they passed. She smiled her thanks at him, and the look in her eyes brought back the taste of her kiss to his lips.

Keep this up, Sixkiller, and you'll be in a world of hurt.

He jerked his mind away from Raney and began trying to put himself into Brassell's skin. What would he be doing in San Antonio tonight?

"You say Brass has very little money with him?"

"How could he have any? Nobody has much hard money, not even Papa. No, Brass will either have to work or beg to survive. And, with his wound, I don't know how much he can work."

"He might get a small advance on this year's crops if he went to a broker who knows him and your papa well."

"True," she said, "maybe we can find that out tomorrow."

"What does he have with him that he could sell?"

Raney ticked the items off on her fingers. "Horse, gun, saddle. I don't know if he has his watch with him."

"What else can he do besides play music?"

"They say he's a pretty fair poker player, but he'd be too scared to wager his horse or gun or saddle, I'm thinking."

"Depending on his judgment of his opponents," Creed said.

He began trying to think of all the gamblers and gambling places he had known in San Antonio in his wilder days.

"You know," Raney said, thoughtfully, "even if Brass does know some dangerous secret, I think he'll feel safe by coming so far from home. And in such a big town, he'll feel even safer. He'll be out here on the streets somewhere and we can find him. You know how to do it, Creed. I just can't wait."

Her voice had such a note of hope in it, and of complete faith that the reunion would be nothing but joyful, that he cringed inside. He was silently praying, one more time, that he would find Brassell and take him into custody peacefully when they reached the other side of the square.

A small crowd gathered around the three musicians, two fiddlers who were tuning their fiddles to the other's guitar. Raney stood with Creed at her back, looking in every direction as if she expected Brassell to appear any minute. The expression on her face was so pitiful that it threw all Creed's prayers to the winds and made him want to punch out Brassell when he found him.

How had a kid that young ever gotten so embroiled in such a stupid waste of manpower? Brassell should have to see what it was doing to his sister. Feuding was an insidious weed that would choke the whole county if he didn't put a stop to it.

When the musicians started to play, they were terrible. They said the song was the old fiddle tune "The Eighth of January," but just by listening, no one could tell it was a tune at all.

"Git a job," one disgruntled listener yelled, and soon the audience melted away.

Raney stood right where she was, oblivious to everything but the chance of finding her little brother. Her yearning eyes were searching everywhere, and she looked so sad, he expected to see tears on her cheeks at any minute.

She was very young and, until recently, very much accustomed to getting her own way about everything. She must have believed, like a little girl, that they would find Brassell the minute they walked out onto the plaza—especially since she believed she had seen him the minute they rolled into San Antonio.

Finally, Creed took her hand and pulled it through the crook of his arm.

"Let's walk around this side of the square," he said, "and head back to the hotel. You've had a long, hard day—all that shopping and then all that eating everything that poor waiter could carry must've worn you out."

For a moment, it was as if she didn't hear him, then she looked up and gave him a smile. She tried to put her heart into it, even if her eyes were still sad. She was game, he had to hand her that.

"Well, thank you so much. I do believe you're calling me a pig, Mr. Sixkiller."

"Not at all." He began to walk her along the edge of the plaza toward the sidewalk so they'd have more room to walk as they headed back toward the Menger. "I'm simply pointing out that indulging in

213

excess of any kind tends to tire a person out."

"Then you surely must be exhausted," she said, "since you've indulged in an excess of philosophizing ever since we met up on the road."

"Are you calling me a bore?"

That made her laugh out loud, which made him feel ten feet tall.

They stepped up onto the rough sidewalk, into the shadows. The new-fangled gaslights were being lit, corner by corner, but between them, the dark of night was growing.

"Hold on to me," Creed said, drawing her closer. "It's not easy to see where you're going along here."

It wasn't only that he wanted to feel her skirts brush against his leg and her arm press against his. He truly was concerned that she might stumble.

She moved even nearer to him as they walked through the blackest part of the way.

"Now that it's getting dark, all these people seem like too many," she said. "I liked our camp last night much better."

"Does that include the food and the table setting, too?"

"No, it does not."

They chuckled over their private joke and walked on to the corner in companionable silence. They stopped in front of a store where the proprietor's sign swung overhead on a squeaky chain. The wind was picking up. Dust swirled even higher in the street.

"Suddenly, I do feel wrung out," Raney said. "It wrenched my heart to see Brass so quickly and then to lose him again just as fast."

"I know."

She squeezed his arm in appreciation for the sympathy. He would enjoy it. All that understanding would be gone when they found Brass.

They waited while a bunch of noisy cowboys rode past, heading out of town. Then, just as they started to step off into the street, a group of four men on horseback came down the alleyway and around their corner.

The streetlight lit them clearly. Raney's quick intake of breath told Creed that she'd recognized them, too.

The Mason brothers, Reynolds Carter, and Loren Hastings. Four prominent–to–fairly prominent citizens of Limestone County. All of them Chicken-hawks. Loren rode his favorite mount, a big white gelding that stood a full hand taller than the other three horses in the group.

They rode past at a long trot, looking toward the plaza.

"I don't think they noticed us," Raney said. "Or if they did, they didn't recognize who we are."

The wind picked up even more and moaned a little between the buildings.

"Right."

Creed put his hand under her elbow as they stepped off the sidewalk and kept it there until they'd reached the other side of the street and started down the long block toward the hotel. His mind was racing in all directions.

It was way too much of a coincidence to try to believe the men were in San Antonio on business, but he said nothing. No sense in alarming Raney unnecessarily.

But she knew.

"It's a busy time of the year to leave a plantation or a ranch to come this far," she said.

"Yes, it is."

"Creed," she said, and her voice broke a little, "those men are Chickenhawks."

"Yes, they are."

"They're here hunting for Brass, aren't they?"

No sense in trying to fool her.

"Could be."

She stopped in her tracks and looked up at him. The light coming through the long windows of the hotel showed the glisten of tears in her eyes.

"They are, Creed. And those are men who used to be friends of my papa's. Before the feud. Important men. They wouldn't be here themselves if hired men could do what they want done."

She was way too smart for her own good. Already

she'd been trembling and tired. This might break her down.

Instead, she lifted her chin and straightened her spine.

"They're here because that other bunch of Chickenhawks couldn't catch Brass," she said. "He does know something, Creed. And it's something they can't risk him telling."

"We could be wrong, Raney. They may have business here, and that's all."

"And I may can rise and fly," she said, "but I don't think so, Creed."

"Yoo-hoo-oo," a woman called. "You two, there."

The high, piercing voice made the hair on the back of Creed's neck stand on end and turned Raney toward it like a giant's hand.

It belonged to Mrs. Scarborough. The doorman was helping her down from the carriage in front of the Menger.

The judge himself still sat in the driver's seat. He lifted the handle of his whip in salute to them and touched it to his hat brim for Raney. Then the stable boy arrived and the judge climbed down.

Creed and Raney moved toward the wide doors, but there was no escape, of course.

Creed's heart sank. There was no way to avoid a conversation and no way to avoid gossip about Raney once they were all back home. Unless Mrs.

Scarborough's loyalty to Raney's mother's memory would make her hold her tongue.

"Fancy this," Mrs. Scarborough said, as they all passed in through the door. "Why, we *never* expected to see *you* two here."

Once inside, she took Raney by the hand.

"We just knew you'd be at your friends' home," she said. "Are you and Mr. Sixkiller here to dine?"

"No, ma'am," Raney said. "We had dinner earlier."

The expression that suffused Mrs. Scarborough's face caused Creed to smile before he could suppress the urge. She looked horrified and shocked and curious and as determined as a cat after a mouse.

"Oh, my Lord," she said, gasping for breath. "Honey!"

She leaned toward Raney and said, in a stage whisper that all four of them could hear, "Raney, you must know that this doesn't look good. Not good at all. Your dear mother would—"

Creed smiled at Raney. She looked properly horrified, too, but he could see the glint of laughter in her eyes.

"Oh no," she said. "Why, Mrs. Scarborough, to think that you would entertain such a thought! No, it's just that my friends are unexpectedly out of town. Mr. Sixkiller and I have taken rooms—separate rooms, of course—here at the hotel."

Creed saw that the judge had a hotel room key in

the watch pocket of his waistcoat, so they were bound to cross paths here again.

"You *have*? You are staying here . . . at the hotel . . . ? You and . . . Mr. Sixkiller?"

Her voice dropped to a whisper on Creed's name.

Somehow, instead of embarrassment, that brought out the mischief in Raney. Creed was glad to see it.

"Well, yes, ma'am," she whispered loudly. "We didn't want to sleep on the ground in the freight yards, you see."

Mrs. Scarborough's eyes grew even bigger.

"Well. Well, of course *not,*" she said. "But sugar, your poor dear mama would want me to see about you. You have no chaperone?"

"No, ma'am, because I came off from home in such a tearing hurry. But"—and she put on a horrified look of her own—"as I said, we are not staying in the same room together. Surely you would *never* think such a thing of me."

The tiny woman clapped a plump hand over her mouth.

"No! Oh, honey, of course not! Not at all! I'm only worried about your reputation. About what people might *think*."

This was enough. The woman could keep on plowing this same ground all night. Creed got them all moving toward the stairs.

"Judge Scarborough," Mrs. Scarborough said in a firm voice as they started the ascent, "we shall have to serve as chaperones for these two. Raney's friends, unfortunately, happen to be out of town."

"Of course you couldn't know whether they'd be at home," she said to Raney, whom she held firmly by the arm, "after all, you had to come on, and quickly, after your brother, so there was no time to send word ahead."

"Even if there had been," Raney said, "there wouldn't have been time to get an answer back before I arrived in San Antonio."

"True," Mrs. Scarborough said, nodding her head up and down like a bird. "Very true. All there was left to you was to stay in the hotel. You did not have a choice in the matter, darlin', and I want you to know that I fully understand."

The Scarboroughs stopped at room twenty and the judge opened the door.

"Good night," Creed said, and guided Raney on past them.

"Good night," Raney said. "Y'all sleep well. Isn't it just the most fortuitous thing that we're all in the same hotel?"

"Oh yes. Well, now, good night," Mrs. Scarborough finally said, and the judge echoed her.

Creed opened Raney's door and escorted her inside, glancing back to see that the hallway was empty. He locked the door behind him and turned to her.

Raney stood stock still and stared at him. He stared back. They burst out laughing and laughed until they were both gasping for breath and the tears ran down their cheeks.

"I will never forget the expression on her face," Raney said, still snuffling into the handkerchief Creed had lent her to wipe her eyes. "If she gossips about me for the rest of my life, it'll be worth it to remember how shocked she looked."

"I know," Creed said. "And the judge was trying to shut her up the whole time but he didn't know how."

"He knew it was a losing battle, that's what."

Raney wiped her face one more time and smiled at him.

"That's the best laugh I've had in a long time," she said.

"I'm glad it didn't make you cry instead."

She made a face at him.

"After all this worry about Brassell? A little thing like damage to my reputation can't make me cry."

"Spoken like a real Cherokee woman," he said.

But she didn't care about her own strength at that moment. She didn't care about anything at all except her brother.

She fixed her solemn blue eyes on him.

"Creed? Do you think we'll find him tomorrow?"

He lifted his hand and brushed a curling strand off her damp cheek. He let his fingers linger in her hair. He had never wanted anything more than he wanted to take her in his arms.

"I can't promise you that," he said. "I wish I could just hear you laugh some more. All I can say is that tomorrow we'll get closer to finding Brassell somehow."

"Creed . . ."

She started to go on, then stopped her tongue and bit her lushly full lower lip. She'd almost said that she wanted him to kiss her. He could see the longing in her eyes.

Watch yourself, Creed. You've been wanting more than a kiss. You have a lot more self-discipline than you did three years ago, but you're still human, man.

"Raney . . ."

A brisk knocking came at the door.

"Damn!"

He strode over to it, flipped the key in the lock, turned the knob, and jerked it open.

Mrs. Scarborough stood there, eyes big as saucers and mouth aghast. Creed looked her up and down.

In one hand, she held a small reticule. Two furry slippers peeked out of its open top. Over her other arm, neatly folded, lay her nightclothes.

Chapter 11

◦─∽◯∼─◦

Raney stared at Creed's back. He'd gone completely immobile. Apparently, he was wary of their visitor.

She moved toward him to see who it was but there was no need, for before she could take two steps, Mrs. Scarborough's piercing voice and then her busy little body pushed past Creed and into the room. Dumbfounded, Raney stared at her.

Raney blinked and looked again. That seemed to be a nightgown and wrapper Mrs. Scarborough carried thrown over one arm. And a bag, with slippers! What was she *doing*?

Creed tried to find out. "Mrs. Scarborough, ma'am—"

She cut through his words ruthlessly, although with a charming, even coquettish tilt of her head and a twinkling smile.

"I've come to help you children out of this *embarrassing* situation y'all find yourselves in," she said. "I felt so *bad* for y'all a little while ago when we ran into each other downstairs—not knowing a *soul* in San Antone who could serve as chaperone to deflect any slanderous tongues that might be out and about in the halls of this hotel! I simply could not stand it a minute longer. I had to *do* something."

In the middle of that little speech, she beamed an even sweeter smile at Creed. But by the time she got to the end of her spiel, she was looking at Raney.

"I'm acting in the stead of your dear, departed mother, Raney darling. I know she would not want you without a chaperone, especially in a city so far away from home."

Creed was looking at Raney, too.

Both of them seemed to be waiting for Raney to say or do something. What she wanted to do was either laugh while she threw Mrs. Scarborough back out the door she came in or cry because she didn't.

But, dear Lord, she had no choice. How could she insist that the woman leave her? That would be the final blow to Raney's reputation. It might be possible to get away with her impulsive search for Brass, but it would never, ever, be forgiven if she refused to be chaperoned.

Especially by the most powerful social arbiter of Limestone County. Raney would never be received in a respectable home again, and she'd be excluded from the social life of the county. Papa would be devastated.

She couldn't believe she could speak in her normal voice, but she did.

"No," she said slowly, "Mama wouldn't want that."

"That's right, sugar. You can rest easy now that I'm looking after you. I'm going to sleep in this room with you and look after you for the rest of this trip as if you were my own daughter."

She paused to give Creed another of her beaming smiles.

"Y'all know, of course, since everybody in Texas knows—everybody who is *anybody* stays at the Menger when they come to San Antone. There's just no telling who might happen to see y'all's situation and take away *entirely* the wrong impression, and I am *not* going to let that happen."

The rest of this trip! Those words kept echoing in Raney's head. She had to make one try.

"Mrs. Scarborough, I do appreciate your thoughtfulness ever so much, but this arrangement leaves Judge Scarborough all alone, and I feel so bad about that—"

The older lady cut her off.

"Now, honey, I'm not taking no for an answer," she said, bustling over to a chair to put down her

225

things. "The judge doesn't mind one bit. In fact, he encouraged me."

She widened her eyes and looked up at Creed again.

"We both of us know that you are an honorable gentleman, Mr. Sixkiller. It's not that the judge or I mistrusts you in the least, I hope you know that. But you are a mighty handsome man in anybody's book and Miss Raney is a beautiful girl. *And* you know, as well as I do, that there is temptation afoot in this world."

Shocked, Raney stared at her. If Mama could hear her friend speaking so plainly—and in mixed company, too—she'd be downright scandalized. Fine chaperone Mrs. S. would make.

Mrs. Scarborough did have the good grace to blush at her own temerity.

Creed raised his eyebrow at her, and she blushed even harder.

"After all," she said, clearly flustered now, "the judge and I were saying that we both remember what it's like to be young."

Creed smiled. "And tempted?"

That flustered Mrs. Scarborough so much that she started shooing him out of the room, even though she couldn't resist smiling back at him.

"Go along with you, now. It's been a long journey, and we all need our sleep."

She was trying to herd him toward the door to the

hallway, but he went to the connecting inside door of the room and opened it.

"Good night, ladies," he said, over his shoulder.

Then he paused and turned to look from one of them to the other with his heavy-lidded dark eyes.

"Don't forget, I'm right here if you need me."

He looked at Raney for two long heartbeats, smiled and winked at Mrs. Scarborough, and then he was gone, closing the door behind him with the softest click.

Mrs. Scarborough started fanning herself with both hands.

"Oh, my darling girl, I can see that I got here just in the nick of time! Oh, my goodness, that Creed Sixkiller could charm the bark off a tree, now, that's just all there is to it!"

She went to Raney, took her by the arm, and led her to an empty chair as if she were helpless or ill. Really, it was Mrs. Scarborough who needed to sit down, which she promptly did, landing on top of her bag and nightclothes without an effort to remove them.

"Get your shoes off, now, sugar, and let's get ready for bed," she ordered, bending over to start unfastening her own high-topped footwear. "I'm telling you, I've had just about all my poor heart can stand for one day. That man is a danger to society, and I only wish I was twenty years younger than I am. I don't care if he's an Indian or not, he's the

227

most man in one skin that there is in Texas, and I don't care what anybody says."

That outburst brought a giggle from Raney. Who would ever have thought it of Mrs. Scarborough?

Mrs. S. popped back up, her laces half undone.

"The judge excepted of course," she said.

Then she frowned, rolled her eyes at Raney, and waved that dutiful statement away. Raney giggled again. She had never known Mrs. Scarborough before. Being around Creed certainly brought out a shocking side of her.

To be perfectly honest, being around him brought out a shocking side of Raney, too.

By the time they had both finished undressing, taking turns behind the Chinese screen in the corner, and had washed up and gotten into bed, Raney's head was spinning and every inch of her body was longing to lie down. And longing for Creed.

It felt strange to be separated from him after all their hours together. All she could think about was the last time he had closed that door between them and the way his voice had made her feel when she was in her bath.

Even in bed, Mrs. Scarborough didn't stop bustling. She was busily making sure that Raney had plenty of room, plenty of pillows, and just the right amount of covers. If only the room had two beds!

"I'll be no bother to you, Raney, dear."

Mrs. S. was whispering now, as if Creed were lying over there in his bed trying to overhear.

Raney let herself try to imagine him at this moment on the other side of that door. What did Creed wear to bed, anyhow? Surely not a nightshirt, like Papa's. There had been no nightshirt in the sparse roll of clothes where he'd found his extra jeans for her.

The image of him in his breechcloth, the dawn sun shining on his perfect body, came unbidden to her mind.

"We can have a big visit, just like a slumber party," Mrs. S. said, as she settled herself on her pillow. "You can tell me how you came to be traveling with Mr. Sixkiller and all about when he was courting you. I was so sorry your papa had to break that off, sugar."

Well, actually, she had broken it off, too. She'd been sorry to lose the excitement of walking out at parties with Creed and letting him kiss her and the thrills that had given her, but deep down, she had agreed with Papa. At that time.

She had not been strong enough to go against him and Mama and do something so shocking as to marry an Indian. She'd never once thought of breaking such a taboo as that. But the real truth was that she hadn't loved Creed then, any more than she loved Leonard now. Creed was right. She hadn't known the first thing about him, back then. She'd learned more about him in these last two days than

229

in the months when they'd been courting because back then, she'd been nothing but a flighty girl.

Now she had different feelings for him. And she had no idea if they were the beginnings of love, either.

Creed was proud of her when she thought for herself. And he was impressed when she did things for herself. That glint of approval that came into his eyes when she'd shown her independence was like the sun shining on her. She had never known another man who liked a woman to think—or do—for herself, and Creed actually encouraged her to do so.

That would never be true of Leonard if he lived to be a hundred. Leonard wanted to control her.

On top of all that, she could hardly think about anything but the way Creed's hard-muscled arm had felt beneath her fingers and the thrill that had run through her whole body when he'd pulled her against him so suddenly out there in the plaza. The feel of his long leg, the thrust of his hipbone, and the immovable protection of his chest all were imprinted in her flesh.

Yes, it was a good thing Mrs. Scarborough had busybodied herself into Raney's room.

Because, if she hadn't, Raney would have been right over there at that door, right this minute, opening it to Creed.

Imagining doing such a thing, imagining how Creed would look and what he would say . . . and what he would *do* caused a burning to start, deep in the very core of her, and it began to spread through her veins, heating her blood without mercy. She threw back the covers and got out of the bed.

"I have to sit by the window," she whispered back to her waiting companion. "I . . . I look at the stars every night and . . . remember my mother. It takes a long time."

"I understand, sweetie. We'll talk tomorrow."

Mrs. Scarborough already sounded sleepy. She was snoring before Raney got the chair situated in front of the French doors where she could see the moon.

Well, the snoring wouldn't keep her awake, that was for sure. Most likely, she would never sleep again.

Not only was she burning all through from thoughts of Creed, she was on fire with fury at herself. Not because she didn't go against Papa and marry Creed.

No, it was because she never even thought about it. All her life she'd just accepted whatever was handed to her, and had done whatever she was told. Leonard was a good example of that. He'd been decided on by Mama and Papa and handed to her just as surely as the judge and Mrs. Scarborough had handed her a chaperone tonight.

Was she going to sit around and let people do that to her for the rest of her life?

The rest of her life might not be long enough to waste any of it. Life was short. Hadn't she nearly drowned on the way down here? Hadn't Mama died way before she became old?

Raney was not going to spend whatever time was left in her life with Leonard.

That truth fell into her heart and glowed there like a star dropped from heaven. She sat still and let its sparks shoot the knowledge into her bones.

The heavenly smell of coffee woke Raney from her dream—a dream about Creed in their camp beneath the live oak tree where he kissed her. When she opened her eyes, it took her a second to assimilate the sight of Mrs. Scarborough and the sound of her happy humming. Mrs. S., in her dressing gown, was seated at the table by the French doors, pouring from two silver pots, coffee and milk.

"It's about time you woke up," she said cheerfully. "We've already had a gift from our admirer this morning."

Raney sat up and pushed her hair out of her eyes. "What? Who?"

Mrs. Scarborough cast a significant look at the door to Creed's room.

"Why, your friend Mr. Sixkiller, of course. He had this tray sent up just now."

Incredibly, in spite of the dinner of the night before, Raney's stomach growled.

"Mrs. Scarborough, does it have any food on it?"

"No, sugar, it doesn't. We are to meet the men in

232

the dining room in an hour. And please call me Miss Hallie. No reason to be so formal with your chaperone."

She got up and, beaming at Raney, brought one of the steaming mugs to her.

"Nothing like coffee in bed first thing in the morning," she said.

No matter how annoying it was that she'd pushed her way into her position as chaperone, Raney could do nothing but smile back at her. Mrs. S. had a good heart. She must, if Mama had been her friend.

Raney held the heavy cup in both hands and breathed in the aroma, then took a sip.

"Perfect," she pronounced. "You made it just exactly the way I like it, Miss Hallie. And thank you for bringing it to me. I just have to have my coffee to start off my day."

Much as she'd like her privacy, it was nice to be fussed over. It made her miss her mama even more.

But she didn't want to go to breakfast with Miss Hallie and "the men." She wanted to talk to Creed.

She held the cup still against her lips. Creed had thought about her; he had sent the coffee up because he knew she loved it. That was so much more thoughtful than anything Leonard had ever done. She didn't know whether Leonard had ever even noticed how much she loved her coffee in the mornings.

Miss Hallie poured herself a cup of coffee, turned

her chair around, and settled in for a chat. Eerily, she spoke Raney's thought.

"Apparently Mr. Sixkiller knows you pretty well," she said, "if he's sending you coffee early in the morning."

The tone she used was not tacky at all. She wasn't being critical, she was only being curious. Creed fascinated her. As, Raney had to admit, he fascinated a lot of people. Herself included.

"He's observant," Raney said. "But then, we've known each other for some time now, and I guess he did learn a lot about me when we were . . . courting."

"I'm surprised your father permitted that."

Raney took another sip of coffee and thought about it.

"I think I misspoke. We weren't really courting, I guess. Papa wouldn't let me go out alone riding or in a buggy with any man, Indian or not. Creed and I were just part of the same social circle."

"Yes. I always say to the judge that there's such a nice bunch of young people in the county. I like to watch you all because our daughter that died would've been your age."

The old hurt lingered, deep beneath the matter-of-fact tone she used.

"I'm sorry. I didn't know you had a daughter."

"Diphtheria took her as a baby. Losing a child really is the worst thing. I pray you never have to go through that, Raney."

234

Raney hadn't thought much about children, but now that she did, she knew Leonard wouldn't be their father. If she hadn't come to her senses about him, she might've found herself the mother to a bunch of selfish, stiff-necked, scaredy-cat little Leonards who would run her completely out of her mind by talking to her day and night.

Miss Hallie gave herself a shake, took a sip of coffee, and changed the subject back to her first choice.

"You know, Raney, there are so many young women in your social group who would give anything for a proposal of marriage from Creed Sixkiller. It's a shame how they throw themselves at him—and with their mamas' encouragement, too."

"That's true of all the Sixkiller men," Raney said. "Most people don't even think of them as Indians. Eagle Jack's wife, Susanna, is white."

Each took a sip of coffee and thought about that.

"My mama agreed with Papa, though, that Indians are different and not good enough for me. Our family is one of the first families of the South."

Miss Hallie nodded. "Not to contradict your dear mama, but I must say that all my life I've observed that a woman who doesn't marry by the dictates of her heart always lives with regret."

Creed's voice echoed in Raney's memory.

You went into that betrothal with your head, Raney, not your heart.

Now here was the judge's wife telling her the very

same thing. It was an affirmation that she'd made the right decision about Leonard.

Raney met the other woman's gaze. That was all Miss Hallie was going to say in words, but her eyes were still talking to Raney.

She felt heat come into her face.

"I'm . . . I . . . it's hard to know what my heart is saying," she said, trying to show appreciation for Miss Hallie's concern but not reveal too much.

What nonsense. How could she reveal too much? She herself didn't know anything.

"Yes. But eventually it will all come clear."

Miss Hallie's voice was so certain that it was a comfort.

"Bloodlines are important," she said, in that same sure tone. "But the finest of lines needs new blood from time to time. Your parents may be forgetting that there are other fine people. The Sixkillers are from an important line of chiefs and leaders among the Cherokee, I hear."

Raney blushed as red as she ever had done in her life. She caught a glimpse of herself in the mirror behind Mrs. S.

"I . . . I'm not . . . Creed and I are not courting again. Not at all. Ours was an accidental meeting, as we said. I'm . . . betrothed to Leonard Gentry, you know, Miss Hallie."

That didn't ruffle Miss Hallie in the least. Raney

was beginning to see that Miss Hallie was not nearly as flighty as she sometimes seemed.

"Yes. But, as my own dear departed mother used to say, 'There's many a slip 'twixt the cup and the lip.' Things change, Raney dear. People change. Texas is in great danger with all these feuds and the Mexican raiders and the Reconstruction and all. It will take strong, smart men to impose order and hold her together."

Miss Hallie was also a good judge of character. She had, no doubt, traded with Leonard at the store and formed an opinion of him. He wasn't strong enough to go bring Brass home or smart enough to know how his refusal would affect Raney.

"Strong, smart women standing with those men will add to their strength and give them heart enough for the task. That's what I'm trying to do for the judge."

Raney felt emboldened by the talk and the coffee.

"Miss Hallie, why is the judge out looking for Brassell? Has Brass done something worse than what I've heard about?"

"Oh no, no, my dear, I'm quite sure that he hasn't. The judge didn't come all the way down here on account of your brother. He has other business here in San Antonio."

"I'm just so worried about Brass that I guess I think everybody else is, too."

"No, that's not the reason we're here. The judge doesn't confide in me about the details, of course, but I could tell by his manner that this business he's conducting is something so very important that contemplating it has shaken him."

She stopped and looked at Raney wide-eyed. "Don't ever let him know that I said that, of course. He'd be terribly put out with me."

"I won't breathe a word."

"When I saw how nervous he was, I insisted on coming along to support him."

"That was very good of you. It's a rough trip."

"Yes. It is. But it beats sitting home alone with nothing to do."

She turned and reached to another chair for the dress she had worn the day before and looked at the watch pinned to the bodice.

"Time is getting away from us, Raney my dear. I'm going to slip down the hall to my room and into a fresh dress. The maid said the judge and Mr. Sixkiller are in the lobby reading the newspapers. I'll come back for you in a little while."

She put down her cup, gathered up her clothes, and tightened the belt of her wrapper. Then she stopped by the bed to give Raney's hand a little pat.

"Don't forget to lock up behind me, sugar."

Then she bustled out the door.

Raney did so, and, on her way back, opened the armoire that held her new clothes. She poured herself another mug full of coffee, then sat cross-legged in the bed, drinking it and looking at her new things to pick out which she would wear.

But she couldn't keep her mind on that. It just kept going over the surprising conversation with Miss Hallie.

She sounded like that Frenchwoman—talking about Raney and Creed as a couple. Why did people get the impression that they were in love?

Raney froze, with the cup at her lips. Could people see those feelings she had for him that she was thinking about last night? Surely not.

A little daydream took her. What if Creed should ask her again to marry him?

If she said yes, it would no longer break her mama's heart.

But it still would kill Papa. He was in a terrible shape already from all the grief he was carrying.

Her sending Leonard away would be hard enough on him. And he would be angry enough with her over that, never mind any mention of Creed.

She leaped out of the bed, her mind racing, set the mug down, and went to the desk with the gracefully carved legs that sat against the far wall.

Leonard had to know, right now, that she was through with him. It was the only honorable thing to try to let him know before she told anyone else.

And it was the only smart thing to do. He would surely get a letter before she could find Brassell and get home with him. That way, Leonard could move off the plantation before Papa had a chance to try to talk her out of changing her mind.

And, more importantly, Papa would hear about it while Brassell was his biggest concern.

Sure enough, there was nice eggshell-colored stationery in one drawer, with "The Menger Hotel, San Antonio, Texas" written in two lines of script across the top, and a pen and inkwell in another. She took them out, arranged them on the polished surface, and pulled up a chair to the desk.

She would tell Leonard and she would tell Creed, since she had already talked to him about her betrothal. He had advised her to follow her heart, and he had a right to know that she did it.

But she would not tell Miss Hallie. That news would only encourage her to continue talking to Raney about Creed, and that was too cruel.

Because, leaving Papa completely out of it—as if she could—the hard truth was that Creed would never ask for her hand a second time. He always did what he said he would do, and hadn't he said, "Never" when she refused him?

On top of that, he would never forgive her when she took Brassell and ran away from him.

No, there was no sense whatsoever thinking about marriage with Creed. She might never get married— certainly she wouldn't if she never met another man whose kisses made her feel like Creed's did.

All she could do was enjoy being with Creed for this next day or two until they found Brassell. She would find ways to get rid of Miss Hallie and be alone with him, no matter what she had to do.

That and getting rid of Leonard were the only two things she could accomplish until she found Brassell.

It was hard to get the lid off the ink without getting any on her new nightgown but she did it and dipped in the pen.

Dear Leonard,

As you can see, I have arrived safely in San Antonio. I am not telling you this for your own peace of mind—since your lack of action has told me that you haven't been worried about me. I am telling you so that you can inform Papa the minute he returns home and relieve his mind. You might also tell him that I have found friends here, so he is not to worry.

I do, however, include a message to you. You are not the man I thought you were. Your behavior, the last time I saw you, can only be called reprehensible. I refer both to your lack of loyalty to me and my family and your clumsy attempt to take advantage of me as soon as you knew both my brothers and my father were away from home.

I will never marry you, Leonard. Please re-

move yourself and your possessions from Pleasant Hill as soon as my father and brother return to oversee it.

Coltrane St. Iberville Childress

Smiling, she added a flourish of a line beneath her name and picked up the blotter. Nothing had felt this good to her for a long, long time.

Nothing except Creed's kiss.

Chapter 12

San Antonio in the morning was only a little bit quieter than it had been at night. A firewood vendor in a creaking cart yelled at his burro, booth owners called to potential customers, a church bell rang, and horses whinnied.

Goat and chili and tortillas and tamales were still cooking in the plaza, and the air was redolent with those food smells all mixed up with a dozen animal smells; the fresh, cool scents of flowers; and dust. Raney took a long, deep breath of it.

"No matter what it smells like," she said, "a person needs fresh air after breakfast with the judge."

"Amen," Creed said. "I never saw anyone who

could eat that much and talk that much at the same time."

"He's nervous," she said. "Miss Hallie thinks so, and now, after listening to him for so long, I can swear it's true."

"Nervous about what?"

"She said it's in anticipation of whatever business he has, here in San Antonio. She came with him to try to help because she could tell he's upset."

"Miss Hallie, huh? Sounds like y'all are getting friendly."

"She's a very nice lady, Creed. She's trying to mother me because her daughter died and she would've been my age if she'd lived."

Creed was only half listening to that.

"Miss Hallie didn't say what the judge's business is?"

"No. She said they didn't come here because of Brassell, though."

Creed put his hand at the small of her back to guide her a little closer to him as they moved over and let three bearded gentlemen pass by. She could still feel his hand there when he let go of her.

"Do you think you could find out?"

"She doesn't know. Most husbands don't talk to their wives about business, you know."

He slanted a quizzical look at her.

"No," he said, "I didn't know. My mother, and

my sisters, too, know as much as they care to know about the running of the Sixes and Sevens."

"That's because they're Cherokee," she said.

As she stopped and turned to look back at the plaza, from the corner of her eye she caught the amused glance he gave her.

"What's funny?" she said. "You're the one who told me about Cherokee women."

"True," he said. "Did you ever notice a difference between you and Maggie?"

"I noticed she was bolder and braver than I was," Raney said, lifting a hand to shade her eyes from the sun as she scanned the square and the people in it. "And I was better at flirting and playing the piano than she was. That's all. She was too little to go to the war when it started, so I never knew she had the right to."

That made Creed laugh. Raney continued to search for a curly, blond head on a tall boy.

"I always expect Brass to be out there in the plaza somewhere," she said. "Since that's where he was for our one sighting of him."

"We'll find him," Creed said. "Maybe today. First, it's the cotton broker, then we'll try Mr. Brackenridge at the bank."

"No, first, I need to go to the stage line office," she said. "Whichever one goes to Fort Worth. I have to send a letter, and I'm hoping someone can take it today."

He stopped in his tracks. "A *letter*. I thought you came down here to find your brother."

She stopped, too.

"You just said we will find him. Maybe today. Those were your exact words."

"Well, we sure as hell won't if we have to trudge all over town to the stage lines looking for someone to carry a letter to Fort Worth."

Creed sounded so suddenly angry that it made her mad. She set her head and faced him down.

"I would think there's only one stage line in question," she said. "I want the one that goes closest to Waco. How many coaches do you think there are going in that direction—running all over Texas, in and out of San Antonio?"

He looked completely disgusted with her.

"Cut me some slack, Raney! We'll have to go get your buggy because it'd take us half the morning to walk over there and back. What letter could you possibly need to send?"

"That's none of your business, Creed Sixkiller. Now, would you please just escort me to the right place, or shall I go back to the hotel and ask Miss Hallie to go with me?"

"Don't tempt me," he said, and spun on his heel to head back to the Menger for the buggy. "If I didn't need you to be the one inquiring of the bankers and brokers into your brother's affairs, I'd leave you with Miss Hallie for good."

"Well, it took you long enough to get me away from her in the first place," Raney said. "I couldn't believe you made plans for breakfast with them."

He didn't answer, so she glanced sideways at him. His jaw was set hard as stone. He glared at her for a moment.

"I was trying to get a handle on the whole situation," he said. "That's why I started with talking to him in the lobby and sending coffee up to you and the missus."

A lightning bolt of disappointment slashed through her.

"Well, you were eager enough to accept our thanks for your thoughtfulness in sending the coffee," she said. "Don't you think that's more than a little bit hypocritical? You basked in the praise for your consideration of others as if you were about to be sainted on the spot."

"What did you expect me to do? Refuse to accept thanks from you and Mrs. Scarborough?"

"Well, no, but I thought . . ."

"But you thought what?"

She clamped her mouth shut. "Never mind. I just never knew you were so devious, that's all."

"Devious?"

"Shhh, people are looking at us."

He walked faster. She had to hurry to keep up.

"I was not devious, I was courteous," he said rapidly, from between his clenched teeth. "And sociable.

How can you have expected me to be otherwise?"

"Well, I'd say that you're not being very sociable right now."

He growled at her. That was the only word for it; he made a dangerous, growling noise. But then all he said—with great sarcasm—was, "I wonder why."

"I'm only stating an obvious truth."

"Yes, Miss Prim and Proper, you damn sure are."

He didn't apologize for cursing, and the imp in her wanted to mention that, but she restrained herself. She didn't want to push him completely over the limit of his patience.

They arrived back at the Menger, and he sent the boy at a run to get the buggy and Tally from the stable.

"We'll be back in Concho before this letter gets to whoever it is in Waco," he said.

"Maybe so," she said, "but I must send it now. This is a matter of honor."

The surprised look he gave her made her smile, but she turned away and tried to hide it.

"You have more curiosity about you than I'd ever noticed before, Creed."

That caused his teeth to clench again.

"The only thing I'm curious about is what the Scarboroughs are doing in San Antonio."

"Well, we spent half the morning with them— that breakfast took a lot more time than mailing this letter will—and you still don't know any more than you did before."

"I know that you've lost your mind," he said. "You were so anxious to get to Brassell that you nearly drowned yourself and a good horse, yet the minute you get a chance to actually find his trail, you have to go mail a *letter*."

"It's a matter of honor," she said. "I told you that. You, of all people, should understand."

"Honor be hanged," he said, "it'd better be a matter of life and death."

"It is."

He gave her a disbelieving glance and started escorting her out of the hotel.

"If we stay in here, we're liable to end up with Mrs. Scarborough again," he said. "I only hope the buggy gets here before she sees us because I'm about out of charm for today."

"You've gone past that," Raney said. "You're already out of *manners*, and it isn't noon yet."

He shot her a look of fierce annoyance that made him look like a very mad little boy. She laughed. She couldn't help it.

Then she sobered. She must try to smooth his feathers so they could get this done and get on to the hunt for Brass as soon as possible.

"I must say, Creed, that you did a beautiful job of helping me explain to Miss Hallie that you had to escort me on some private family business. For a little while there, I thought she was going to stay glued to me for the whole day. The judge was really encouraging her, too."

"He wants us to find Brassell for him," Creed said darkly.

"But he knows you'll find him because you never quit. He knows you'll bring him back to Concho. No, it must be true that he has other business here, as he told Miss Hallie."

"Think what you want. You certainly *do* what you want."

"This won't take a minute. Then we can move around town on Brass's trail even faster because we'll have the buggy."

For the rest of the time until the boy brought the vehicle to them, Creed paced and Raney concentrated on watching the plaza. She didn't see one person who looked the least like Brassell.

At last Tally brought the buggy rolling to a stop right in front of them. Creed gave the boy a coin, lifted her up onto the seat in a flurry of skirts, climbed in, and had Tally moving before Raney could catch her breath. He didn't even have to ask directions. He'd known all the time which stage she needed for the letter.

She watched the streets and the walkways for Brassell all the way—up and down the dusty streets, across another plaza, and onto another street leading south. Finally, Creed pulled up at a corner store marked by the names of the proprietors on one side: Kapp and Munzenberger.

"I can manage," Raney said, "if you want to stay here."

"Wait." He was growling again.

He got down and came around to hand her down.

They went into the dim interior that held as many different smells as the plaza, but not the same ones. Creed escorted her to the man behind the counter, who was weighing out some hard candy for two children.

"Mr. Sixkiller," he said, and smiled at Raney. "What can I do for you fine folks today?"

"Mr. Kapp, how are you? Miss Childress has need to mail a letter."

Raney stepped up to the counter and reached into the pocket of her skirt.

"I'm hoping there's a stage going north today, Mr. Kapp. Could that be true?"

She laid the letter on the counter.

He picked it up and read the address aloud, "Mr. Leonard Gentry, Pleasant Hill Plantation, Concho, Texas."

Then he peered through his tiny eyeglasses at Raney.

"Nearest big town would be Waco. Am I right?"

"Yes, you are."

"The stage'll be leaving for Fort Worth this after-

251

noon. The driver will make sure the mail connects to Waco. Fare'll be five dollars, miss."

The sound of that amount went right through her like a knife. She gasped.

"Five dollars! Why, I don't even know if I have that much . . . I had no idea."

What if she couldn't mail the letter after all? Raney pulled her snap purse out of her reticule, emptied it onto the counter, and began to sort through its contents.

"Permit me," Creed said.

He handed the fare to Mr. Kapp and swept Raney's money back into the gaping top of her purse.

With a nod to answer the storekeeper's word of thanks, Creed dropped the purse into her hand, put his other arm around her, and hustled her out of the store.

She knew he was angry. His irritation had turned to anger when Mr. Kapp spoke Leonard's name. Even though she hadn't been looking at him and he hadn't made a sound, she had known it that instant.

"Get away from me," she said, as their feet hit the dirt outside. "You had no right to take over my transaction."

"Mailing the letter," he snapped, "is enough delay without losing another day counting out the fare."

"I'll add it to the amount Papa needs to pay you."

"Forget it."

He set her firmly on the seat and climbed in after her.

Raney looked at him. He had no right to be so high-handed with her.

But his pique gave her a twinge of satisfaction. It stemmed from more than his hurry to look for Brassell. He only became truly furious when he found out she'd written to Leonard.

If he would behave decently, she'd tell him why. She had caused this delay and furor so she *could* tell him why.

She kept her gaze on his grim profile. He ignored her. He picked up the lines and pulled the team around.

He slapped the lines on their backs, called, "Ha!" and they pulled. He drove out into the street and turned back toward the Alamo Plaza and the Menger.

Finally, he turned and looked Raney in the eye as he spoke.

"Life and death, you said. Matter of honor."

"It is."

He thought about that as he drove between a mule-drawn cart hauling water and a fancy carriage coming from the opposite direction.

"He's not coming," Creed said, "not even if he knows where you are. I thought you had more pride."

"I do," Raney said. "This is about *my* honor. *My* life or death."

He looked at her. He waited.

"I wrote to tell him I won't marry him. Not if he were the last man on earth."

He stared at her for a moment, then he smiled.

"That should be plain enough."

"I had to mail the letter before I told you. That was only right—to tell him first."

"We may get back to Concho before the letter does."

"If we do, I'll tell him in person," she said.

"Raney, you've been worried about your papa having a heart attack. This may do it."

"I can't help it if does," she said. "Papa picked Leonard, but I'm the one who'd have to kiss him for the rest of my life. I'm not going to do it."

He gave her a long, speculative look before he turned his attention back to the horses.

"What brought this on right now?"

"You."

He turned to her, fast. She couldn't read his eyes.

"You told me to choose with my heart."

He waited, his gaze on hers.

"And Judge and Mrs. Scarborough gave me a chaperone the same way Mama and Papa gave me a fiancé. That's the last time anybody gives me anybody."

Creed threw back his head and laughed.

Raney watched him, then she had to look away. She wanted to touch his face. She wanted him to turn to her and let the laughter fade into a smile that would still be lingering on his lips when he bent his head to kiss her.

She imagined how that would feel while she stared at the small band of musicians on the next street corner. Finally, she realized what she was seeing. Whom she was seeing.

She grabbed Creed's arm. "Over there! Look! Creed, it's Fiddler and his friends."

Creed was already angling the team toward the side of the street. He'd seen them, too.

Fiddler gave Raney a big smile and a flourish of his bow, but he didn't quit playing for the four or five people who'd gathered around until the song was done. Then he came to the buggy and greeted them both. Raney could hardly hold her tongue until he was done.

"Mr. Fiddler, have you seen my brother yet?"

"Not yet, missy, but I'm searchin' for him every place we play. If he likes music, he'll hear us and come up to get a closer listen sooner or later."

"Could y'all please come play on Alamo Plaza? Creed and I saw Brassell there when we first came into town—he was at the cockfight—and I'm thinking he'll come back around there soon."

Fiddler nodded. "Well, then, we'll meander over that way after a while," he said.

"We're staying at the Menger," Raney said. "I'm in room—"

Creed interrupted. "We'll check at the desk for

messages," he said. "Thanks for keeping an eye out."

They chatted for only another minute, then drove away.

"It wouldn't have hurt anything to give him my room number," Raney said. "Especially since I'm not alone there. Brass needs to know—"

"If Fiddler finds Brass, the boy will find you. You can't put too much stock in Fiddler, Raney. I've tried to tell you that. You don't know him and you have no idea whether you can trust him or not."

Raney felt as if he'd stolen her hope.

"I can tell," she said quickly. "I know by my woman's intuition that Fiddler is a man who can be trusted. Plus, Creed, it's our best chance. Brass loves music and he'll be drawn to it no matter what trouble he's in."

"Raney, listen to me. What we need to think about right now is every place in this town where Brass would be recognized. He's bound to have seen someone who knows him. We can't put all our eggs in the Fiddler basket."

"I don't know very much about Papa's business at home or in Concho, much less here in San Antonio. This is a big town."

They spent the rest of the morning and a good deal of the afternoon going to the places Raney could recall did business with her family. She thought of four: the cotton broker, the bank, the mercantile, and the lawyer.

In every one of those establishments, Creed was his usual determined self, and he persisted until they spoke with someone there who had, in the past, done business with one or another of the Childress family. If Brassell had come seeking help or credit or a loan of money, that person would have been the one he'd have asked to see.

Creed asked questions, then he introduced Raney. She explained—without mentioning that Brassell was on the run from jail—that the feud was heating up, that Brassell was young and foolish and wounded, and that he had told his friends he was coming to San Antonio.

Her heart was in her throat every time she finished her plea. Every time, her hopes were high that Brass had been there and that the person who was sitting across from her at that moment with sympathy in his eyes and a concerned frown on his face would know some bit of information that would lead her directly to him.

Always, though, the answer was no.

When Creed escorted her out to the buggy after the last one, the lawyer, had been of no help at all, a creeping fear started to take over her insides. She set her jaw and scoured her mind for more places to try. In spite of that, tears sprang to her lashes.

What else could she do? What if Brassell didn't come to San Antonio, after all? He might've been telling a lie to keep Creed from finding him again.

As Creed went around to get into the driver's seat, she pulled a handkerchief from her pocket and dabbed at her eyes. He saw her.

"Don't get discouraged, Raney. We'll find him. Remember I always get my man. You said it yourself."

The light tone of his voice held an underlying sympathy that made more tears come.

That was stupid. If he did get his man, one thing for sure was that he'd have no sympathy for Brassell. The boy would be headed back to jail if she didn't figure out a way to save him from that fate. *Finding* Brassell would be wonderful, but it would be only the beginning.

Dear Lord. How could all this have happened with Papa and Trent gone? How could it all be her responsibility?

She wiped her face and thought she was done crying, but a big sob escaped her.

"I thought you were tougher than that," Creed said, as he picked up the lines. "Are you the same woman who fords swift creeks on her own?"

Remembering that terrifying time, instead of making her proud and confident, this time made her want to let go, collapse on the seat, and cry her heart out. After the hard trip, the surprise chaperone, the sudden revelation about Leonard, the strain to get his letter mailed, the realization that Creed considered it unlikely Fiddler would happen across Brassell, and her high hopes of the morning that kept getting dashed, she just wanted to give in to a spell of nervous prostration the way Tante Marie used to do.

No, what she wanted to give in to was her need for Creed to hold her.

The truth was that the strong feelings for Creed that kept sneaking up and attacking her were the biggest reason she wanted to collapse. She *needed* him to hold her.

"We've only just started," he said, as he drove out into traffic. "Don't give up."

She wiped her face once more and put her hanky back into her pocket.

"I'm not," she said. "It's just that in every one of those places, I think I somehow expected all the talk about Brassell to make him appear."

"He will. We'll find him."

They went to the freight yards, where people without money for a room slept under their wagons, and to every livery stable on that side of town. Brass probably wouldn't spend his meager money to stable his horse, but he might have asked for a job at one of them.

No luck.

"We haven't eaten since breakfast," Creed said. "Let's go back and check the livery of the Menger, just in case, and then we'll go to the rooms to wash up. We'll make new plans over supper."

"If we don't have to sit and listen to the judge," Raney said.

Creed groaned. "Maybe we'll be too early for the judge and the missus."

"I hope they've gone to visit some friends and they'll be *very* late."

"Keep on thinking it."

They fell silent as they drove through the falling dusk, made strange by the lights and the smells and the sounds and the bustle of the many people surrounding them. As they turned a corner, Creed's thigh came against hers.

He left it there. She didn't move away.

His long saddle muscles flexed, and even through her skirt and petticoats, she felt his heat. His power. Deep inside, at the core of her, she felt them.

"Creed, I want some extra time to wash up before dinner. I think I'll wear my other new dress."

His leg stayed against hers.

"How many dresses did you buy, anyhow? I may have to get a job to pay your Joske's bill before we leave town."

She laughed.

"Only two. And two skirts and blouses. And a hat—"

"Stop! Stop! I don't even *want* to know. It worries me too much."

He drove up to the Menger, leaped out of the buggy, and gave the lines to the boy who came running out to them. When he lifted her down from the seat, his hands lingered on her waist even after her feet stood on the ground.

As they came in from the twilight, the lobby seemed very brightly lit. It was busy, too, and they had to wait a few minutes until one of the desk clerks could help them.

"Any messages for Miss Childress?"

"None," the man said. "And none for you, sir. Sorry, Mr. Sixkiller."

Raney fought the disappointment in the pit of her stomach that threatened to spread its tentacles through all her veins.

"Fiddler's only had a few hours since we saw him," Creed said comfortingly as they climbed the stairs.

"I wish you hadn't said that," Raney said. "It tells me you don't have any other ideas and neither do I."

"Let it go for tonight," Creed said. "Put on your new dress, and we'll go dancing."

He opened the door. The lamp was lit but the maid must have done it because Mrs. Scarborough wasn't there.

Raney breathed a sigh of relief. It would be good to have a few minutes all to herself.

"Will thirty minutes be enough time?" Creed asked. "Or do you want to lie down for a little while?"

261

"Give me an hour," she said, glancing up at him, "but it's to dress my hair. I may be a crybaby, but I'm not an old lady who has to go lie down every whipstitch."

They smiled into each other's eyes.

"All right then," he said. "An hour it is."

It was after he'd closed the door between them and she had taken off her hat and gloves and started unbuttoning her blouse that she saw it.

A wrinkled, folded piece of paper lying beside the closed door to the hallway, gleaming white against the dark hardwood floor.

Chapter 13

Raney ran to the piece of paper. It must be a message slipped under the door.

Her hands were shaking as she picked it up and unfolded it. Tears threatened again. She was too tired. She was too scared that she'd never find Brass and that this would be only another hope of this long, disappointing day dashed to bits.

It wasn't Brass's handwriting. Her gaze flew to the signature. Fiddler.

She went back to the beginning of the surprisingly clear, ornate script that flowed across the ratty piece of paper, which was almost too small for all the words.

*Miss C. I lied to you this morning, for your
brother swore me to secrecy re Mr. Sixkiller.
Brassell is well. Meet him at the hotel livery
stable tomorrow at noon. Yr. Friend Fiddler*

Happiness fired her blood. She slapped the note
to her heart with both hands and held it there. Brass
wasn't in pain or dying from his wound. Brass knew
she was here. She would see him tomorrow!

A cold thought stopped her breath. What if it
weren't true? Creed was right in saying that she
didn't know Fiddler. This could be a trick or a joke
or a way to get her out of the hotel alone.

No matter, she would be at the livery stable at
noon, as she'd known she would from the instant she
read those words. What choice did she have? What
other chance to find Brassell? None. She and Creed
had exhausted every other possibility of finding him.

Besides, the livery stable at noon could not be a
terribly dangerous place. Other people besides Brass
would be there, and always, in San Antonio, there
were people in the street.

But noon! How would she get away from both
Creed and Mrs. Scarborough?

She'd think of something. Right now, she wanted
to let the good news sink in, after nothing but bad for
so long. Brassell was all right. He was fine. He would
meet her. This time tomorrow they'd be together.

Thank goodness, she had visited the livery with

Creed this very afternoon, so she knew exactly where it was. Brass, no doubt, had chosen it as the meeting place so she wouldn't be out on the streets alone for a long distance.

And . . . he'd chosen it because he'd seen Tally and the buggy there. He and Raney would be leaving town the minute they met.

Creed would never speak to her again.

Raney walked to the bellpull and rang for the maid. She would have warm water to wash with and help with her hair and someone to press her new dress. She would look as beautiful as she could for her last evening with Creed Sixkiller.

So she could feel strong enough to enjoy it. Already, a bittersweet ache was rising in her heart but she wouldn't let it take her. Life was short. This would be her last time to share a social occasion with Creed, and she was going to make the most of it.

Her heart clutched. She would lose Creed again, and this time it would be worse because she was just beginning to know him.

But as she lit a candle from the lamp and burned the note in the washbasin, she knew that wasn't the only reason. She pushed it away and refused to think about it.

The musicians playing in the dining room struck up a rousing rendition of "The Yellow Rose of

Texas" while Creed was escorting Raney down the stairs.

"You promised me dancing, didn't you, Mr. Sixkiller?"

He looked down into the October-sky blue of her eyes. She tilted her head flirtatiously, and the smile she gave him made him want to kiss her.

"I did," he said solemnly, "and I always keep my promises."

The Scarboroughs were right behind them.

"Judge Scarborough? Did you hear that? Perhaps we could take a whirl on the dance floor, too."

"I haven't danced in twenty years and I don't intend to start back now. Can't you recall, Hallie, how I always stepped on your feet?"

The judge was in a grumpy mood with his wife, evidently, but he had been extremely friendly to Creed and Raney when they all met upstairs in the hall. He had wanted to hear all about their day and whether they'd made any progress in the search for Brassell.

"Yes, I do, now that you mention it. In fact, the very memories have made my poor toes begin to hurt. Something about this festive evening must've made me lose my head. Can you ever forgive me?"

Mrs. Scarborough kept her tone more wry than sharp, but there was an edge to it. The judge must've already tried her patience while they were dressing for dinner.

Creed didn't care. All he wanted was to be rid of them both. After dinner, he'd do that somehow and take Raney out onto the plaza where a fiesta was taking shape. Through the long windows and the doors as they opened and closed, he glimpsed a mariachi band climbing up onto a wagon bed and a lot of brightly dressed dancers. The smells of roast goat and chili and barbecued beef floated into the Menger with a new group of revelers.

While they crossed the lobby, which was full of well-dressed people and an air of excitement, the judge held forth to all three of them with a boyhood tale about being tricked into eating goat meat unawares. Creed started racking his brain for a way to dominate the conversation during dinner.

"Twelve thousand people and always something going on in San Antone," the judge blathered ponderously, as the maître d' showed them to a table near the open door to the patio garden. "Your brother is a needle in a haystack here, Miss Raney."

Raney said, "Yes, sir, we've found that out today."

Creed held her chair for her and bent to speak into her ear while the judge was seating and talking to his wife.

"What do you want to bet we find Brass before dinnertime tomorrow, though?"

"Or before breakfast, even," Raney said, keeping her voice low.

They shared a conspiratorial grin. He wanted to kiss her.

"Don't you get discouraged, Raney dear," Mrs. Scarborough said, once they were all settled around the table.

She cast a reproving glance at her husband. "A needle *can* be found in a haystack, and here we have just the man to do it. Mr. Creed Sixkiller."

The lady beamed at Creed while the judge scowled at her. Then he turned to Creed.

"If that's so, then would you get to it, Sixkiller?"

He was attempting to sound jovial, but he sounded impatient instead. That made Creed sure, once again, that the judge was in San Antonio because of Brassell Childress. It was inconceivable, but it must be true. So far, trying to lead him to talk about it hadn't revealed one clue. Maybe, if he goaded the man, he could find out what was really going on back in Limestone County.

"Sounds like you don't trust me to bring the boy back," Creed said. "If you think you can do a better job of it, Judge, jump right in the middle of it. I'm needed on the ranch, anyhow."

Both women gasped, and the judge's ruddy face paled a shade.

"No, now, don't get your dander up, Sixkiller. I didn't mean that—"

Shouts and screams erupting in the lobby interrupted him. Every head in the dining room jerked around to look in that direction.

One voice sounded clearly over the noise of running feet and jingling spurs. "Stop in the name of the law! Billy Tate Burnham, you're under arrest."

Burnham, notorious for killing cattle for their hides and men for no reason, burst into the dining room, waving his six-shooter above his head. He threaded his way among the tables, heading for the doors to the patio that were open to the garden not a dozen feet behind Raney's chair. His desperate eyes flicked to her, then to the doors again.

The sheriff, or whatever lawman he was, was doing his portly best, but he was way too far behind to do any good.

"Ladies," Creed said, without taking his eyes from the outlaw, "when I stand up, dive under the table. There may be gunplay."

Raney heard the words, but she couldn't take them in. All she could think about was the fact that Creed didn't wear his gun to dinner. Creed was unarmed. The man not only had his gun drawn, the best she could tell, he had his finger on the trigger.

As she had the thought, he fired a shot and, on the other side of the room, a piece of a chandelier broke in a shattering of crystal that came showering to the floor. When the sound of it died away, the only sounds left in the room were the running bootheels

269

on the marble floor and the sheriff and the outlaw panting for breath.

She couldn't take her eyes off Billy Tate Burnham. It was true she was afraid to look at Creed and see him take an impossible chance, but it was also true that she couldn't move. The inside of her skin felt like a sheath of sleet, freezing harder with every second that passed. They passed like hours. Like days.

Dimly, she heard scuffling sounds out on the patio, but they seemed miles in the distance.

Her eyes finally did move enough to widen, though, when the wretched bad man looked straight into them with his bloodshot stare. He glanced at the door, then back at her and motioned with his free hand for her to get up. Close, he was so close now. Her brain finally froze, too, when he reached out for her as he ran.

Creed. It was a silent scream from her spirit. *Creed. Help me.*

Now she was the one in danger. Burnham was coming for her. He wanted her for a hostage.

And she couldn't move to help herself if he stuck the gun right in her face.

But he didn't. He disappeared. He hollered out, and something hit the floor with a clatter, and Creed's big body flashed across her vision. By the time she was able to turn and look, the two men

270

were struggling like panthers fighting, rolling over the place. They fought and struggled on toward the doors, bucking and kicking and wrestling, but Creed never lost his hold on Burnham's gun arm.

Then Creed made some kind of move with one leg that partially pinned his enemy down and, when the outlaw reached to poke him in the eye, Creed ducked his head, drew back his free hand, and hit him in the face with his fist. Burnham's gun went flying and even before it had finished skidding along the slick floor, the sheriff and some men who rushed in from the patio were all over them.

She couldn't turn away. She couldn't see Creed anymore but she couldn't turn away. Her heart was racing like a horse in the wind.

"Raney, darling, oh dear Lord, I think that horrid man was reaching for you. *Honey!* Oh, what would've happened if Mr. Sixkiller hadn't been here—"

But Creed appeared from out of the circle of men. His eyes were on hers and he was coming to her. She jumped up and ran into his arms.

He held her for a long, long moment in silent relief, his body speaking to hers as plainly as if he'd used words, and then people were surrounding them, crushing in to thank Creed for capturing Billy Tate Burnham, asking to shake his hand and to know his name, telling Raney how lucky she was

271

that Creed was so brave, and on and on. It took a long time for things to settle down and for them to have the dinner that the manager of the Menger insisted on serving everyone for free.

After that, they danced and Raney clung to him. She melted into Creed's big hand at the back of her waist and let him draw her nearer and nearer to his body until they were dancing scandalously close.

His heavy-lidded gaze lingered on her lips and, shamelessly, she stepped into him even more until the saddle muscles of his thighs brushed against her legs. While the sweet strains of the fiddles rose and fell, they floated across the shining marble floor without ever setting a foot down.

Long after midnight, she was clinging to her pillow and wishing it were Creed. Her eyes would not close, they would only watch the moon, sliding down, now, toward the west. Even the carnival that was San Antonio from noon to midnight had fallen into a condition that a person could almost call quiet.

She had less than twelve hours before she would meet Brassell, and she felt at least twelve years older than she had been when she read Fiddler's note. Now she'd realized that there was a choice she could make when she met Brassell: she could take Creed with her.

They had searched for Brassell together and they

could find him together. She could let him take her brother back to jail. That way, at least she, and Brassell, too, would see Papa and Trent and Pleasant Hill again someday.

But she had thought about it and thought about it and decided that she *could* do that, but she wouldn't. For one thing, she'd told Creed at the very beginning that she'd never agree to his jailing Brass again, and her self-respect demanded that she keep her word.

For another, she wouldn't be that disloyal to Brassell. He hadn't felt safe in that jail and had taken terrible chances to get away. And the Chickenhawks had come all the way down here after him, so he'd been right about not feeling safe. She would take him home and hide him until this feud could get all sorted out. Eventually, Brassell would tell Papa all he knew and Papa could take care of it.

But until she and Brass could get to Papa, what would she do without Creed? What would *they* do?

She knew how to work Papa's old six-shooter and she could hit the broad side of a barn. But a man like Billy Tate Burnham was a lot smaller than the side of a barn and he moved a lot faster. Even with his glasses, Brassell couldn't shoot and hit much of anything.

Now she knew firsthand how many and how terrible the dangers were that lurked along road between here and Pleasant Hill.

It wasn't courage that had made her leave home all by herself in the dark. It was stubbornness and anger. Courage was what people had who knew the dangers ahead of time and struck out anyway.

Courage was what it would take for her to go off alone with Brassell when noon rolled around, now that she knew there were men like Billy Tate Burnham who could be in her face and reaching for her in an instant, creeks that ran so hard and swift underneath the calm surface of their waters that they could suck a horse and buggy under in the blink of an eye, and men like Creed Sixkiller who could kiss a woman for one heartbeat and melt every bone in her body.

Men like Creed Sixkiller who could hold her without saying one word and make her feel she was safe from all harm.

Courage was what it would take for her to leave him, knowing that she forever would be losing every chance to be with him.

And knowing that Creed would never give up on finding Brassell and never forgive her when he did.

Courage was what it would take to see him one more time and give him the apology she owed him. Courage was what it would take—and help from a thousand angels in heaven—to talk to him again and then turn around and walk away.

She had to do it, though. Honor demanded it.

And when she was an old, lonely woman, she would have nothing left but her honor.

Stealthily, Raney threw back the covers and got to her feet. Miss Hallie had taken a long time to fall asleep, but she was sleeping so hard now that she didn't even snore. She just took long, deep breaths that came as regularly as the clock's ticks. Raney took a step on every breath, then stopped at the chair, picked up her wrapper, and slipped her arms into it. She pulled the belt tight and tied it before she opened the French doors to the balcony. If Creed was sleeping as hard as Miss Hallie was, he would never hear her knock.

Gently, she opened her doors and stepped out into the moonlight. It washed the black wrought-iron of the railings in gold and shone into her eyes to blind her. She closed the doors behind her by feel and turned, touching the wall as she moved along the balcony toward the next set of French doors, the ones that opened into Creed's room.

The moon's shine pulled her up into it while the tile floor held her to the earth, its surface smooth and cool against her bare feet. A free, daring feeling came into her, up there in the air above the scattered lights of the city.

"Driving all over Texas without a chaperone is one thing," drawled Creed's low voice, "but sneaking around San Antonio in your nightdress is something else again."

She whirled. A small, orange ember burned in the darkest corner of the balcony overlooking the street. A whiff of his sweet, spicy tobacco came to her on the low breeze.

"Spying on people in the dark isn't exactly socially acceptable, either," she said, walking toward the tantalizing aroma and the big, dark shadow that was Creed. "I'm afraid that you, too, need a chaperone to sleep in your room."

"Are you volunteering for the job?"

"Creed!"

He chuckled. That sound was another thing she'd want to remember when she thought about him.

"Forgive the assumption," he said, standing up to pull out the other wrought-iron chair at the small, round table, "but you appeared to be on your way to my room."

He flashed a significant grin at her. "What else could a man think? Beautiful woman, slipping around in her nightgown, her hair still up so he could take it down . . ."

"Creed, stop it this minute."

His hand brushed her shoulder when she sat down. She felt it through the wrapper like a touch of fire. Her whole body trembled.

"I tend to lose my head in the middle of the night," he said. "What excuse do you have?"

She laughed. "I've been out of my head since I left home . . . no, since long before—since I let myself say I'd marry Leonard. That's all I can tell you."

He smiled down at her, and she wanted to reach up and touch his face, nearly hidden by the dark.

"Sorry I have nothing to offer you but tobacco."

"I don't use it."

Then, teasing him, trying to bring back the laughing times they had shared over his smoke signals, she said, "I didn't know a person could smoke a peace pipe all by himself."

"I didn't know we were at war," he said.

"We aren't."

Not yet. Not quite yet. We have a little while left.

He sat down and leaned toward her across the small table. The moonlight caught and held him. Her breath caught in her throat.

He was barely wearing his shirt. The tail was out, it was unbuttoned, and when he moved his arms, his broad chest rippled with muscles. Her fingertips ached to stroke his skin.

But she couldn't touch him. Not until she kissed him good-bye. She was not leaving him without one more kiss to remember.

Before then, though, she had to say what she had come to say.

He sensed that, as usual. He waited. He turned his chair, lifted his long legs, and propped his feet carelessly on the railing, ankles crossed, puffing at his pipe.

He wore no belt, and the waistband of his jeans

hugged his hard, narrow waist. She wanted to slip her arms around it inside his shirt and hold on for dear life.

She couldn't say it yet. She needed to work up her courage to bring up that old bad time between them.

She needed to look at him for a little while so she could imprint him on her memory.

"When I said that about the peace pipe, I was talking about Billy Tate Burnham," she said, making herself say the name and recall her fear at the way the outlaw had looked at her.

That was one step taken toward courage.

"No need for the pipe," Creed said. "It was never personal between me and Billy Tate."

"It nearly was between him and me," she said. "I'll never forget the way he looked at me. If it hadn't been for you he might've used me for a shield."

"Might have. Big words. We never know what might have been but we always think we do."

Suddenly, she was in no mood to sit around and talk philosophies and what might have been. His dark eyes flashed in the moonlight. Her heart was beginning a slow, pounding rhythm.

All her instincts as the belle of Limestone County were stirring. Creed wasn't bad at flirting himself, as he had already proved tonight.

"You noticed my hair is still up," she said, "do you like it pinned up this way?"

"Raney," he drawled, "I have never seen your hair pinned any way at all that I didn't like."

There was a smile not quite hidden in his voice. He was gently making fun of her coquettishness.

"I like the dress you wore tonight, too. It's the same color as your eyes."

"I thought it was amazing that it fit me, too. I wish I could look for some more. I never get to shop much in a big town."

How to get away from Mrs. Scarborough by noon came to her then, as the decision about Leonard had done. She pushed it away, to the back of her mind. Right now, these last moments with Creed were precious. She wouldn't waste them thinking about when he'd be gone from her life.

"Maybe someday we—" Creed said, then he stopped.

He knew, too, that there could be no future for them together. In that instant, she wanted one. Wanted it with all her might.

This was unbearable, to sit here and torture herself by watching his flashing eyes and teeth in his dark face. By listening to his rich, low voice. She would apologize to him, kiss him good-bye, and go back to her room to wait for morning.

He was watching her, too. She was sitting in the moonlight while he was in the shadows. She could feel his gaze drift over her face and come back to linger.

Now. Now she would say it and leave him.

"Is that some of the Grandfather Medicine in your pipe there? Or is that only for incantations?"

He went still.

"It can be used for deliberations as well as for religious ceremonies."

"Are you deliberating about how to find Brassell? Since it isn't dawn yet to do an incantation?"

He didn't move.

Finally, in a wry tone, he said, "At least you were listening to what I told you."

She waited, getting her words exactly right so he would not misunderstand.

"Yes, I was. And finally, I listened to my own intuition, too."

"What are you saying, Raney?"

"I'm saying I'm truly sorry for accusing you wrongly about the ceremony in the creek that morning," she said. "I followed the sound of your voice, thinking that you were talking to someone. The minute I saw you, though, my instincts told me that you were praying."

He cocked his head and threw her a sideways glance. He waited.

"I didn't listen to myself, though. I remembered that Papa always said some Indians can conjure magic and put spells on people and even kill them from a distance like the people who do gris-gris back in Louisiana."

He waited.

"It was a terrible shock when I heard you say Brassell's name," she said. "That just took my breath away."

He didn't say anything. He didn't move.

"It scared me so much," she said, "because I knew you wouldn't be asking for a blessing for him."

"It'll be a blessing for him when I find him," he snapped.

She ignored that and clung to her purpose.

"I knew it was a prayer all the time. I knew it wasn't a curse."

He sat silent and still, considering her. Considering whether she was telling him the truth.

"I've learned something," she said. "This has made me listen to my own self and it'll make me not accept everything Papa says as the truth for me."

Creed considered that, too.

Raney felt weak all over, she wanted to go to him so much. He didn't believe her. He would always hold it against her that she accused him of doing evil.

She had to get away from him before she burst into tears. Before she threw herself at him and begged for forgiveness.

Forcing strength into her legs, she stood up and leaned toward him across the table.

"I'm sorry you can't forgive me, Creed, but I can't help that. I've told you the truth."

281

Turning away from him was the hardest thing she'd ever done, but she did it and started walking away. The tile was icy cold under her feet now and her eyes were blurring with tears. She started toward his French doors, realized they were the wrong ones, and headed toward her own.

His big hands took hold of her shoulders with a gentle strength that made her knees go to water, and he turned her around to look at her face in the moonlight. He moved his hands over her back and down to her waist, stirring every inch of her body with his callused palms through the silk of her robe while his eyes burned into hers.

He didn't say a word. He just shook his head slowly as if he could hardly believe she was standing there, held in the span of his hands. Then he rested one of them at the small of her back and used the other to lift her chin.

"Raney," he said in a hoarse whisper, "I forgive you."

A sweet madness swept through her. With an incoherent little cry of joy, she reached up and locked her hands behind his neck as his lips met hers. His mouth was hot and deep. She thought he had kissed her before now, but he had not.

His kiss held a lushness she'd never known, and it heated her blood more than what seemed possible. That heat melted her to him.

He seemed to know that, because he loosened his

hand and let it roam over her back and up her spine to her hair while his tongue roamed in her mouth and teased with hers. Then he tore his lips away.

"I've wanted . . . to do this . . . since I saw you . . . at your door . . . in your . . . blue, blue dress," he said, in a husky voice.

He punctuated the words by pulling the pins from her hair. Very, very slowly, one at a time, he pulled each of them out and let it fall with a tiny chinking noise to the tile floor. Her hair tumbled to her shoulders.

Creed thrust his fingers into it as if he were taking possession of her.

She unlocked her hands to stroke his face. Her thumbs traced his beautiful high cheekbones.

"Oh, Creed," she whispered, and stood on tiptoe to kiss his eyelids.

He shook out her hair and caressed her head with his strong fingertips. When a curtain of curls fell onto her face, he pushed them away with his cheek and blew them away with his breath so he could find her mouth again.

Creed swept her up against him and she latched on to him again with all the strength in her two arms and they kissed, straining to get closer together, until Raney was up against the wall. He suckled her mouth with a primal power that held her as breathless as the night surrounding them.

His kiss was a force like none she'd ever known.

It poured a heat into her blood that drove her heartbeat through her bones.

No, it was Creed's heart beating that she felt. Creed's heart, in perfect rhythm with her own.

She couldn't take it all in—all the feelings, all of Creed. She couldn't imagine more, but she wanted more. She welcomed the rough, unyielding stones on her tender back. They were all that held her to the earth with Creed's body hard against hers and his mouth consuming hers.

The one ragged breath of air that she managed to drag into her fanned the flames inside her like a blowing wind. He pulled her off her feet and crossed his arms behind her, cupping her bottom in his hands. Instinctively, Raney wrapped her legs around him.

He grasped the back of her head and told her without words what he'd like to do next. Then he tore his mouth loose from hers and let her down, taking her shoulders in his hands to set her away from him.

"Go," he rasped. "Go in, Raney."

She stood, stunned, her lips throbbing, her head spinning, her mind befuddled, her entire body aching, screaming for more. For more of Creed.

She felt intolerably bereft. She reached for him.

But he shook his head.

"I can't resist you, Raney. I can't be responsible. Go."

He led her to her doors and opened them.

"See you in the morning," he whispered into her hair.

She didn't dare turn to face him. If she looked into his face again, *she* couldn't be responsible.

So, over her shoulder, she whispered, "Good-bye, Creed."

Chapter 14

Raney started in, then she stopped in the middle of the doorway. Every fiber of her body resisted walking away from Creed.

What was she doing, anyhow? Letting someone else make a decision for her, when it was her life it would change the most. Her life, which would be that of a lonely old maid because she would never find another man who could make her feel the way Creed made her feel.

Never. She knew that now.

She needed to know him as much as she possibly could, so she could remember everything about him when the nights were long and cold and she was old. Another thing she wanted to remember was that she had made her decisions on her own.

So she took a step back and closed the doors again, very, very softly, so as not to disturb Miss Hallie. When she turned around, Creed had not moved.

He still didn't. He looked at her.

"I want you to make love to me, Creed."

"Raney . . ."

She lifted her hand and laid her finger across his lips. Neither of them had spoken louder than a whisper. The sound was gone in that instant because the soft words drifted away in the dark. Words were the most unnecessary things in the world.

Standing there, with the sleeping city spread out around them and the moon sliding down, she felt the first hint of morning coming into the wind. Time was passing. They were together. Here. Now.

Raney's pulse beat faster. The night was cooling fast, but her flesh and her blood were heating like the sun at high noon. Creed was doing that to her. He was all the sun she needed.

The breeze blew her robe back from her legs and lifted Creed's shirt away from his body. She moved closer to him until the rough denim of his jeans rubbed against her bare legs and her breasts brushed his naked chest.

Desire flared hotter in her.

His lips burned her finger. She wanted his hot skin against her hot skin. All of it.

She traced the edge of his lips with her fingertip and

then ran it along the shape of his hard jaw. She would memorize him so she could come back to this night in her mind whenever she wanted and find this moment and all the others that were about to follow it.

Her finger trailed along the side of his neck and down over his broad chest. His eyes narrowed with pleasure. A shudder went through him.

Raney smiled. She had never known she could hold such sway over him. She had never felt so strong.

"I mean it, Creed," she murmured.

His eyes burned in the dark. He cupped her face in his hands and bent his head to hers.

"Raney, honey, you don't even know what you're talking about."

"I want the memory of making love with you to carry with me forever, Creed. That's what I'm talking about."

He kissed her, short and sweet, not lingering even a little. Creed Sixkiller was a tough man. He'd made up his mind not to take her virginity and he was the one who, once set, never changed his intent.

But this time he would. She had the power.

"You'd regret it later," he said.

"I'd regret it much more if it never happened. All the responsibility in the world is not yours, Creed, even though you always think it is. I love you for trying to take care of everyone and every situation, but this is my call."

He searched into her eyes, the moonlight playing on his face. Then he kissed her again. Swiftly.

She murmured against his lips, "I'm beginning to think you don't want me."

With an incoherent growl, he swept her up into his arms.

"I want you," he said. "Do you need proof?"

She twined her arms around his neck.

"Yes, I do," she said, giving him a short, quick kiss to match the ones he'd given her.

He carried her to the doors to his room, kicked them open, and strode across the room to his bed. He laid her down. She reached for him.

"You are going to have to prove it to me, Creed Sixkiller, because after the way you've been behaving, I am terribly prone to doubt."

After that, she could say no more because he was on the bed, too, and his mouth claimed hers with no intention of letting it go. His hands began to move over her with a hunger that held no hesitation.

A wild, new thrill raced through her. What had she done? Whatever it was, she was glad of it.

Her nipples hardened even more, crying out for his touch. Deep inside, the ache of desire burst into a torturing need that shook her to the core.

He stroked her tumbled hair, then caressed her neck and her shoulder and her arm before he cupped her breast in his palm and rubbed it against his bare chest. Moaning into his mouth, she tore his shirt off his shoulders and one arm but then she let it hang from the other because she could not bear for his hand to move away from her breast to let the cloth fall.

She could not bear for his mouth to move away from hers, either, and when he broke the kiss, she cried out in protest. He stopped that by moving to her other breast and suckling it through the thin cotton of her gown.

Raney gave a long, shuddering gasp. The shock of these new, wonderful sensations made colored sparks fly against her black eyelids. A tingling excitement shot into every part of her.

When he raised up to push her robe off her shoulders and lifted her to pull the gown over her head, she helped him in a desperate haste. Then the sensual languor he was creating in her pulled her prone again and she fell back against the bed.

With his big, callused hands, he stroked her skin, every inch of it he could find. He kissed her everywhere; he murmured about how sweet she tasted and trailed his tongue along her lips until she met it with hers and took it in to suckle.

When he tore his mouth from hers and moved it to the other breast, she opened her eyes for the thrill of seeing Creed pleasure her so. She ran her hands through his hair and stroked his muscled shoulders.

Finally, her growing desire gave her strength to stop caressing his back so she could start unbuttoning his jeans. He toed off his boots and left her breast to start making a trail of fiery kisses down her throat and down between her breasts to her womanhood, which now was weeping for his touch.

She dragged in another long breath with what energy she could spare and undid his buttons one by one, her fingertips and her knuckles brushing the fascinating hardness of him, straining against the cloth. Moaning, he finally began to hurry her and she let him help her push the jeans off his hips. Her hands explored as much of him as she could reach as he pulled away, shoved the garment all the way down, and kicked it off.

Skin to skin at last, as their mouths came together in an instant, they melted into each other for their whole lengths. He rose over her and anchored her head in his hands to deepen the kiss.

Raney copied the motions of his tongue, returning each firm thrust with one of her own, and when he entered her she came to him with a welcome that held no fear. She wanted to remember every moment, and she would, but after one heartbeat, after he had filled her and she had taken him in, living those moments made her forget that this need and heat and closeness with Creed would not last forever.

It made her forget everything but him.

He made her feel things she never knew existed to such an extent: passion and power and perfection.

And in the white-hot rush that carried them, clinging together, right off the face of the earth, he made her know lust and love and life.

Later, lying together with their arms and legs tangled, melded into one by their sweat and what they had just done, Raney learned how to name the feeling that held them, lying there still and sated, inside and out. It was like coming home.

The sun rose slowly, as if giving them time to get used to the idea of daylight a little bit at a time. Raney watched the sky change from gray to pink.

Soon Miss Hallie would be awake and raising the alarm because Raney wasn't there. She had to go.

That seemed the most impossible task she'd ever faced. Harder, even, than rescuing herself from the quicksand and the creek.

Creed slept on his stomach with one leg twined in hers and one heavy arm across her as if to make sure she would be exactly there when he awoke.

She couldn't get out from under without waking him, so she made herself do it.

"Creed?" she said. "Creed? I have to go now. Let me up."

He raised up, shook his hair out of his face, and looked at her with his eyes as alert as if he'd never slept. He cradled her head in one hand and kissed her thoroughly. She kissed him back as if she would never leave him.

Finally, she tore her mouth away and sat up as fast as she could. Her treacherous hands were tangled in his hair, and she freed them without touching him anyplace else.

Well, except for cupping his cheek for one tiny second to caress his cheekbone with her thumb while she looked into his deep, dark, beautiful eyes.

"If Miss Hallie finds me here, we will be in so much trouble," she said. "Don't touch me again or we'll be lost."

He leaned on one elbow and looked at her. Up and down, every inch of her.

Blushing, she made herself get up and out of bed to look for her clothes. Wrapper. Gown. That's what she had been wearing.

She picked up the wrapper and stuck one arm into the sleeve.

"Are you going to wear your gown on top this time?"

That low drawl was an instrument of seduction in itself.

The desire that had flashed to life the minute she woke flared again. She looked at him, lying there in the warm, tangled sheets with his head propped on his hand, watching her dress as if she belonged there, in his room. In his arms.

How could she leave him? She loved him.

The truth stunned her. It wasn't just desire that made her feel so connected to him. It was more, way more, and it was in her now, in the marrow of her bones. Last night she had given him part of her heart and part of her soul.

The new sunlight reached into the room and painted a glow on Creed's bronze skin. She had to hurry and get out of here—not just because of Mrs. Scarborough but because of her own state of mind.

Raney made herself tear her gaze from his, snatched up the gown, and pulled it over her head. Hurriedly, she put on the wrapper and tied the belt.

"I think I'll have a dressmaker come in this morning," she said. "Or I'll go to her. Does the Sixes and Sevens have credit at the dressmaker's shop around the corner? Maybe Miss Hallie might go over there with me to order a handmade dress or two. I might as well get some more clothes while I'm in a town big enough to offer a dressmaker who knows the latest styles."

When she met his gaze again, he was waiting for her.

"You look better in nothing at all."

"Now, Creed," she said, fleeing to the French doors but not yet touching the knob, "please just answer my question."

She turned to face him. Courage. She had to build her courage before noon.

"Any merchant in San Antonio will trade with you on the name of the Sixes and Sevens," he said. "I'll go over there if you have any trouble, so order anything you want. It's a good time for that because I'm going to look for Brassell this morning in some places a lady can't go."

Guilt stabbed her in the heart.

"Perfect," she said. "I'll be praying you'll find him."

She reached behind her and took the cool brass knob in her hand.

"Bye, Creed."

He looked at her so long with his sleepy-lidded eyes that she had to hold on to the knob extra hard to keep from running back to him.

"See you this afternoon," he said. "Buy something blue."

"Thanks for the loan."

Raney turned the knob, opened the door behind her, then turned and ran without closing it after her. She felt strangely breathless when she opened the door to her own room.

Buy something blue.

Creed was falling into the same fantasy she was. He, too, had forgotten about Papa.

He was going to be so furiously hurt when she betrayed him.

Miss Hallie was sitting on the side of the bed, rubbing her eyes.

"It's a beautiful morning out there on the balcony," Raney said, trying to act as if that were the only place she'd been. "You should go out, Miss Hallie, and watch the sunrise."

But Miss Hallie shook her head and started taking the braid out of her hair.

"I need to go see about the judge," she said, sleepily. "Lay out his clothes and see about his breakfast and all that."

"I'm going to have breakfast brought up here, so I can think about my wardrobe," Raney said. "Later this morning, I want to go around the corner to Madame Robicheaux's to be fitted for the latest styles."

She shrugged carelessly, hoping Miss Hallie wouldn't notice that she was practically holding her breath. "I thought I might as well do that while I have the opportunity."

But Miss Hallie was waking up. She tilted her head and sent Raney a long look.

"More new dresses? For your trousseau? Have you and Mr. Gentry set a date for your wedding?"

Clearly, Miss Hallie was worried about her. In just a few hours, she'd be a whole lot more worried, and Raney hated to do her that way.

"No," Raney said slowly, trying to comfort her without telling too much. "And I'm still thinking about what we talked about—choosing with my heart instead of my head, Miss Hallie."

She did not dare go farther right now because if

Miss Hallie started talking about Creed again, Raney might blurt out her real feelings for him.

I love him. I love Creed Sixkiller.

She wanted to go out onto the balcony and shout it to the world. At the same time, she wanted to throw herself flat down on her face on the bed and sob her heart out.

In just a few hours, Creed would hate her. And *that* was what would go on forever.

"Well, I'll be glad to go with you to the dressmaker's, Raney dear."

"You could get some new things, too."

"That's an excellent idea. I'll tell the judge he needs to give me some money."

Miss Hallie stood up and, with brisk motions, put her hair up in a loose bun and stuck her arms into her wrapper.

"I'll be back," she said. "Let me go get the judge off for the day. He said he has a meeting this morning. I wonder what Mr. Sixkiller will be doing. Will he want you to help look for your brother?"

"Creed said—last night when we were dancing, he told me—he's going to look for Brassell today in some places not fit for a lady."

"Then it's probably our only time for shopping. I have faith in him. It won't be long until he finds Brassell and you all will be on the road home."

"How long will you and the judge be here?"

"I don't know, darling. But I wouldn't think too much longer."

Before she left the room, she came to Raney and smoothed her hair back from her forehead just like Mama used to do.

"Don't worry about anything, sugar," she said. "Just relax and enjoy your breakfast."

That was like Mama, too. Miss Hallie had sensed the turmoil inside Raney without her saying a word about it.

Raney stared after her as she left. Miss Hallie was so thoughtful that she stopped and rang for the maid to come to Raney before she went out the door into the hallway.

Her kindness made it even worse that Raney was going to deceive her so.

Everything fell into place for the deception, though, as if it were meant to be. At Madame Robicheaux's, behind the main parlor where the dressmaker showed her styles and fabric samples, there were four small fitting rooms where Madame's assistants measured the customers and fitted muslin patterns to them.

At eleven-forty that morning, according to Mama's watch that Raney wore, she and Miss Hallie finished choosing fabrics and styles and were taken to the little fitting rooms. They were separated by one already occupied, and Raney's was on the end nearest the entrance.

"Remove your clothing down to your chemise and step up onto the riser, *s'il vous plaît, mademoiselle*," the girl assigned to Raney said, taking her tape measure from around her neck.

She wore her name, Monique, embroidered on her smock and the slightest touch of rouge on her lips. She looked like a fun-loving girl. Raney could only pray that she was an understanding one, too.

Raney reached into her reticule—stuffed with a clean blouse and Creed's jeans, which she had never returned to him, and her canteen. She pulled out a whole dollar in coins that she had wrapped in a fine embroidered handkerchief and put the little bundle into the apprentice's hand.

She held the hand in both of hers while she gazed straight into Monique's wide eyes with her strongest persuasive look.

"There's a dollar there," she whispered. "I need to slip out the back way. Can you show me the door and give me a few minutes before my friend knows I'm gone?"

The girl raised her brows. Her green eyes sparkled. *"Vous avez un rendezvous?"*

"Oui," Raney said. *"Un rendezvous d'amour."*

If only it were true! She'd give anything.

Anything but Brass's freedom and Papa's peace of mind.

The girl peeked outside the curtains, indicated that the coast was clear, and gestured for Raney to follow her. Miss Hallie was talking to the girl who was measuring her, and other voices were murmuring in the other cubicles. The bell above the door rang when a new customer entered, and Madame went to greet her.

Raney followed the girl down a short, dark hallway to a door that opened onto the alley that ran behind the shop.

"I will wait until your chaperone is almost done with the mea-sur-ing," Monique said, with her heavy French accent, "then I will go to make my pencil sharp again and she will find you gone."

"*Merci,*" Raney whispered. "*Merci beaucoup, Monique.*"

Raney hoisted the strap of the heavy reticule onto her shoulder and began to run, thankful that her new traveling skirt was a divided one for riding and not so full as a real dress. The alley had piles of garbage and smelled terrible. She could see the side of the Menger, though, when she reached the street, and that stopped her for a moment.

Only for a moment. She crossed the street quickly, threading her way through the traffic that wasn't too thick, thank goodness, and walked fast toward the livery stable. She stayed close beside the wall of the hotel so it would be harder to see her from above.

Creed had left through the hall door to his room

while she was eating her breakfast. She heard him and peeked out into the hallway as he reached the top of the stairs. Probably he had not yet returned, but she was taking no chances.

She forced her mind to think ahead and not back. If her riding hat was still under the seat of the buggy, that would be great. If not, she needed to buy one before they left the town.

A fist of fear clutched her stomach. Brassell had better have *some* money, at least. It was a long, hard trail that lay ahead of them.

She squared her shoulders as she turned the corner behind the hotel. They could do it. She and Brassell had both managed to get themselves to San Antonio in the first place, hadn't they? Well, then, they could get home.

The sight of the livery stable sign swinging back and forth above the sidewalk made her heart race. At last! She was about to see Brassell.

She began to run again, dodging the two little boys running toward her, intent on some errand of their own. At the door, she slowed to a more sedate pace. It wouldn't do to be all sweaty and disheveled if she had to charm the proprietor into letting her have her rig without paying its rent.

Raney wished she'd paid more attention to the arrangements Creed had made at the desk, but she believed that the livery charges would be added to the hotel bill. That shouldn't be a problem, though, for she planned to tell yet another lie to add to all her other sins and say that she'd only be going for a drive and would be bringing her rig back later in the afternoon.

Tally was hanging his head out of his stall, and he nickered to her as soon as she came into sight. Halfway down the wide middle aisle, a boy of about twelve was sweeping shavings into a stall. The buggy stood out back in the small wagon yard.

Where was Brassell?

The strap was cutting a trench into her shoulder, so she dropped the heavy bag in front of the stall and stood there to catch her breath while she stroked Tally's nose and looked around. Tally nudged at her hand and blew his hot breath on her.

She couldn't see or sense another person anywhere in the stable. Everybody else who worked there must have gone to dinner.

The stable was dim in the corners. The air felt chill with that odd coolness of noon when the sun rode high and distant overhead. A shiver ran over Raney's skin.

She wished Creed was here. But she'd just as well forget that wish because Creed would never be here anymore.

She opened Mama's watch and looked at its round face. Both hands rested straight up at noon.

"Psst, Sister!"

At first, she thought she'd imagined the faint

303

sound. No matter where she looked, she saw nobody but the one boy.

The voice came again, above a whisper now. And above her.

"Raney, are you sure nobody followed you?"

She looked up. Brass lay full length along the rafter that ran over the stall. Cobwebs and moldy dust and Brassell. He was grinning down at her with a string of a spider's web hanging from the brim of his hat.

"Brassell Childress, you come down from there. I cannot believe you climbed up there. You'll have that mess all over the buggy!"

"You sound just like Mama," he said.

Raney's heart broke for him all over again. Her eyes filled with tears. He was only a kid, only sixteen, and Mama's baby. He didn't know what to do without her—no wonder he'd gotten into all this trouble.

But she felt an uplift in her spirit, too. She was doing the right thing. She'd made the right decision. She was going to bring a lot of good from the sacrifice she'd made.

As Brassell swung off the beam and hung by one long arm before he let himself drop to the ground, she realized fully for the first time that it all rested on her now. Men, even with all their strength, couldn't find their way by themselves. Helping them through this situation was going to make her as strong a woman as her mother had been.

Maybe it would also make her wise.

Brassell landed in a crouch in the aisle. He straightened up and enveloped her in a bear hug.

"Honey," he said, when he let her go, "let's get out of this town."

"Hitch him up," she said. "I'll be right back."

She went to the stable boy and told him she was going for a drive, but he could not have cared less. She could've saved herself one lie.

"Yes'm," he said, and kept on sweeping.

Brassell was already at the buggy with Tally in one hand and her bag in the other before she could get there. Together they took the harness from the wall and hitched the horse to the buggy. Even Tally was ready to go, prancing around in place like a two-year-old.

Brassell set her up in the seat and drove out into the street where he stopped to get his horse. He untied him from the hitching rail and tied him to the back of the buggy while Raney looked at San Antonio for the last time.

At least, for a long time.

On her way here and in this town, she had changed forever. She had become a woman and she had learned to think for herself and she had fallen in love.

She looked up at the second-floor balcony of the Menger where she and Creed had been last night. She could recall exactly how it had looked in the moonlight.

Those were the doors to Creed's room. She could remember exactly every moment of her time with him.

She would never forget even one of them.

Chapter 15

Creed's only purpose in riding back to the Menger at sundown was to let Raney know what progress he'd made in his all-day search. That, and to change into his other shirt, which he had left to be starched by the hotel's laundress. Some of the high-stakes poker games required the players—and spectators, even—to be well-dressed, and he would continue his rounds tonight.

But his little voice of truth wouldn't let him get away with the excuse. It whispered that, even after three years, he was still well known in that night-time world of the gamblers and the exclusive clubs and he would probably be admitted just as easily in what he was wearing. And his voice was right.

The real reason he was threading his way through the crowded streets of San Antonio just when all the nighttime revelers were coming out to crowd the streets was Raney. He wanted to see her. He needed to see her. He might be in time to take her to dinner, with or without their chaperones, and after that little respite he'd be off looking for Brassell again. At least he'd found out that Raney's brother was alive and gambling as recently as last night. That news would make her happy.

When he arrived at the hotel, however, instead of having the boy hold Marker at the front doors, he sent him back to the livery. If he did go to dinner with Raney alone, perhaps they could talk for a while.

Creed strode across the lobby, inquired for messages with a glance and a raised eyebrow as he passed the desk, nodded in answer to the clerk's negative shake of the head, and bounded up the stairs two at a time. Mrs. Scarborough stepped out of Raney's room the instant he put the key in his own door.

Her face was as white as a field of cotton.

"Oh, Mr. Sixkiller, thank the good Lord you're here," she said, and promptly burst into tears. "But you're alone! Is Raney not with you?"

The words hit his ears and traveled through them into his blood like tiny shards of sleet.

"No. I thought she was with you. Didn't you two spend the day shopping?"

"She slipped away from me," she said, in a voice

fraught with chagrin. "I finally got it out of the shopgirl. Raney told her she had a rendezvous and left by the back door."

Creed stared at her. He couldn't seem to help himself.

"When was that?"

"Around noon. '*Un rendezvous d'amour*,' was the way the girl quoted Raney. Naturally, I thought it might . . . uh . . . forgive me, but I thought . . . mmn . . . after the way y'all were dancing last night . . . that it could possibly be with you . . ."

Creed froze at the word "*amour*."

"She told me she sent a letter to break her betrothal," he said, more coldly than he'd intended, "perhaps Leonard has come looking for her to try to make her change her mind."

Mrs. Scarborough began regaining her color.

"I doubt that very much," she snapped. "That man doesn't have the gumption of a tree frog. All he cares about is squeezing two bits until it makes a dollar."

"Is her rig gone from the livery?"

"I sent a hotel boy over there to look and he came back to say that there was no buggy of that description there."

"I'm going to see if anybody over there knows anything," Creed said. "I'll be back shortly."

He took the stairs two at a time going down, too. As he went out through the patio garden and across the alley, he tried to tamp down the jealousy and, most of all, the fury that had boiled to life in him.

And the guilt. He should never have taken her. Was she sorry that she had slept with him?

Taking twenty-year-old virgins into his bed certainly wasn't his usual style. And Raney was so innocent! He'd known she'd had no idea what she was asking for when she came out to him on the balcony dressed in her nightgown and wrapper.

You're twenty-eight years old, Sixkiller. You ought to have more sense.

Did it all go back to the old Indian prejudice? Raney herself used to think an Indian wasn't good enough for her. Hadn't she told him that very honestly when she turned him down three years ago?

Ideas like that became, in time, feelings that lived in the bone. Raney had never heard anything else her whole life from her beloved papa except that the Sixkillers were fine enough to have as friends but he wouldn't want her to marry one.

Well, she needn't have worried—if that was what had driven her away. He'd told her three years ago that he would never ask her again, and he wasn't one to go back on his word.

The troublesome thing was this *rendezvous d'amour*. Who else did she know in San Antonio?

His mind whirled. Had she lied about what was in the letter she sent to Leonard? Had she asked him to come to her instead of sending him away?

Had Leonard had time to get the letter? Had he read it, refused to accept Raney's decision, and come to try to persuade her to change her mind? Or, God forbid, to take her against her will?

Maybe she agreed to meet him only out of courtesy. But why had she told the shopgirl that she was meeting her lover?

He pushed all his feelings aside before he arrived at the stable, except for the urgency that was making a drumbeat on his heart.

The owner had gone home for the day, and the first two employees Creed questioned knew nothing, but he finally found a boy who had been there when Raney took her horse and buggy.

"Was she alone?"

"No sir. A fellow was with her."

"What did he look like?"

The boy leaned on his broom and stared off toward the street as if he could still see them driving away.

"Older than me. Nice boots."

Creed waited patiently but the kid didn't say any more. He seemed to live in another world. He couldn't be more than twelve years old.

"How much older than you?"

"A lot. He was 'bout sixteen or seventeen. Nice hat, too."

Brassell. Creed would bet Marker on it. Raney was a sneaky little minx. Resourceful, too.

"Did you see his hair?"

311

"Yellow and curly," the boy said.

Creed thrust some coins into his hand. "That's my horse there. Saddle him for me. I'll be back in five minutes."

The only reason it took him ten minutes instead was that Mrs. Scarborough almost fainted from relief that Raney was with her brother and fear that the two of them wouldn't be safe on the road alone, so Creed had to call the maid and make sure she had smelling salts. He packed his gear while they were waiting for the maid, though, and left Miss Hallie in good hands.

He would always have a soft spot in his heart for her, based on what she'd said about Leonard. The lady was a good judge of character.

But as soon as he was on the Nacogdoches Road, also grandly called El Camino Real, which was the main trail leading from San Antonio to the north-east, his thoughts all turned to getting to Raney before she and Brassell left the main road somewhere to angle back toward Concho. He tried to harden his heart against the pain of remembering her in his bed.

Her body had told him that she was loving him.

Had she come to him purposely intending to ask him to make love with her for some reason other than making memories? She must have already laid plans to meet Brassell because she mentioned going to the dress shop.

She had lied to him. Had she persuaded him to take her to his bed hoping to soften him up so he wouldn't jail Brassell if he caught him? Or to distract him from the hunt?

How could she?

The question brought him a grim little smile. She had told him from the minute he found her on the road, barely outside Limestone County, that she would not let him jail her brother and that she would take him home to hide.

On that subject, at least, Raney Childress was a woman of her word.

Raney was torn to pieces. Half of her—mind and spirit, at least—was thrilled to have Brassell, with his eyeglasses firmly on his nose, sitting beside her, driving the buggy for her and pouring his heart out to her while they raced toward home up the Camino Real. The other half of her mind and spirit, and *all* of her body, longed for Creed.

She could touch the tip of her tongue to her bruised lips and still taste his kisses. Creed would never kiss her again.

A terrible empty feeling blew through her and sucked the strength out of her shoulders. She let them sag back against the seat.

Creed would never hold her again. His arms had felt like her heart's safe home, and she would never have that feeling anymore. Her heart would never have a home.

How could she ever quit loving Creed, even if she

tried? What other man would try to teach her to be strong and to think for herself, the way he did—and be proud of her as she grew? What other man would wait patiently and listen to her talk until she found for herself what she was really thinking and feeling and wanting to do?

The wind was picking up as the sun went down. It'd be a while yet until dark, though, since the days were rapidly getting longer. Raney reached under the seat for her hat to tame her wildly blowing hair.

Brassell grinned at her as she tied the stampede strings beneath her chin.

"Ain't you proud of me, Sister? I bet I'm the only man that ever led Creed Sixkiller on such a wild-goose chase and stayed free."

The bitterness of loss rose in a lump in her throat. What had she done? Brassell was her own flesh and blood, yes, and she loved him. And it was not just important for her family that she bring him home, it was essential. Papa couldn't live with another loss.

But, oh, dear Lord, Brass was such a little fool and he had cost her her happiness.

Assuming that Creed would ever put aside his famous pride and ask her again to marry him.

Assuming that there could be such a miracle as Creed loving her the same way she loved him.

"We're not home yet, Brass. Don't get too cocky. And don't say 'ain't.' "

He threw her an annoyed glance.

"You sure are full of rules and regulations, Rane. Don't you know you're dealin' with a bad, long-ridin' outlaw?"

"Well, *you're* dealin' with a desperate, dangerous woman," she said. "You've put me through more grief than any sister ought to have to bear. Now you can just tell me what this is all about and I mean now. Don't try to give me any more excuses."

"How long do you think it'll be before Creed comes after us?"

"And don't try to change the subject."

She crossed her arms over her breasts and glared at him with her best bossy, big-sister look. It had always worked on Brassell's tender feelings.

His eyes slid away from her stare.

"I can't tell you—for your own good. If you knew, you'd be as much a target as I am."

He glanced back over his shoulder at the stagecoach that had been behind them for some miles.

"Think about it, Brassell. If some of the Chickenhawks are on that stage and they see us together, aren't they going to assume that you've told me already? They'll shoot first and ask questions later."

"I'm riding a streak of luck right now," he said. "I've won enough at poker to keep me and have some left over. I've stayed out of Creed's clutches. We'll get home all right."

"Well, while we're doing that, I have to watch out

for myself as well as for you, don't I? Who's the danger?"

He narrowed his eyes and thought about it. He shook his head.

"I'll watch out for you, Raney. I'm the man, even if you are older. Besides, none of them is so low-down he'd shoot a woman. They'd just threaten you to see if you know. If you don't know it, then they'd give up."

"That doesn't make a lick of sense. What if they thought I was lying? What would they do then?"

"They wouldn't," he said comfortably. "You can't lie worth two bits, Rane. You never could. If you knew the secret and tried to lie about it, even their horses would know."

"Speaking of horses, maybe you should let Tally slow down a little. He hasn't had much exercise lately."

"He wants to go."

"He's barn sour, Brass. He knows he's going home, but we don't have to let him kill himself trying to get there tonight."

Reluctantly, he pulled Tally to a slow trot.

"Brassell, you had better tell me the whole story."

"Not until we're home. Not until you have more than just me to protect you."

Maybe if she changed the subject, she could catch him unawares when she came back to this one.

"How did Fiddler find you?"

"I was listening to them playing in the square. I'd

just won twenty dollars at craps and I was feeling good and I asked a Mexican girl to dance. Fiddler seen me and called me over."

"*Saw* me," she said. "Honestly, Brass, your grammar's no better than a field hand's."

Brass pretended to ignore that.

"The little fiddlin' man told me that he *saw* you and Creed and you asked him to come and play in Alamo Square," he said. "I paid him to take the note to you because I sure didn't want to run into Creed Sixkiller before I could get out of this town. He said he charmed the maid to find out which was your room."

He glanced around at her and said slyly, "I sure do hate to leave it, though. Good ol' San Antone has a lot of pleasure pots, all right."

That idiocy just flew all over Raney.

"I think you mean flesh pots and I'm sure that's why you ran to it in the first place," she snapped.

"Ain't the only reason," he said. "I didn't want to come home where y'all could quiz me like this."

"If you don't want to talk to your own folks, then why don't you just stay in San Antone?"

"Because Creed Sixkiller would find me, sooner or later. I heard he went to Monte's Poker Parlor last night, looking for me."

"Forget the poker parlors. What you'd better be thinking about is where you can hide on Pleasant Hill that Creed can't find you."

Brassell heaved a big sigh.

"Oh yeah, he'll be on our trail, all right," he said, "but I've got a few tricks of my own. And when we get home, I'll go down to the fish camp. He'll never find me there."

"If you'd done that in the first place instead of running off down here to be on your own in the 'pleasure pots' of the big city, you'd have saved us all a lot of grief."

Mainly me. You'd have saved me from losing my happiness. I would never have known what it was.

Raney gave up on Brass then, and let herself think about Creed. He *would* find her, either on the road or at home after she had hidden Brassell. She would see him, she would probably talk to him. But he would never look at her when his eyes were heavy-lidded with desire, the way he had done last night. And his words to her would never be in those velvet tones that were a caress to her skin and sweet music to her ears.

Never again would she lie in Creed's arms.

The light was failing. There was no way now to deny it.

"We have to find a camping spot, Brass. Look up there ahead. See that little hill with the trees at its foot? The way they grow, there's most likely to be a creek, and there's protection on two sides and firewood. I'm getting chilled."

She wore the light jacket that, thank goodness, she'd had the foresight to put in her reticule. Regret stabbed her. If only she hadn't had to leave all her pretty new things! She especially wanted the blue dress that Creed had liked so much, but there had been no way to take more with her to the Madame Robicheaux's than she had done.

"Besides that, I need to rest," she said. "This road has more ruts than a washboard."

"Just be glad it's dry," Brass said wisely. "When it's raining, it's impassable."

Raney leaned back against the seat. She felt jolted into bits, body and mind, but it wasn't all from the road. She needed to collapse in the back of the buggy and cry herself to sleep.

Only then did she remember that Creed had furnished her blankets all the way down here. She glanced back at Brass's horse as if she could see into the bedroll tied to the back of the saddle.

"Brass, how many blankets do you have?"

Brassell was slowing Tally even more, getting ready to drive off the road into the long, dark shades of the three live oak trees Raney had pointed out. Instead of watching where he was going, though, he was peering through the dusk at two oncoming horsemen who were veering across the road toward them.

Brass reached for the handgun he wore. Raney snapped open her reticule and began feeling around for Papa's old weapon.

"Hello! Is that the Childress buggy there? Raney? Son, is that you?"

Could it be Papa? His voice sounded like a long-lost memory. It seemed she hadn't heard it for years.

"Papa!" Brass called. "Yes! And I've got Raney right here."

As if he had come all this way to rescue her instead of the other way around. Brass had always been full of himself.

"Thank God," Papa said fervently. "I've been worried sick about you both."

Raney's arms went weak and she sat slumped in relief with her arm still in the bag on her lap. Thank goodness. It wasn't all on her shoulders anymore.

They all met on the road, and Papa rode around to her side of the buggy.

"I have to see you with my own eyes," he said. "Sugar, you can't know how scared I've been that something bad would happen to you."

The other horseman was right behind him. Raney caught a glimpse from the corner of her eye and whipped her head around to look.

It was Leonard! Not Trent. She had leaped to the conclusion that if Papa was one of two riders, the other would be her brother Trent.

"Hello, Raney," he said. "You should've told me you were going to go off by yourself. I would've come with you."

Shock stiffened her spine. Her resentment of Leonard's neglect surged up and took on a whole new life.

"Don't worry about it," she said. "I traveled with Creed Sixkiller."

Both Papa's and Leonard's mouths fell open at that. They followed as Brass drove off the road and into the camping spot Raney had chosen.

She hoped that news hadn't been too abrupt for Papa's heart, but she'd had to strike out at that mealymouthed Leonard. The very *gall* of him to hook up with Papa and come to find her when she'd told him in no uncertain terms to get out of her life.

Her mind raced. Leonard and Papa had plotted during all those miles from Pleasant Hill to here to make her change her mind.

Then it hit her. The letter hadn't yet reached Pleasant Hill. There had not been time for that.

She set her jaw as the buggy rocked to a stop. Well, she'd just tell the news to the two of them right to their faces. They could waste their breath on her from now until Christmas but she would not marry that milquetoast. It embarrassed her that she had ever said she would.

Papa dismounted and came to lift her down from the buggy into a huge hug that took her breath away. It was great, no matter who his companion was, and she threw her arms around his neck and kissed him on the cheek.

"I'm so glad to see you," she said.

She kissed him again.

"If anything had happened to you, I could not live," he whispered to her.

"I'm fine," she said. "Don't worry about me anymore, Papa. I can take care of myself."

It was true. The thought lifted her heart as she turned to face Leonard. Papa left them to go around the buggy to Brassell.

"Raney," Leonard said, opening his arms for a hug, "I am so glad to see you."

She laughed as she avoided his embrace.

"You've got a lot of nerve, Leonard, I'll hand you that," she said. "For a cold-footed coward."

He put on a shocked look.

"What are you talking about?"

"Looks like you were scared to take to the road until you had Papa to come with you. That's pretty sad. Papa's getting old and he's got heart trouble but he has to protect you."

Leonard paled with anger, then he forced a smile to his lips. "Raney, I'm afraid you're a little bit featherheaded from all the traveling."

He looked past her at Papa.

"Mr. Childress, let's make a fire right away. Raney needs to eat something."

That flew all over Raney. "Don't try to take care of me now," she said. "It's way too late for that. Believe it."

She turned her back on him and walked away into the trees. By the time she returned, the three men had built a fire in a fire ring that was already there. Evidently, this was a well-used resting place.

"Daughter, we have coffee and jerky and some ham biscuits Etty packed for us. Do y'all have anything better?"

She and Brassell had nothing to eat in the buggy, unless he had something in his pack. This was the first time food had entered her mind since she'd made her plans to meet him.

The irony of it made her smile. Maybe she wasn't so good at taking care of herself after all.

"Not unless Brass has something with him," she said. "We just hooked up at noon today."

"I have jerky, that's all."

So the four of them sat around the fire on the horse blankets and ate ham biscuits and drank coffee while the horses grazed on the fresh grass and night fell. It was nice to have Papa and Brassell on either side of her and to be with family again, but someone was missing.

Creed. She *missed* him. A wave of pain washed through her with that silent admission and another followed with her next acknowledgment of truth.

She loved him beyond time. She loved Creed Sixkiller with every fiber of her being, and she always would. So how long would that love hurt her heart like this? If the answer turned out to be forever, how long would it take her to get accustomed to the pain?

Papa motioned for her cup and poured her another one.

"Let's make a second pot," he said. "I want to hear the whole story now."

He looked from Brass to Raney. "Two whole stories."

"It's getting really dark," Brass said. "Let's move out of the firelight."

Papa sent him a sharp look as Brass moved into the shadows.

"What's all this trouble about, son?"

"I've been begging him to tell," Raney said. "There's a bigger reason than Brassell being a Peckerwood that the Chickenhawks are so bound and determined to kill him, and we need to know what it is so we can protect him."

She looked up into her father's eyes. His face looked older than usual and very haggard with the firelight playing on it. She could just strangle Brassell for adding to Papa's worries. The least he could've done was go home to hide on the plantation like any normal boy would have done.

"Brass knows what it is, Papa. Make him tell us."

"That was the very reason I didn't come home when I escaped from jail," Brass said. "I knew if I did, y'all would get it out of me somehow."

Raney made her plea to Papa, too.

"If any Chickenhawks see us together now, they'll think he's told us whether or not it's true. If

324

they're shooting at him to keep him quiet, they'll be shooting at us, too. We need to know why, so we can do something about it instead of sitting around like a bunch of ducks on a pond."

Papa sighed heavily as he fixed another round of coffee.

"That's right," he said. "Move into the shadows, everyone."

When they did, Leonard walked close to Raney. Way too close. He spoke quietly.

"Sweetheart, let's go back here in the trees for a minute. I really need to talk to you and—"

"No, Leonard. I don't want to hear it."

She sat down beside Brassell at the foot of a tree. Leonard, the stubborn stump, sat beside her.

Papa joined them and said to Brass, "Then tell us everything but the secret, why don't you? This all started with the Chickenhawks invading a meeting of the Peckerwoods?"

"Yeah. A bunch of them rode in and sat around the edges of the crowd, yelling insults and interrupting all the speakers. Unbeknownst to any of us, somebody sent for the Sixkillers and they and their crew got there by the time words turned into bullets."

"You were shooting, too?" Papa asked.

"We all were!" Brass said indignantly. "It was self-defense."

"And Creed arrested you for that?"

Brass had the good grace to hang his head. "No," he said, "for cold-cocking him. From behind."

Papa shook his head. "Son, son," he said, "when will you ever learn?"

"His men were arresting a lot more Peckerwoods than Chickenhawks."

Brass was pouting now.

"So he arrested you and took you to jail and you escaped and went to San Antone."

"Yes sir."

Brass told his adventures—at least some of them—in the big city and bragged about his gambling winnings while they all listened carefully for a clue to the secret but found none. His voice shook at little when telling the scariest parts about being beaten up by some disappointed robbers and threatened by some drunken soldiers. Raney felt sorry for him, but she still was so angry, too, that she could slap his face.

She concentrated on those feelings and tried not to think about Creed. When Brass was done, she told her tale as succinctly as possible—leaving out selected portions of it, of course.

"So you and Sixkiller didn't leave Pleasant Hill together?" Leonard asked, in a nasty voice.

"No, we didn't," Raney said. "We met on the road in the middle of the night."

"Well, you didn't have to take up with him and travel with him for days," Leonard said. "As your betrothed . . ."

She interrupted him ruthlessly. "You are no longer my betrothed. I will not marry you, Leonard. I will never marry you."

As she spoke, she was more aware of Papa's listening to her than of Leonard.

"I sent you a letter from San Antonio that told you that. I don't want to see you anymore, Leonard. I want you to move off Pleasant Hill and never come back."

Leonard, for once in his life, was shocked into silence.

Papa said, "*What*?"

"*What?*" Brassell said, like an echo.

"I'm not going to marry Leonard," she said. "That's all."

"*Why?*" Papa cried.

"Lots of reasons. I don't love him, being the most important one. I realized that when *he* didn't love *me* enough to come after me when he found my note."

"I thought you'd turn around and come right back and be there when I got home from the store that evening," Leonard said.

"And when I didn't?"

"Then it was too late," Leonard said. "You could've been anywhere in Texas and I didn't know where to look for you."

"That might wash if it weren't for the fact that you knew Brassell went to San Antonio and I went after Brassell," she said. "Don't forget you had a store to run."

"And a plantation to see to," Brassell said. "Leonard was in charge while we were all gone."

"*You* were supposed to be in charge, you little dolt," she said. "But you were too busy running around getting into feuds and trying to get yourself killed."

"That still doesn't mean that you shouldn't marry Leonard," Brass said.

"That's right, Daughter," Papa said, sputtering in his haste to find something to say that would change her mind. "You have to forgive and forget in any marriage. You gave your word."

"*You* picked Leonard, Papa," she said gently. "I was a silly girl, used to doing whatever you told me. I didn't know what I was saying."

Papa gave a terrible snort. "You didn't know what you were saying when you wrote that letter. You didn't know what you were saying just now."

"Yes, I did. I still say it. I'm not going to marry a man I don't love."

"You most certainly are going to marry him," Papa roared. "I've invested a small fortune in that store of his, I've given my word to his father and mother, and our families have been friends for five generations."

A knife of despair cut through her heart.

"Not one of those reasons has anything to do with me and my happiness," Raney said.

"You're too young to know what happiness is," Papa said. "You're a silly girl, just as you said."

"I said I *was* a silly girl when I agreed to marry Leonard. I'm a woman now and I know what I want."

She'd never known a man's voice could be as catty as that of the tackiest woman who ever lived, but Leonard's was.

"And Creed Sixkiller is what you want," he said. "Isn't that right, Raney?"

She'd never known she had it in her to take defiance to such a level, but she'd started out telling the truth, and she was going to finish telling it if they *all* died of heart attacks right there.

"Yes," she said. "But he'll never marry me. I've betrayed him now."

Chapter 16

Creed and Marker kept on moving at the same pace after night fell. They had their rhythm and they had their reason and they had long been believers in the old ranch saying that if you let the dark or the weather hinder you, you'll never get your work done.

Man and horse knew well they had work to do. Creed considered how simple and yet how difficult that work was: capture Brassell and jail him again, then get to the bottom of this feud. That was the only way to bring order to the county so he could stay at home on the ranch and tend his own business instead of the public's. He must think about all of that instead of about Raney.

He could do that. His mother said that since the moment of his birth he had been all or nothing in everything he did. She'd said that most often—and always with a sorrowful shake of her head—during his wild years of drinking and womanizing and gambling.

Those years had ended only three years ago. The shock of Raney's rejecting him and her father's prejudice had made him turn to sobriety and respectable girls and heartfelt learning of the old Cherokee ways and hard work.

Hard work was his refuge. It held such satisfaction for him at the end of a long day of giving all he had to the land and the animals and, through them, to the good of his whole family: the tired ache in his muscles that brought deep sleep and the sense of having accomplished good things that pervaded his bones.

He shook his head. He was a different man now, different from the one who had ridden off to town and its pleasures thinking that he'd have a much better time than if he stayed home to help his father and brothers. That man had taken the Childresses' prejudice and used it to make himself stronger. That strength would get him through the hurt that Raney had seemed to love him but had not.

Leaning forward in the saddle, Creed patted Marker's neck. He should be thankful. At least he had a horse he could trust. He threw him the reins, left the road up to him, and began to clear his mind.

All generative power resides in thought.

He could hear his grandfather's voice saying that the first day he began to teach him about Cherokee medicine. So he would turn his thoughts to finding Brassell.

First, he would send the most powerful *idi:gawe:sdi* for traveling that he knew out into the Earth Mother and the sky and the air. It was one of the longer ones but the fact that its form fell into seven parts meant that it possessed extra authority.

> *Listen! Ha! You have just come to hear,*
> *You Provider who rests above!*
> *Ha! Now You have just come to place my feet*
> *   in the right pathway.*
> *Ha! Let me be keeping out of sight.*
> *Ha! You have just brought my soul*
> *   as high as the treetops!*
> *In front of me the Red Mountain Lion*
> *   will be going, his quick head reared.*
> *On White Pathways I am making*
> *   my footprints.*
> *You have just come to trace my footsteps.*
> *   Listen!*

After Creed had thought the incantation four times, he said it four times. His spirit became peaceful.

He would find Brassell. He would find Raney,

too, but that would make no difference. He would not let the sight of her reach all the way to his heart.

The moon came up even bigger and brighter than the night before, and the miles fell away beneath Marker's hooves. In the past, they had caught up to many a fugitive who was riding a fast horse, and a buggy was slower and less likely to be traveling at night. If Raney and Brassell had stopped to wait for daylight to see the rough road, he would find them by midnight.

And so he did. He saw the shape of the buggy in the moonlight and then the four horses grazing nearby. His breath caught in his throat. Why four horses? Had some Chickenhawks found Raney and Brassell?

If so, it wasn't the same bunch he'd seen in San Antonio unless Loren Hastings had changed horses. The big, white gelding wasn't there.

He slowed Marker to a barely moving walk while he looked over the terrain. Beyond the three big live oaks that sheltered the camp, smaller trees grew in scattered clumps near the bottom of the hill and all the way up the side of it. He had his choice of several vantage points.

Several yards past the camp, he stopped his horse, stood in the stirrup with a soft creak of saddle leather, and swung to the ground in the road. Then, keeping to every shadow he could find, he led his horse to cover on the north side of the little camping spot. From there, he could see their horses better.

Besides that, he could see the road coming from San Antonio and anyone else who might be following Brassell.

Creed ground-tied Marker and moved closer to the silent camp. He studied every part of it, including the horses. When they grazed into an open spot where the full light from the moon washed over them again, he recognized Robert Childress's favorite mount, a tall, sorrel Tennessee Walker. A sigh of relief escaped him. Raney was safe. Robert and Trent must've come to meet her and Brassell.

Now he must figure out how to take Brassell without having to hurt anyone.

He picked a place at the foot of a tree and sat down cross-legged with his back against the trunk, looking down into the dark camp. He couldn't even see where the people were sleeping—couldn't tell whether Raney was in the back of the buggy or under it or out in the open.

This looked like one of those situations when he'd need to surprise his quarry in his bedroll. At dawn.

With Raney there, he wanted to be sure there was enough light for everyone to identify everyone else when the shooting started—if it did. He would slip into camp in the darkness of false dawn and be waiting to spot Brassell's curly head sticking out of his blankets when the first light came.

He took one last, long look around, then pushed his hat to the front and leaned his head back against the tree. He would doze lightly to relax his muscles, but his mind and his senses would stay alert. Before dawn, he'd wake and stretch, find the best position inside the camp that the moon could show him, and be in it when Brassell opened his eyes.

The sound of wheels on the road hit his ears like gravel thrown against a window glass. The moon shone directly in his eyes because it had drifted low in the western sky. The dark was getting blacker everywhere.

The buggy, or whatever it was, was coming from the south, from San Antonio. It sounded fairly light—it was no freight wagon or stagecoach, either of which might travel at night out of necessity, but which was very unlikely. There were too many banditos and highwaymen roaming around Texas for anyone to take chances he didn't have to take.

The thing that set him on edge was that this vehicle was moving so slowly. While he listened, it stopped. He waited for it to appear in the farthest place on the road that he could see but it didn't.

He didn't hear it anymore.

The air wasn't still anymore, either.

But the small animals were. No nightbirds called, no skunks or rabbits stirred.

Silently, Creed got to his feet.

Marker had his head up, his ears pricked, and he was watching something. Creed eased around to the other side of the tree and followed the look. A Lucifer stick flared, down on the road, and something flashed—a gun or the side of a bridle bit or a concho on a saddle. Then the light vanished and he heard the creak of leather, a hoof strike a stone.

He loosened his gun in its holster.

The moon drifted out from behind a cloud, and he caught a glimpse of men and horses. Men on foot, leading their horses up this way.

Creed went to Marker, took the reins, and led him a little farther up the hillside to hide behind a clump of mesquite. He found a good vantage point, put his hand over Marker's muzzle, and waited.

The dark was deepening. It was almost time for the sun to rise, but he wouldn't be down below in the camp to greet it. Somebody else had come to see Brassell, and he needed to see to them.

He knew who they were as soon as the big, white horse loomed out of the night.

This was beyond serious. These men had businesses and ranches to run and families at home, yet they had ridden all the way to San Antonio and then stayed there because Brassell had said he was going there. They could not mean any good by climbing up onto a hillside above him in the dark, furtive as thieves and rifles at the ready.

The four of them faded into the brush just in front of Creed, with Loren Hastings and his horse taking the same tree that Creed and Marker had sheltered under only a few minutes before, the place with the best view of the Childress camp. Loren was known to be an excellent shot.

Of course, if they'd followed Brassell here, they knew that Raney was with him. These were respectable men. Surely they'd take care not to shoot a woman.

Trouble was, Loren was the only one Creed could see—part of the time. The other three had faded away into the brush scattered all over the hillside. There'd be no way to get them all by surprise, unless he did it silently, one man at a time, and that could never be until daylight because he didn't know the terrain well enough.

His heart beat a little faster. He backed Marker, an inch at a time, a little deeper into the brush and moved away from him to protect him from stray bullets. One good thing about making any noise— the Chickenhawks would think it was made by one of their own, since none of them could know exactly where all the others were.

They obviously weren't trained to hunt by an Indian grandfather, because all of them were getting restless by the time sunrise began. Creed heard enough rustlings and scratchings to have an approximate location for the other three as the new sun rose.

He tried to imagine their plan. They would wait for the camp to begin stirring, then take shots at Brassell until one of them killed him. They would mount up and ride down to the road before the

Childresses could collect themselves enough to shoot back, and they'd be miles away before Raney's pitifully distraught family could even load the body into the buggy.

Whatever the secret was that poor Brassell carried with him must be an earth-shaker, at least in Limestone County, for respectable men like these to feel compelled to do murder. Of course, they were all deep into the feud. Feuds were nothing but one murder after another.

Raney woke with a start from a dream. She'd been in Creed's arms, in his bed in the Menger Hotel, and she'd been pressing her lips to the sleep-warm skin in the hollow of his neck and reveling in the scent of him while he sang, very, very softly, a Cherokee love song in her ear.

She opened her eyes, but she lay without moving under the pinkening sky of early, early morning. She had never heard Creed sing. She didn't even know if he *could* sing.

He hadn't so much as hummed in her ear while they danced at the Menger, and he never had at any of the socials where they had danced in the past. Creed had a beautiful baritone singing voice. She just knew it.

A cat's claw of truth raked across her heart.

She would *never* know it. She would never be with Creed again, much less when he was in a mood to sing.

The rattle and creak of wheels broke into her thoughts, and she realized that was what had waked her. Who was there? Chickenhawks?

She sat up so fast, she nearly hit her head on the back of the seat. A buggy was driving off the road and straight to them. Dear Lord, it was the Scarboroughs.

"Hello, the camp," the judge called, over the rattling of the wheels. "Have y'all got the coffee made?"

Papa sat up, fast, blinking against the light, getting his handgun out from under the edge of his blankets as he spoke. "Who's askin'?" he called back.

They rolled right on in, and the judge stopped the team just past Raney's buggy. He was staring in astonishment at Papa and rightly so, since he and Miss Hallie had expected to find Raney and Brassell alone.

"I thought you were in Fort Worth, Robert."

"I was," Papa said dryly, "but I came back."

Miss Hallie beamed at Raney.

"Honey!" she said, "I'm so happy that your papa found you. I've been worried sick about you."

"I'm sorry about slipping away from you, Miss Hallie, but I was trying to protect Brassell from jail."

"Has Mr. Sixkiller not caught up with y'all yet?"

"No. I was expecting him to come after us but then when we met up with Papa, I didn't worry anymore because Papa can take care of all that."

Papa could be the one to talk to Creed, to try to

persuade Creed to keep Brassell out of jail. If it came down to it, he could be the one to go with Creed and Brassell to the jail and arrange for bail. But that would be all that even Papa could do.

If only someone could take care of Creed's feelings about me.

Raney could barely get the words out, but she had to know.

"Miss Hallie, was he very angry with me?"

Miss Hallie looked at Raney as if she knew exactly what Raney was thinking and feeling.

"He was angry, yes. But he was worried about your safety, too."

"What did he say?"

"Well, it wasn't so much what he *said*. I could just tell by the way he looked and acted."

Raney had to know. It would never make a difference now, but she had to know every detail.

"Didn't he say *anything*?"

"He didn't come in until dinnertime. I was hoping that the rendezvous you mentioned to the shopgirl was with him—because I did notice how you two were dancing that evening—and I told him that. He said perhaps Leonard had come looking for you."

Shame stabbed her. No, it was regret. Keen regret. It was a burning hot and a bitter cold invasion of her mind, and it felt inextinguishable. Regret might possibly be the very worst feeling of all.

Creed's estimation of her was so low that he thought her capable of making love with him one night and going to Leonard the next day.

He probably thought that she regretted that night in his bed. He probably would never again believe one word that she said.

But that didn't matter. She'd never have a chance to talk to him again.

"He was devastated at the thought of the dangers that could befall you on the road, Raney. I could see it on his face, and you know how he can hide his feelings most of the time."

What if there had been hope? What if Creed loved her, too, the way she loved him and might ask her to marry him one more time? What if that was what would have happened if she hadn't run off with Brassell, who—if Creed didn't catch up with him, an outcome that she could not even imagine—would probably only go home and get in the feud again and end up in jail again or worse.

What if she had given up a lifetime of happiness for her silly brother who wouldn't even be able to appreciate the sacrifice she'd made? And for Papa, who had ordered her never again to mention the words "Creed" and "marry me" in the same sentence. Papa couldn't even see that she had begun to grow up and think for herself. He didn't think she had any right to do so.

She threw back the blanket and got up. She had to move, had to get down from here and try to change her mind off onto something else.

"Y'all get down, Miss Hallie. Stay for breakfast."

As she turned to climb down over the wheel, she glanced over at Papa, Brassell, and Leonard, who were all on their feet and beginning to move around. She turned her back on them to step over the side of the buggy, and the whole world exploded. It took a second for her to realize that what she'd just heard was the hard, fast, sharp sound of shots.

One of them hit the iron rim of a wheel with a loud, echoing twang.

Papa started yelling.

"Daughter! Get down! On your stomach! Get down! Stay in the buggy!"

Raney fell the rest of the way out of the buggy and threw herself to the ground under it. Miss Hallie screamed, one of the horses whinnied, and more shots cracked.

"They're up there," Papa yelled. "Boys, get the rifles and keep them busy."

He fired again. Then, when Brassell had gotten to a rifle and started shooting back at them, Papa ran, crouched over, to his saddlebags for more ammunition.

"I'm goin' up there," he said. "I'll get around behind them."

* * *

When the rifle fire started coming from the camp, Creed bent double and ran from his hiding place to a clump of brush closer to Loren Hastings. He didn't want to shoot the man in the back, but he had to stop this.

He should've acted sooner, but with four of them scattered all around him, he had to be careful. The Childresses were no match for these Chickenhawks, and he couldn't help them if he was the first one shot.

One of the Chickenhawks behind him fired a shot that whistled right by his head. He dropped into a squat and sat on his haunches, which greatly hindered his ability to see.

A round flew in from below to hit the dirt at his feet. Another one followed it. Robert and Leonard must be better shots than Brassell was. Too bad he couldn't know if they had seen him moving up here or they were just lucky.

The only thing he had a hope of accomplishing at the moment was disarming Loren. He needed to do it now, too, before somebody got killed. Pray God nobody had, yet. Raney was down there. These men wouldn't target her intentionally, but shots could go astray.

So could honor and good intentions and the code that said a man could never shoot a woman go astray if the shooter was desperate. What if the Chickenhawks wouldn't take the risk that Brass had told Raney the secret?

Creed tightened his jaw, rose to a crouch, and aimed at Loren, who was busy reloading his rifle. His round knocked the long gun from Loren's hand.

Loren screamed and dropped to his knees, cradling his arm and twisting his neck around to look toward Creed.

"You idiot," he yelled. "Carter! Is that you? Can't you see who you're shootin' at? Help me."

Somebody started crashing through the brush toward the wounded man, but Creed didn't wait to see who it was. Still bent over, he ran back up the hillside to his old hiding place.

If the others all came to see about Loren, he might be able to get the drop on them and round them up without shooting any more.

Toby Mason was the first one to get to Loren. He started taking off his belt to use for a tourniquet and Creed began moving his gaze in a wide sweep over the hillside, willing the other brother to show himself.

A rock rolled and bounced—off to his left and down the hill a little. He whipped his head around to look.

Robert Childress was climbing the hill, trying to move quietly while making as much noise as a herd of wild horses, aiming to get behind everyone. Above him, Josh Mason lay on his belly beneath a mesquite tree, aiming down at him. He had Robert in his sights and he had started the squeeze on his trigger.

Creed raised his own gun, aimed by instinct, and

fired—a split second before Josh's round left the barrel. He stayed to the brush and ran toward him, ignoring the thorns and thickets while he barreled on through. Sure enough, Josh was shocked but not hurt. He saw Creed coming and tried to get up, snatching for his handgun at the same time, but Creed was too fast for him. He threw himself on him and knocked him back to the ground.

Josh struggled like a yearling steer until Creed hit him in the jaw with his fist.

"Sixkiller, you saved my life."

Robert Childress stood over them, panting, his face flushed. His blue eyes, so like Raney's, fixed on Creed's.

"I find myself much obliged to you."

Creed nodded, while he was getting up as fast as he could.

"Tie his hands and go get his gun," he said. "Then cover me. I'll go for the other three."

One of the other three yelled, "There! There he is. Now!"

Two rifles fired from the hill in quick succession before Creed regained his feet. He dug his heels in, widened his stance, and slammed his rifle butt against his shoulder.

"Throw 'em down," he yelled.

Reynolds Carter started to turn around.

"Face the front. Throw 'em away and drop to the ground or die."

They did as he said.

He strode down to them and held his long gun ready in one hand while he kicked their guns away.

"Don't shoot up this way anymore, boys," Robert Childress yelled. "We've got 'em."

Creed looked up and saw him jerk Josh to his feet by his shirt collar, hands bound behind him.

"All right," Creed said, to the other three, "get up and march downhill. Right now I still have my love of justice by the law, but I could lose it any minute. If either one of those women is hurt, I'll shoot you sons of bitches and leave you where you lie."

He and Robert together herded the four prominent citizens of Limestone County down to the camp, where he saw Brass and Leonard, both apparently unharmed.

"Get a rope," he called to them.

"Hey, now," Loren said, "you surely won't try to hang us without a trial."

Creed ignored that and kept looking for Raney. Finally, he saw her, up in the buggy with the Scarboroughs, on her knees, frantically working over someone. The judge, who had fallen over into Miss Hallie's lap.

Loren Hastings stopped in his tracks.

"Carter, you ass, you've gone and killed the golden goose, goddamn it," he blurted.

"Will you stop picking on me? Toby was shooting at the same time I was."

"They were shooting at Brassell and hit the judge," Raney called, over her shoulder. "One of you men bring us some water."

Creed motioned for Brassell to do it. He went for his canteen while Leonard and Robert tied the three Chickenhawks into the same rope. Then Creed crossed the campsite to the Scarborough buggy.

The judge was pale as death already, but his eyelids were fluttering. When he saw Creed, he parted his dry lips.

"We . . . would've been here . . . to take Raney home," he said, so low that Creed had to strain to hear him. "Would . . . n't we . . . Hal . . . lie?"

"I don't know what you're talking about, Horace," she said. She was as pale as her husband, whose blood was soaking into her dress and Raney's.

Raney was holding the heel of one small hand on his chest wound to try to staunch the flow. Her arm was shaking.

"Here," Creed said, "rest a bit. I'll do it."

"I'll try to get some water down him," she said, and waited for Creed's hand to be next to hers, ready to take over the job, before she let up.

That was wasted effort because the judge had already bled almost too much to live.

She went to get the water from Brassell.

"When would you take Raney home?" Creed asked.

"After . . . they killed Brassell," he said. "We had it planned. They wouldn't have . . . hurt her, too."

Creed looked at Miss Hallie.

She was as white as paper. Tears began to roll down her face. She shrugged her shoulders to show she didn't know any more about this than he did.

"You insisted . . . on coming with me, Hallie," the judge murmured. "And Raney was . . . with Brassell. So we had to . . . change . . . plans . . ."

"Loren Hastings called you the golden goose," Creed said.

"Because I'm . . . a Chickenhawk," the judge said. "We . . . 're taking over the . . . uh . . ."

He paused to cough, although he barely had strength enough to do it. ". . . . uh, Limestone County."

"I can't believe it!" Miss Hallie cried. "Horace, you never told me!"

"Of . . . course . . . not," he said, mumbling to himself as much as to her. "You'd . . . clean my . . . plow."

He opened his eyes all of a sudden, and stared up at her.

"I'm dying," he said clearly. "Hallie, remember the good times."

Creed watched a dozen different expressions fly across her face.

"Yes," she said, at last. "I will. I'll remember the good times."

The judge took a great, shuddering breath, and then he was gone.

•

Chapter 17

~~~~

Raney got back to the buggy with a cupful of water just as the judge drew his last breath. She had been beside Mama when she died. She knew death when she saw it.

"Oh, Miss Hallie, I'm so sorry. I really thought maybe we could save him."

Miss Hallie's face was a mask. The tears she'd cried were drying on her cheeks. She didn't have a sign of any new ones.

"No, honey, *he* was the only one who could've saved him. He got what he deserved for planning what he did for your brother."

Raney looked to Creed for an explanation, but he

351

only cut his eyes at Miss Hallie to say he didn't want to talk in front of her.

"I saw that, Mr. Sixkiller," she said. "You may speak freely. Everyone in the country will soon know that all the respect people held for the judge was completely misplaced on a dishonest, *murdering* old reprobate."

A hiccupped dry sob racked her, and Raney offered her the cup of water, but she shook her head.

"I need to be alone," she said. "Help me out of here."

Creed lifted the judge's body off her lap while Raney took her arm and helped her climb down out of the buggy. She started to give her a hug to comfort her, but Miss Hallie stiffened even more.

"It wasn't a half hour ago that we drove in here, and everything was still true," she said. "Now it's all false. Including the past."

Gently, she put Raney's supporting hands aside and, blood-soaked skirts swaying, walked away toward a thin copse of trees that grew at the bend of the creek. She kept her back straight and her head high, but the hesitant, faltering way she took each step made her look as lonely as anyone Raney had ever seen.

Raney turned back to see Creed carrying the judge around the buggy to lay him out in the back of it. She went to help move the bags and suitcases to one side to make room.

"Creed, what was she talking about?"

"The judge was a Chickenhawk. He was working with the Mason brothers and the rest of them to kill Brassell to keep him from telling the secret."

Stunned, she stared at him.

"The *judge* was trying to kill Brassell?"

He laid the body down and folded the judge's hands on his chest.

"Yes," he said, turning to her, "and Miss Hallie's the one he's nearly killed. She didn't know anything about it."

"Poor Miss Hallie! That's why she said the past was false."

In dismay, Raney clapped her hands to her breast, and the blood drying on them stuck them there. Her whole body stuck where she stood. She wanted to move a step forward and be in Creed's arms.

Oh, she wanted Creed to hold her. This terrible news could not be true.

Creed will never hold you again, you ninny. He will never trust you again.

"You mean we were down there in San Antonio trying to save Brassell from the Chickenhawks and having dinner with the head Chickenhawk all the time? Telling him everyplace we looked for Brass and everything we found out?"

Creed nodded.

He might not trust me, but he wants to put his arms around me. I can feel it. I can see it in his eyes.

"How's the judge?" Papa called. "Daughter? Are you sure you're all right? We've got these bastards tied down."

"You'd better wash up," Creed said, his tone turned suddenly to a bitter one that cut her like a knife. "I'll go get you some water."

"No," she said, snapping out her words in the same tone he'd used, "don't bother. See to your prisoners instead."

He hates me. He despises me even though he wants to hold me. It must be true. Just as I expected.

But still she couldn't keep from watching Creed walk away from her. With his smooth, sure stride he approached Leonard and Brassell and the upstanding citizens of Limestone County who were now being tied together with a rope as common criminals.

Papa was waiting for her answer. Papa was looking at her—she could feel his gaze on her. Still, she couldn't take her eyes from Creed.

This is only the beginning. This is only the very start of learning the enormity of my loss.

The realization sucked the strength out of every nerve in her body.

The only way she could comfort herself was to think that Creed's famous pride would've made him keep his word and never ask her a second time to marry him, whether she had run off with Brassell or not.

But then she remembered that night in his arms, and she couldn't be sure that was true.

Raney waved to Papa that she was fine, then she went to her buggy to get clean clothes. Just washing up would not do. She had blood all over her sleeve and her blouse and her new riding skirt, and it probably would never come out—blood from trying to save the man who'd been trying to kill her brother.

Life was so full of irony that a person could hardly stand it. Why hadn't she ever seen that before?

She went to the creek, at the bend where the trees grew thickest. Miss Hallie was there, standing on the bank so stiffly, her body looked as if it could never sit down again. She was staring down into the water.

Raney didn't bother her, and Miss Hallie gave no sign she knew anyone else was in the world. Raney chose a spot downstream so the water wouldn't carry the color of blood past the dear lady's eyes, found a spot protected by some bushes, and stripped off her ruined clothes.

She had no soap. Of course not. She hadn't even thought of it in her haste to stuff everything she could into her reticule without making it bulge too much for the trip to Madame Robicheaux's shop.

That seemed a hundred years ago, now. A thousand. At the moment she'd packed that bag, she had been drunk with the taste of Creed's mouth and the feel of his hands on her skin.

And Miss Hallie had been full of confidence that her husband, the judge, was a just and honest man. She had trusted him.

She glanced around to check on her, but Miss Hallie was gone.

The first thing Raney must do when she was cleaned up was find out what she could do to help her. Miss Hallie shouldn't have to bear humiliation piled on top of sorrow.

Raney spread out the clean side of her skirt to kneel on and, wearing only her underthings, submerged her arms and hands in the water. She scrubbed as hard as she could with her bare hand to remove the dried blood.

"You'll need soap, dear."

Raney jumped and turned to see Miss Hallie approaching, carrying soap and towels. She was still walking with that strange, stiff gait.

"Thank you, ma'am. It's awfully sweet of you to think of me at a time like this."

"There's certainly nothing else I *want* to think about," Miss Hallie said.

Her voice sounded strange and stiff, too.

"I am so sorry for your loss," Raney said. "This must be such a hard time for you."

Miss Hallie handed her the things she'd brought.

"That man who died is not my husband," she said.

Raney felt helpless in the face of the bleakness in Miss Hallie's eyes. She cast about in her mind for something to say.

"He loved you, though. He told you to remember the good times."

356

"Right now, I can't recall any of them."

Miss Hallie stared off into the distance, so Raney turned back to her task, soaping her arms and rinsing them in the cool creek water.

Finally, Miss Hallie picked up her discarded blouse, bent over, and dipped it into the water to get the blood out. Her movements were that of an old, old woman.

"Thanks for helping me," Raney said. "And thank you for volunteering to be my chaperone, Miss Hallie. I truly don't know what I would've done without you on this trip. I hope we can exchange visits every week after we get home."

"You may not want to see me after we get home. I'll be disgraced."

"Miss Hallie! You most certainly will *not* be disgraced. No one will blame you for what the judge has done."

"There's always guilt by association."

"No! People love you for who you are."

The older woman sat down suddenly, heavily, in the grass beside Raney.

"Raney, honey, I don't even *know* who I am. If I lived with the judge for all those years and didn't know him at all, how can I be as observant, as astute, or as *smart* as I thought I was? I thought I knew his heart and I didn't."

"Men can fool us," Raney said wisely. "If we love them, we can be blinded to their real feelings."

Like thinking they might possibly love us back when they don't.

Tears sprang to her eyes, but she blinked them away. Miss Hallie. Miss Hallie was the one she must think about now. That would keep her from thinking about Creed.

"Horace wasn't my first love. I never loved him the way I loved Jedidiah, but after we were married for a while, I did begin to love him in a different way."

"What happened to Jedidiah?"

"He got killed. We were betrothed—when I was about the same age as you are now. He was killed by a falling log while he was building a house for us."

"How terrible! That must have broken your heart, Miss Hallie."

Like mine is broken now, over Creed.

Miss Hallie looked at her with eyes that burned.

"It did. I thought I would never stop crying."

Raney dropped the towel and reached out her arms to her friend.

Miss Hallie leaned into them and hugged her, but she didn't cry.

"If you could break down and cry right now, too, you'd feel much better, ma'am."

Raney listened to herself in wonder. She couldn't believe she was speaking so boldly to an older woman and patting her on the back as if she were a child.

"Finding out about Horace dried up every tear in my body," Miss Hallie said. "I know that life can change fast and in shocking ways, but this has been such a shock, it's sent me way past tears."

They pulled apart and sat back on their heels.

"Listen to me," Raney said. "If anyone—or everyone—in Limestone County society cuts you dead, I won't. I will be your friend forever."

The older woman smiled a shaky smile. Then, with a little cry, she threw her arms around Raney.

"Thank you, darling. You are a brave, brave girl."

"And you're a brave woman. Remember what you said about how Texas needs smart, strong women? Well, you're one of them, Miss Hallie, no matter whether you have a man to stand beside or not."

"I want to think so, but when a woman doesn't know her own husband—"

Raney interrupted her. "There's no shame in that. He lied to you and he'd always told you the truth before, so you had no reason not to believe him."

"He may have lied about other things, too."

"You'll find out soon enough," Raney said, using the calming tone Miss Hallie had used with her in San Antonio. "Anybody can get fooled if the other person works at it hard enough."

Miss Hallie was staring off into space again.

"My whole place in the community was as the judge's wife," she said. "That's not only gone but it's false as well, and they'll not let me forget it."

"Didn't you tell me to listen to my heart about whom to marry? Anyone who would say that knows that bowing to the opinions of other people is no way to run a life."

Miss Hallie turned and smiled at her. Raney saw the first spark come back into her eyes. She tried to blow on it and get a flame.

"You're a person of your own and you always have been," she said. "Did you know that Cherokee women make their own decisions and they can even go to war if they want to?"

Miss Hallie blinked.

"No. I didn't know that."

"Well, it's true. You don't know how much you've helped me be stronger and be a person of my own, just in those few, short days. You could do that for lots of other girls, too, Miss Hallie."

An idea hit her as she heard herself say those words.

"I know, you could start a school! A school for girls. Like a charm school, maybe, but yours would have smart, strong, and brave added to the manners and deportment."

Miss Hallie chuckled. She actually chuckled, and Raney felt so much better about her.

"If I did that, could you come and be a guest lecturer from time to time? As an example?"

She glanced at Raney's change of clothes—Creed's jeans lying on the ground with the lacy blouse, both freshly washed by the Menger.

"And fashion? Could you talk about appropriate dress?"

It was Raney's turn to laugh.

"I'll do it," she said, picking up the jeans. She stood up and stepped into them.

"You don't have to wear those pants," Miss Hallie said. "I brought all your new clothes."

Raney stopped in the middle of buttoning the buttons and stared at her.

"You did that for me even though I ran off and left you like that?"

"I forgave you when I knew you were with your brother. I was still worried but not as much. Do you want me to go get you a dress?"

Raney resumed buttoning. "No, thank you. I'm more comfortable in these for traveling. If I'm going to be a woman of my own, and I am, I won't worry about what anybody thinks."

"That sounds very smart and brave," Miss Hallie said.

"I won't have a man to stand beside, either," she said, even though the words made her heart hurt.

She put on the lacy blouse, picked up her wet clothes, and held them away from her until she could get them to her buggy. Miss Hallie walked beside her back into the camp.

Raney dropped the heap of wet clothes into the back of her buggy and took Miss Hallie by the arm.

"Let's make some coffee. That'll make us feel better."

Papa was stirring up the fire, but no one had

started the coffee. He looked at Raney, then looked again.

"Daughter," he said, in a low tone as if he wanted to keep this private, "please come here."

He dropped the poker, straightened to his full height, and frowned down at her.

"What is the meaning of this scandalous mode of dress? You are wearing men's pants. I won't have it."

"I'm a woman grown, Papa. I'll decide what to wear."

"But that is not acceptable. Not in good society. You know that well. And if you and Leonard are to repair the rift you caused—"

"Papa, it breaks my heart to know that you hold that hope," she said.

Her interrupting was every bit as shocking as wearing men's pants, but she could not bear to hear one more word about repairing her rift with Leonard.

"Please give it up. I will never marry Leonard. I've decided never to marry at all."

Papa looked so shocked and sad that for a moment she regretted telling him her decision. It would've been kinder to let him come to a gradual recognition of the fact as the years passed.

"What kind of talk is this? The belle of the county to be an old maid? And by her own choice?"

He was horrified.

"I won't live forever, you know," he said. "You must have a good man to look after you, Raney."

"I can take care of myself, Papa."

He searched her face, shaking his head, his tired eyes looking totally bewildered.

"Sweet girl, this terrible trip has unsettled you completely. Never mind what you're wearing for now. Once we're at home for a little while, you'll be your old self again."

He patted her shoulder and gave her another wrenching look.

"I must go and offer my condolences to Mrs. Scarborough now," he said. "I'll drive your buggy today so you can get some rest."

"Thank you, Papa."

It would be a terrible irony if she'd gone through all this agony to bring Brassell home in order to prevent a heart attack for Papa, and then had given him one herself with her newly independent thinking. She needed to let Papa get used to it a little bit at a time.

Creed was standing over the prisoners, questioning them. Raney walked over to him.

She had to speak to him—she couldn't touch him anymore so at least she had to look into his eyes. Once they got on the road, he'd ride out ahead, and after they got back to Limestone County, he'd be gone.

"Where are Brassell and Leonard?" she asked.

He swung around to face her. His dark eyes met hers without telling her a thing. Then, slowly, his gaze followed the lace neckline of her blouse and the shape of her body, all up and down. He made her feel every inch of the tight jeans against her skin and remember every time his hands and his lips ever touched her.

"Gathering the horses. Don't you have any other clothes?"

"None appropriate for traveling."

"There are a lot of men here."

She looked at him straight.

"None of them have anything to do with me. Or my choice of clothing."

"I do. Those are my jeans."

"I'll return them when I'm done."

She turned and walked away, an unbidden smile playing at the corners of her lips, her heart beating like a hammer, her ears vibrating with the low tone of his words.

There are a lot of men here.

He didn't hate her. He was jealous.

Creed watched her go. He tried not to but he couldn't turn his head—no more than he'd been able to look away from her when they sat beneath the tree watching for a smoke signal answer from Eagle Jack. That thought brought the taste of her kiss to his lips.

But even more than the taste of her, he liked the change in her. She truly didn't give a rip what anyone might say about her wearing pants. Judging by what he'd just overheard, Papa no longer held sway over her. The belle of Limestone County was thinking for herself now.

A cold hand clutched his belly. How could he let

her go? How could he ever forget her? They had been through too much together.

She hadn't really betrayed him when she left San Antonio. All she'd done was act out of family loyalty. She hadn't been lying to him with her body and her words that night she spent in his bed. He'd seen that same caring in her eyes just now before she turned away.

But what could he do? He had vowed never to ask her again to marry him.

She might actually say yes if he did so now. Maybe, though, he should wait a week or two and see if her newfound independence stayed with her. Once she got back to Pleasant Hill, she might go back to being the girl she used to be.

If she did that, she might go back to Leonard. He should do something now.

No, he had vowed never to ask for her hand again, and he couldn't go back on that. A man was only as good as his word, and he had a reputation to uphold.

Raney's hands were shaking as she measured out the coffee. Noticing that fact made them shake even more. Good heavens, what would she ever do? Just being around Creed made her hands tremble. What did this bode for her life as an independent woman? Why, if she didn't get hold of herself, Miss Hallie would never invite her to speak to the students at the girls' school!

Which would be fine but a poor substitute for even one hour as Creed's companion. They'd been through too much together for her to just forget him.

Creed might be jealous, but that didn't mean he would ever ask her again to marry him.

Even if he did, there was Papa. Papa, who was still talking to Miss Hallie and getting her a box out of her buggy to sit on.

She watched them from the corner of her eye while she put the coffee on so she wouldn't think about Creed. Papa was a very charming man and Miss Hallie was actually looking at him. It was good for him to actually do something for someone else once in a while.

When the coffee was hanging from the rack to boil, Raney went through the food stores and found enough to give everyone either a ham biscuit or jerky for breakfast. There were probably some items of food in the packs still on all the horses, and all this would get them to the next town, whatever that was, where they could buy more.

Brassell and Leonard came back, leading the prisoners' horses and Creed's.

"We need to get on the road," Leonard called. "What are you doing, Raney?"

"Fixing breakfast. We're not going until I've had coffee and Miss Hallie has had at least a bite or two of something to settle her."

When they'd ground-tied the horses, Leonard came over to speak to her privately.

"This little adventure with Creed Sixkiller has given you a lot to overcome, Raney," he said. "Your reputation for one—which wearing those pants in such a shameless fashion is not helping—and for another, your attitude. It's not your place to try to run this outfit. Your Papa, your brother, and I are here."

"Leonard," she said, turning to look at him as she finished dividing up the food, "don't you worry about any of it, my reputation, my pants, or my attitude. None of it reflects on you in the least, since we are not connected anymore. Why don't you mount up and run right on back to your store?"

"Over here, Gentry," Creed ordered. "We're giving each man a hand free for eating. Keep the other in the rope."

Yes. Creed was jealous, but it didn't make one bit of difference for her happiness in the long run.

Creed sent Brassell to get the food for the prisoners, and Raney gathered up all the tin cups she could find and began pouring coffee. Finally, they were all sitting on the ground around the fire eating the sparse breakfast.

"What have you found out, Sixkiller?" Papa said. "Enough to stop the feud?"

"Looks to be so," Creed said. "The feud's a cover for the real purpose of the Chickenhawks."

"What's that?"

"They formed as a land-grabbing bunch. They've been scaring people off their land and then getting the deed to it for nothing or next to it. They bribed the judge with cash and land titles and livestock so he'd refuse to hear the case of anybody who tried to protest through the law and so he'd let their men off easy when I took them in."

Miss Hallie gasped. "Why, Horace told me he was making some good business investments."

Creed nodded to her. "He was, ma'am. They just weren't legal ones."

"How did you know about this, Brassell?" Papa demanded.

"Thank goodness, I can talk about it," Brass said, "now that I'm safe."

"But you're not free," Creed said dryly. "You have to answer for jumping me from behind and re-sisting arrest."

Brassell turned to stare at him open-eyed. "But the judge is dead," he said. "Who's gonna try me?"

"We'll get somebody," Creed said. "Be glad he won't be a Chickenhawk."

"Brass," Papa said, commanding him to speak.

"I saw him at the rally that day," Brassell said. "Meeting a couple of Chickenhawks back in the woods there before the speeches started. I was so surprised to see them counting out a lot of money and giving it to him, I tripped over a sassafras root and they turned around. All three of them saw me."

Papa put his hand to his head as if to say that if he ever got Brassell raised enough to take care of himself, it would be a miracle.

"I'm surprised they didn't kill you then, son."

"They tried. They chased me and they shot at me but they couldn't quite get the job done."

He turned to glare at the prisoners. "Could y'all? Admit it, now. Y'all couldn't shoot a possum out of a tree."

"Who were they?" Creed asked.

"Mr. Hastings and Mr. Carter. They took after me, but I ran like a deer, I'm telling you. I didn't trip another time, that's for sure."

"Being younger and faster saved you."

"And I wasn't ashamed to run, either," Brassell said. "I just nearly froze once when I looked back and saw their guns pointed right at me. That scared me bad."

"I know that feeling," Papa said. "Up there on the side of that hill a while ago, I felt as scared as I've ever felt in my life."

He set down his biscuit on the tin plate and went on. He needed to tell the whole story more than he needed to eat, Raney could tell. Papa wasn't as much of a talker as the judge had been, but he loved to tell a good story. And this one truly had shaken him. He stroked his goatee with a hand that trembled a little.

"I thought I could get around behind them and blast two of them, at least, before they spotted me," he said, "and before they killed some of us down here—but when I heard a shot and looked up, I had a split second of seeing that muzzle yawning at me. Josh Mason's face was behind it grinning like a gargoyle. He was aiming to kill me, sure."

"Oh, Papa!" Raney barely breathed the words.

"But Creed fired that same instant Josh pulled the trigger and spoiled his aim."

"You had to have help," Creed said. "You were making as much noise as the Union Army. Rocks and gravels were raining down off that hill with every step you took."

Papa shook his head at his own foolishness. He turned to look at Raney.

"Daughter, did I tell you that Creed Sixkiller saved my life?"

"He's *made* my life, Papa."

Papa stared at her.

"What do you mean?"

"I mean I would've lived my whole life without knowing what love is," she said, "if it hadn't been for Creed."

A stunned expression came over Papa's face, but

it was nothing compared to what it would be the next time she spoke.

She had to do it. She had to say it because Creed never would. He put too much stock in his word and his reputation, plus he was stubborn. Not to mention his enormous pride.

There was absolutely no sense in wasting both their lives because of his male pride.

She turned to look at him. His gaze was already on her, waiting for hers. Listening for more. His lips were slightly parted as if he, too, might say something.

What would he do or say when she was finished? Was she embarrassing him? Was she about to embarrass herself to the nth degree?

No. Whatever happened, she wouldn't be embarrassed. She had to say this or die. It would be wrong for him not to know and it would be wrong for her not to speak. If she tried to keep the words inside, they would choke her.

"I had never loved a man before," she said simply. "And I'll never love another."

Creed watched her, his dark eyes steady and wondering, slowly filling with light.

"I know you'll never trust me again," she said to him. "And I can't help that because I did what I had to do. But I have to ask you something anyway."

He looked at her.

She looked at him for a long moment more, trying to read his thoughts.

"I love you, Creed," she said. "Will you marry me?"

Silence fell over the camp like a smothering hand. Her heart stopped in her chest.

Creed's face told her nothing, but his eyes smiled.

"If that's the only way I can get my jeans back," he said.

The shock gave way to laughter that rippled around the fire. Creed looked at her for a long moment more, as if making sure that she was there and she was real, then he set his cup down beside him and stood up without touching a hand to the ground. He walked around the circle to Raney and held out his hand.

She took it, and he helped her up to stand beside him.

He put his other arm around her and turned to face her father.

"Mr. Childress," he said, "I hope you can give us your blessing."

Papa's face was paler than usual, but he stood up and straightened his shoulders.

"I give it," he said. "And not just because you saved my life, Sixkiller. If we're all going to survive, we need more men like you. Men who live by the code and never quit. I'd be honored for my blood to commingle with yours."

Brassell let out a whoop.

"A weddin'," he cried. "That means parties and dances and socials by the bushel."

Miss Hallie clapped her plump hands.

"I'll give the biggest one," she said. "I'll give y'all the biggest party Limestone County has seen since before the war. And I'll use the Chickenhawks' money to do it."

But Raney had turned in his arms to look up at Creed, and he was bending his head to kiss her. It was a long time before they could reply.

There's good cheer and lots of cuddling by the fire for readers of these great new Avon Romances coming in December!

My Own Private Hero by Julianne MacLean
An Avon Romantic Treasure

To avoid the scandal and heartbreak she's seen her sisters go through for love, Adele Wilson agrees to marry the first landed gentleman her mother puts in front of her. Her strategy seems to work, until, on the way to seal the deal, she is overtaken by Damien Renshaw, Baron Alcester, and her plan suddenly falls by the wayside of desire . . .

Wanted: One Special Kiss by Judi McCoy
An Avon Contemporary Romance

Lila has traveled far from home with only a vague plan to make her dreams come true. Instead she finds herself in a small coastal Virginia town, taking care of adorable twin boys for an overworked physician father whose charm seems to be pulling Lila in. Falling in love was not the idea, but once this attraction gets sparked, even the best laid plans don't have a chance!

Must Have Been the Moonlight by Melody Thomas
An Avon Romance

Michael Fallon is the most exciting man Brianna has ever known—and now he's her rescuer! But when Michael unexpectedly inherits the family dukedom, the marriage of convenience Michael proposes is anything but, and Brianna suddenly finds herself falling in love with the very man she vowed never to trust with her heart.

Her Scandalous Affair by Candice Hern
An Avon Romance

Richard, Viscount Mallory, is stunned when he sees a family heirloom on the bodice of a woman he's only just met. The Lover's Knot, as the broach is called, has been the Mallory obsession since it was stolen fifty years ago. Now Richard is determined to know how Lady Isabel acquired it, and if a few kisses will do the trick, then he's up to the challenge . . .

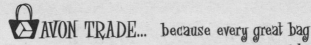

Avon Romantic Treasures

Unforgettable, enthralling love stories,
sparkling with passion and adventure
from Romance's bestselling authors